T0150559

A LETTER
MARKED
PERSONAL

J.P. Donleavy

A LETTER MARKED PERSONAL

THE LILLIPUT PRESS
DUBLIN

First published 2019 by
THE LILLIPUT PRESS
62-63 Arbour Hill
Dublin 7, Ireland
www.lilliputpress.ie

PBK ISBN 978 1 84351 697 2
HBK ISBN 978 1 84351 766 5

A CIP record for this publication is available
from The British Library.

10 9 8 7 6 5 4 3 2 1

The Lilliput Press gratefully acknowledges
the financial support of the Arts Council/
An Chomhairle Ealaíon.

Set in 12 on 15 pt Fournier by Marsha Swan
Printed by Drukarnia Skleniarz in Poland

BOOK I

ONE

HE WAS one of the nicest guys you'd ever want to meet and had reached an age when he could take solace from the fact that he no longer had the whole wilderness of his life ahead to worry about. Especially in a business where sometimes you had to hurt people and you blamed yourself for wondering if you'd hurt them enough so that they couldn't hurt you back. But one of the facts of life he well and truly had learned was that adversity does get rid of loneliness. And then makes you really lonely.

He was living more than comfortably in New York City during a period when pornography was getting respectable, exercise had come into vogue and guys and girls were jogging all over Central Park. If you saw a little group of people you thought had collected to sympathize with a mugging victim, it was often the mugger himself who'd been apprehended by a small crowd of fit and decent New Yorkers and more than a female or two among them. He once witnessed such a gathering and instead of

an ambulance for the victim, a paddy wagon came along to relo-
cate the culprit to jail.

'Hey, what the hell happened.'

'He tried to steal the lady's handbag. She held on to him.'

In short, this king of cities was becoming a better place to
live and merited its reputation as the world's capital of money
and entertainment. Not to mention beautiful women. In fact as he
peered out of the window one day, breaking the law with powerful
binoculars, he focused on a spidery window cleaner high on a
skyscraper, then zoomed towards a street corner near one of the
first bargain erotic lingerie stores he had established, spotting in
the distance a stunning female creature whose mere existence by
the store inspired him to feel he was engaged in one of the best
businesses in the world.

He savoured the comfort that this was a metropolis where,
if you didn't stand too close to the edge of the subway platform
and if you gently minded your own activities and mumbled
'Have a good day' in as many directions as it might be called
for and made a heap more than a few dollars and kept to routine
and didn't let computerized bills drive you out of your mind,
life could, at least for quite decent stretches of time, be sweet.
As his had become with a still pretty wife and three children
grown up and gone off into their own lives with the youngest just
graduated from college, while Muriel, their mother, was free to
attend a plethora of social activities between her beauty appointments and fitness classes. And they both knew, as seasoned New
Yorkers, that you needn't say please to tell someone to get the
fuck out of your way.

From the thirty-seventh floor of his newly built apartment
block, he could watch the air traffic of helicopters and planes
vectoring across the sky. Walking from room to room was a
constant pleasure as was looking out over the city with a map and
then, consulting a detailed guidebook of buildings, finding out

what he was looking at. North to where the trees of Central Park ceded to Harlem and where, in this increasingly democratic New York atmosphere, white people might venture. But south to Wall Street, anybody of any colour or creed could try to make money, placing their bets on stocks and bonds and sitting on their asses waiting and hoping for a kill, but most ending up losing their shirts in a bust and, if they were stylishly dressed, having to cash in their cufflinks as well.

The thing he liked best about being comfortably rich was lounging in bed while Muriel was at a yoga class. He waited for Ida, the maid, to bring breakfast and then watched from his propped-up pillow as the sun arose over Long Island and gradually hit the towers of Manhattan. It was his best time of day for inventing lingerie language to knock the market for a loop, and he never failed to find it awe-inspiring to come up with a name, like Japanese hug-and-tug silk knickers, for his latest creation. But then looking east to Brooklyn, where there were plenty of chimney stacks, he felt less inspired. The stacks were a reminder that whoever was sending up those smoky fumes maybe wasn't glamorous but was probably making money. Maybe even lots of it.

Then in the early evening, when he came home after his workout at the Game Club, it was Martini time. Into a shaker full of ice cubes, he poured his careful quantities of gin and vermouth and added a couple of squeezes of lemon. Filled a Baccarat glass and played Mozart and Mahler on the piano. On a third drink, he toasted old friends and lovers gone till the tears came, then cast his eyes west over Central Park to dream past the Hudson river to Weehawken and speculate upon the future locations that still lurked out there for a lingerie boutique or two. And from that side of the river, one thing was for sure, it was limitless expansion.

He would occasionally contemplate having a big mansion and estate one day. Away from the fumes and grime, the fire engines and police sirens reminding him of injury, murder and death. Plus, what the hell, it would really show them that he'd made it in New York, which you could easily think of as the lingerie capital of the world. With all his bank loans paid off, his credit rating purring, he'd even tested establishing outlets in the smaller boondock towns far out west where, price reduced, you could sell a heap of silk chemises, lace-trimmed camisoles and housewives' see-through boudoir wraps.

Meanwhile, the daily feasting upon the panorama of this soaring megalopolis was a treasuring preoccupation. It made him feel that a city he had arrived in as a bit of a hick was now his personal preserve to enjoy. A place in which he always felt that there was nothing he wanted and could pay for that he couldn't get. And what he didn't want or didn't like, he could easily avoid. Or at least have the offenders whacked. Like the multiplicity of sneaky knock-off artists nosing rat-like in his new-season lingerie designs. Which, why not admit it, he purloined himself out of the erotic stratosphere of Paris and Milan to race back home with and put them on his own cutting tables. But that part of the business also provided the deep satisfaction he got from beating the competition with his own obviously superior quality and style and leaving them standing scratching their privates next to a mountain of inventory. But what a persistent endless bunch of conniving buggers they were.

He liked to choreograph his day. Following breakfast in bed and reading all the news that was fit to print, then taking a bath in the British manner, a Radox muscle soak, his ablutions done and further indulging in leisurely grooming, he carefully chose a shirt and tie to sport with his Savile Row suit and finally descended as an anglophile to the lobby of Midas Towers. Even on a sunny day always carrying a tightly rolled umbrella. Avoiding eye contact, tapping his way through the building's damn nice lobby. Four sumptuous leather sofas flanked by palm trees in large ceramic pots. A selection of papers and books to read. The latter being tomes that no one in their right mind would want to open never mind steal. And no visitor could avoid seeing the sign engraved in brass on the concierge's desk,

ALL VISITORS STRICTLY MUST BE ANNOUNCED

The management maintained that using the word strictly added an air of exclusivity. Which not even the police could ignore for less than three minutes before they drew their guns. One thing he'd learned early in the practice of business was to make damn sure you always knew who was coming to see you, plus have more than a hint of their agenda. And to put a stop to all wishful thinking that the folk coming were rich, charming and good-looking investors ready to back you to the hilt. Of course all they really wanted to do was board your gravy train.

Another big realization was that in trying to be the latest in New York was a waste of time. Because you were already old hat as soon as you were the latest. However, he was among the first to sign up for this ultramodern condominium Midas Towers, publicized as 'Better Than Tomorrow's Best'. And there was no doubt that the apartments were palatial without any sign of stinting.

Sometimes it amazed him that where he lived could matter so much. He still kept and spent time semi-secretly in his first down-market windowless office near the Flatiron Building, where he hung out alone for endless hours daydreaming and listening to music. And what the hell, it was always a bolthole for times if they ever got really bad. And if times stayed good, then it was a reminder of his long struggle up the ladder of success. But aside from his socialistic sensitive feelings, he was proud of where he currently lived. In the lobby of Midas Towers, he could gaze at the fresh flowers in vases on the marble-topped tables and sniff their scent while being lulled by the fountain of water spouting from the mouth of a stone cherub. He especially liked the idea that a waiting visitor, or more likely his wife, anxious to get to the theatre on time, could, instead of being irritated, read an out-of-date copy of *Who's Who in America*. He supposed too that the little verbal amusements provided by the Irish doormen, who were not that keen on his British affectations, were thrown in at no extra charge.

'Good morning, Mr Johnson. So nice to see you looking just as well as you did yesterday when it didn't rain.'

'Ah, but it does from the fountain there. If you stand too close without an umbrella, the spray would ruin your shoe shine.'

Of course this play-acting was just to reassure himself, even in these safer times, and with now somewhere like an eagle's eyrie to peacefully lay his head, that he could continue enjoying all that he had fought so long and hard for without some son-of-a-bitch street marauder relieving him of his life if he refused to be relieved of his valuables.

Nathan Langriesh Johnson, one-time door-to-door lingerie salesman, founder and chairman of Nathan Johnson Lingerie, had reached the top and intended to stay there.

TWO

NATHAN WAS PROUD of his wife and their accumulated years of faithfulness, his grown-up children already past coming to grips with the world. And his dedication still intact to them all. His existence entirely for their benefit. Even digging into his pocket to pay their parking fines. But he could get philosophical enough in his occasional depressions to recognize that no matter how all-encompassing love and devotion were, there still existed the other side of the coin. Which when you didn't know why you were feeling so goddamn far down in the dumps, you realized you were. Then thinking maybe you wouldn't be much admired or loved if you started to limp, blow your nose or fart at the wrong time. Or really worse, go bankrupt or give into temptation to cheat in the shape of a stunning female human being. There in front of him nearly every five minutes during fashion shows, with at least one of them immediately available for the asking.

He had to contend with such temptation in two upcoming shows, one in Paris and another in Milan. Travelling alone and staying at damn nice hotels. Front-row seating along the catwalk. Italian women had such expressively pleasant faces. He could later, gathered for champagne, say, 'Hi honey, you looked really great, here's where I'm staying.' He knew that if he didn't care that his solemn marriage vow in forsaking all others would have to be fatally broken, he'd be in bed with this dazzling piece of ass. Yet he held fast. Ready to resist absolutely, so if any such creature appeared on the scene, all he'd do was smile and nod.

Yet even with its emotional risk foreign travel was what he most loved. Simply to watch others in another culture enjoy life. Plus, in Paris, it wasn't all that bad to have breakfast alone in bed. The French had a big head start on the road to pleasure by simply accepting life as it is. Just as it went by you on the boulevard as you sipped a late afternoon aperitif. Planning where you'd dine that evening and crowning your day with fraises du bois in some fabled restaurant. Continuing the pleasure with an Armagnac and coffee in a neighbourhood bistro. Fellow habitués nodding their approval as you savoured a moment. Then, comfortably leg-weary, back to sleep at your hotel to awake to breakfast. Three thousand miles away from home. Perusing the *International Herald Tribune*. And that the bad news you left behind in America was now far too far away to concern yourself with.

For there were, back in New York, some of his friends for whom he felt sorry. Held in parlous straits by the legal pincers of a once-optimistic marriage. Now facing a bitch who, finished with her castrating, was making sure there was no peaceful place left for men to lay their heads. His own smaller domestic considerations seemed like nothing to trouble about. Such as on sunny days sporting his brolly, one of the few things that made Muriel noticeably cringe. He made it even worse when he would point out that it provided others with a little entertaining glimpse into the more secretly sophisticated life of the city. If it were in fact a sunny day, and with his tightly rolled umbrella pecking his way along Park Avenue, it would get a smile or two from those court tennis players popping in and out of the Racquet and Tennis Club. Or indeed, if you were up near their part of town, the Knickerbocker or Union Club men.

Already a member of the Game Club, which was more devoted to athletics than social ascendancy, he never found himself deeming it useful to belong to any of these more exclusive clubs, as much as the idea attracted him. He guessed anyway it would be unlikely he'd ever be proposed for membership. He read enough to know that these so-called chaps or blokes missed nothing about the right way to be wrong in how you dressed or behaved. But there was something about the sexual overtones in designing and manufacturing lingerie that you didn't boast to those of the stuffy socially registered that it was your line of trade. However, he took a certain satisfaction that his tightly rolled umbrella produced in these gentlemen such a simpatico sense when he walked by. As if you might be hearing words spoken on an English grouse moor. Damn high bird and well shot, sir. But Muriel, ever downright blunt and practical, thought that they more likely would be saying, what a goddamn asshole.

Boy, that was no fun to hear. But the umbrella situation did at least remind one that one was a confirmed social climber, having made a study of every rung of the ladder. Being rich was the first step. The next was being very rich. But he had learned that every rung above you had, as you reached for it, some fucker aiming his footwear to stomp on your fingers. And his umbrella did once start a conversation. A guy, giving him an appreciatively amused look, did at the same time run into a fire hydrant. He commiserated with the chap, perhaps too much out of good manners, and suddenly I'm telling him I'm in lingerie. Well, not in lingerie, but in the lingerie trade. And you never saw a guy so pleased to hear it. He was a transvestite who knew all about harness bras, thigh straps, lantern-sleeved shifts, bodices, and high-voltage coloured microskirts. The guy accepted his card.

'Nice to make your acquaintance, sir. I've actually been to one of your stores.'

Those last eight words were beautiful to hear. Of course it was to such as this aficionado that one owed more than a small part of one's annual profits. Which, as it happened, were being computed at present by his eccentric accountant Reginald, who reminded him that the number thirteen had recently become significant in his life.

'With that contract signed, Nathan, it makes a total of twelve stores. I'm not superstitious, but maybe it's a good idea to avoid any needless invitation of bad luck. Don't set up a thirteenth store somewhere without opening up a fourteenth at the same time.'

Reginald also suggested that perhaps it was time, as they had just added a swimwear line, to go upmarket across the board and call some of his more erotic lingerie sleepwear instead. Which would allow for the stores to be more elegantly regarded. Although he hoped it had already been noted he was a man of dignified steady routines. Taking his walks. Dedicated to finding architecture he could appreciate everywhere and anywhere in the city. And having a concern for the genuinely homeless. Only chasing those irascible bastards who suddenly in the street took to insulting him and his umbrella. And only losing his temper during the annual panic he felt monitoring his tax liabilities.

'Nathan, a couple of little numbers here, a couple of little numbers there. Cut travel expenses a bit, and the IRS shouldn't start growling too loudly at us.'

Although he didn't much like Reginald's reference to the 'too loudly' bit, he trusted his accountant to act correctly in all things financial and to be a board member of the company. But he wasn't going to be like other superstitious New Yorkers in avoiding this bit of notional bad luck, magnified all over the city by there being no thirteenth floor in apartments and hotels. Even so, he thought he should waste no time and maybe fly to Texas to open a thirteenth store in Houston and a fourteenth in Austin, where rumour had it there was a coterie of lingerie fetishists, who might throw a welcoming party.

Then maybe even call the outlets 'The Thirteenth'. Anyway, it was well known how brash New Yorkers could be. But coming as he did from an upstate town where his family, from all of whom he'd grown estranged, had a brush factory for a couple of generations and owned a little bit of property as well, he would have to be regarded as gracious. He felt his own modest social bona fides gave him a degree of vested interest in this otherwise rude city. In college he at least ended up pledged to the second-best fraternity and even kept unrevealed their mildest secrets from Muriel.

'Muriel, why can't other guys' wives be like you.'

'Well, maybe they are. They may just need better husbands.'

It got his gorge when he overheard in the steam room of the Game Club some member, whose face was unidentifiable in the mist, saying, 'The guy who invented the harem was a genius. No lawyers, no bullshit, just I'll have that one, maybe in triplicate, tonight.'

He found himself on the verge of saying, 'Hey buster, why didn't you wait and find and marry the right one?' And here he was in a business where nubile young women were frequently a temptation. Yet wearing a gold wedding ring and keeping his distance with a degree of courtliness not always appreciated by ambitious models, one or two of whom dropped heavy hints, especially at fashion shows, that maybe they were ready to open their legs to advance in their profession. And to those amenable girls, he would invoke equally heavy hints of observing his principles of dedicated faithfulness to his wife.

Of course from his gold ring, they probably knew it. Although, because his business depended upon it, he let it be known that he took a twinkly-eyed interest in the passing drama of attractive women coming that season to New York and not least from the Midwest state of Iowa. One of whom, modelling his swimwear and lingerie, was, with her unusually long, softly smooth-skinned legs, a statuesque charmer. Suddenly flashing her come hither look that instantly incited a warming glow between your legs. In photographs, unless told to smile, she wore a smouldering sulky pouting look. My god, did this sell lingerie. But on longer observation there was a sense of sadness, a look of loss and loneliness in her face. When seen first standing in front of his desk, looking for a job, she did say she was a hick from out west and actually shook a few hayseeds out of her hair. Which fell on a new store's lease he was just about to sign.

'That's right, Mr Nathan, I'm from Iowa. Sorry, I mean Mr Johnson. How much more of my clothes do you want me to take off. Everything underneath is real.'

She had, along with the most beautiful hands, ankles and feet, a body that made him draw in his breath and try not to have it heard too loudly as he exhaled. As she put her black skirt and blue sweater back on, a gentle sorrowful softness came into her voice as she described the most dire disaster in her life.

'They blew up my dog Gesundheit with a shotgun for crapping on their lawn. I told them I hoped they had crabgrass growing there for the rest of their lives. I know it has nothing to do with this job, but that's why I came to New York. So I wouldn't have to get to know my neighbours. Like the kind who shot my dog.'

And Nathan backed away. Realizing this girl with her beauty could get any job she liked in New York. Moisture in her eyes made them glisten a strange green.

'Do you mind, Mr Johnson, if I ask if you are an egotistical reactionary. You know the kind. Who for no reason flies the American flag on his front lawn.'

He thought, holy Christ, with no front lawn, how do you answer that one? Then having put on her coat, she picked up a dog's leash draped over a battered Gladstone bag. He could just make out a tag that read *Gesundheit*. She seemed embarrassed as she looked up and saw his tears. Still welling. And one dropped. He had a dog too, which when he was a boy someone had shot. Putting the small hole of a rifle bullet in its head instead of the large devastation of a shotgun. Then from her suddenly changed expression, it was almost as if she had confessed the worst thing in her life.

'Sorry about the question, Mr Johnson. I really am. It was meant to be funny, but I guess it's not. But these people who shot my dog were egotistical reactionaries and thought the sun shined out of their asses. I guess I also came east because I lived so far from the ocean and wanted to walk the beach and collect seashells. Anyway here I am loyal and reliable and without an agent, doing forty-two sit-ups a day and, while going to acting school, trying to work my way up in the job market, and too honest for my own good. So let's have it straight. Any chance of a job.'

'No problem.'

Although taken aback by her bluntness, he could hardly get those two words out fast enough. But boy, he would sure have to watch his step. As models went, most were, given time, such a goddamn huge problem before they really became an intolerable pain in the ass. If they weren't prima donnas on the make, then they were unreliable the instant they thought it suited them and thought they were destined to aspire to better things than lingerie.

'And Mr Johnson I'm not one of those people who'll soon be telling you sad-faced that my agent just phoned to tell me the good news of a better job.'

He believed her. And she said to call her Iowa. And to excuse her a moment to powder her nose. Which gave him plenty of time to think. Here was someone who might contradict what in his business could give a bad impression of women. There were girls, and now he had to think of them as having hayseeds in their hair, who, perhaps not quite like this Iowa girl, crowded aplenty into New York. Girls who still hadn't lost all their innocence and to whom you could be considerate and kind, as you might be to your own daughter, but of whom you had to be scrupulously careful in other ways. With this Iowa, as he began to practise calling her, he found she could make him laugh and it left him wanting to spend more time in her company. She had, along with her wit and verve, a tenderness that could glow like embers in her strangely sad green eyes.

'You see, Mr Johnson, I don't want to appear too familiar, but I believe in a love that distance never breaks, nor other lives can ever intrude upon.'

And that was Iowa. From whom he immediately found he had to hold himself emotionally steady when she said those words. Especially during her training period over the next few weeks because he thought he once detected a sudden look of affection in her face. He had to remind himself to keep hands off. For as more weeks passed in close proximity, he was finding it harder and harder to not fall in love. Particularly as it had already happened. Which meant not accepting an invitation to dinner at her apartment when by chance they were at a lingerie fashion shoot on her side of town. It was getting late in the evening and she, it seemed mischievously, winked.

'Hey, I'm a damn good cook, especially of spinach and sirloin steaks. What about it, pops. From all these books around the place, I know you love architecture and looking at different buildings. Come on over to my apartment. It's in an authentic bunch of brownstones and practically right around the corner and halfway down the block.'

It was the first time he'd ever been called 'pops', which shook him. But then he'd never before been invited anywhere so enticingly. And somehow architecture and calling him pops took care of having to tell him to his face he was an ancient old fool. Even though at the Game Club, he could do fifty sit-ups to her forty-two. Nor had he ever so disappointedly refused an invitation he was so desperate to accept. If she in turn were crestfallen, she gave no sign. He knew a lot of male folk were under the impression that the lingerie business, for all its bitter competition, could be a bit of a lark. But this was not one of its moments. How could he say he had a jealous wife? He was corruptible and nothing could be further from the truth that he did not want to go. And that was the not-inconsequential conundrum.

Trying to not let her know he was hanging on her every word. Then she reached into her pocket, held out her arm and chuckled as he watched what seemed to be a bean jump in the palm of her hand.

'You see, pops. A Mexican jumping bean. You try to figure out which way it's going to jump, and that will test your ability to predict the future. Here, it's a present for you.'

Meanwhile watching too many times and guessing wrong which way his Mexican jumping bean would jump, he was trying discreetly to delve into her past. The first shock was that she briefly worked as a salesperson for an undertaker and quit when asked to model as a scantily covered corpse in a coffin. Then as a hat-check girl in a semi-fancy restaurant. She moonlighted occasionally as a singing nightclub waitress earning enormous tips but constantly getting fired.

'Pops, I guess you want to know why I've taken this pretty low-paying job and never lasted anywhere very long. At least when I wasn't wearing much. And I hope it's not going to be a problem for you, I always got fired because I wouldn't shave off the hair in my armpits.'

'No problem.'

Again it didn't take him long to put those two increasingly popular words together. After having her brownstone address checked out and knowing which were her windows, he let her witness his signature on a couple of leases. The prospect of arriving in her street on the West Side with an armful of flowers and a bottle of champagne alone provided many a moment of pleasant fantasy. Looking up to see her face looking down. Maybe she could be impressed by watching him step out of the longest limozine in town. No, maybe not.

'Iowa, I imagine that not many of your evenings are free.'

'Well, pops, I get dated a lot. So I sometimes prevaricate to exactly say thanks but no thanks. And I don't explain that I'm just a hick, still in my emotional bare feet. I'm good at humility. But all I really want is to stay alive long enough to torture myself one day with motherhood. That's right, I'm nuts. But I don't like to seem ungrateful when they ask if I'd like to own the Empire State Building or have a palace built for me in Mexico, with a swimming pool in my boudoir and closets full of clothes.'

'Iowa, you could have nearly anything you want in this town. And omit the word "nearly".'

After some of their conversations, he felt like he was standing in his emotional bare feet. Wondering which finger was the one she was wrapping him around. And holy Christ, when she sat cross-legged in a diaphanous black chemise, a white horizon of tooth in view between her parted lips, the hardened lingerie man flipped his foot-thick cast-iron lid. And although this had become a dangerous dream, being one of her suitors with his less lavish lingerie gifts declined, it was, for all its disappointment in Iowa's case, the sweet side of the lingerie business. Because the other side was the ripping off and wholesale larceny by either staff or suppliers and if not that, then the logistical design deadlines always descending and frequently finding yourself quoting to yourself as one of his most ardent competitors did, 'This business is in fact a fucking nightmare without the fucking.'

The ardent competitor was, according to more than rumour, getting plenty of fucking and all he, Nathan Johnson, could safely do was dream. Or think that maybe Iowa, as they got to know each other better, did have a solution. Suggesting, hey gee pops, don't look like that at me, all sad and down-in-the-dumps miserable, cheer up and get out your jumping bean. Watch it jump and laugh. But of course what he really did when down in the dumps was what he always did.

He retreated to his hidey-hole. Marking time in his secret office listening to Mahler and then in a moment of courage emerging from the lair and, starting from the Flatiron Building, commence to walk the fifty city blocks down Broadway, which went straight as an arrow to Bowling Green and Battery Park. From there take a ride on the Staten Island Ferry. Cross the grey waters of Upper New York Bay. Seagulls criss-crossing the sky. Then on return the same buildings rearing up anew against the heavens. It was nearly pleasant to feel sorry for yourself.

'Hey, pops, none of my damn business, but where do you sometimes disappear to.'

'Ah, Iowa, if I told you, you'd stop wondering, and I'd be disappointed that you had no reason to think of me anymore.'

But he had now to be conscious of showing Iowa too much attention. Making excuses for having her summoned somewhere to be alone with her. And he dutifully practised resisting the temptation. Reminding himself that there were, although few, compensating occasions with Muriel, when he was glad to be with her in her less shyly demure moods. She would be tight on too many Martinis and peeling off the latest of the firm's black satin leotards.

'See any tits today as good as these, Nathan.'

'Honey, none as ripely and appetizingly beautiful as yours.'

That kind of action, if he were to be realistic about the timeframe, could have been somewhat longer than a year or two ago. He knew too that Muriel wasn't past using, as Ida the maid did, a vibrator to occasionally amuse herself. Nevertheless, his divorced friends thought it was astonishing that, married as long as they were, they could still behave so affectionately and sensuously and show each other such genuine warmth. Which their friends should have realized was because they meant it. Leading him to have embellished in capitals on all the jewellery he gave her,

TO MURIEL

AND HER BEAUTY

IN BODY AND SPIRIT.

Every year now, for at least the last six years, he took real pleasure in buying her a new, personally customized Buick convertible with *To Muriel* engraved on the dashboard. He took quiet satisfaction too that on the occasions of giving her presents, and without even opening them, she would always smile and rush to throw her arms around him with a kiss. There wasn't much of that kind of reaction going on among his friends, especially one of whose wives, having opened her present and seeing a diamond necklace and bracelet, asked, 'How much are these pieces of crap really worth, Harold.'

And Harold, who happened to be a good actor, his shoulders heaving and his hands up clutching his face, broke down in tears.

'It bankrupted me, honey, and we're broke.'

Trouble was it was true. By an impetuous raising of his hand at a Sotheby's auction, or was it Christie's, Harold was the highest bidder and kept confirming it by raising his paddle and shaking his head up and down. The gems he bought trying to please an ungrateful wife were the real thing, provenance proved, originating from the French crown jewels. And for this poor pal, Nathan had to guarantee a bank loan.

'Nathan, you've saved my life, you really have. If there is ever anything I can do for you, please just let me know.'

The wife, finding out the jewels were real and worth more than their apartment, the ownership of which was in her name, sold them and the apartment pronto. A dealer then robbed her blind over the jewels. She beat it to Monaco, set herself up in a suite at the Hôtel de Paris. As the last of the money ran out, she boarded a Hollywood film-producer's yacht and sailed out of Harold's life, to finally get dumped ashore on the island of Trinidad. Meanwhile, Harold became Nathan's hottest lingerie rep and reorganized his sales team. On the side, he made a pot of money overnight currency trading, moved to Monaco with an Asian beauty and was rich enough to buy and sail his own yacht. You never knew where justice was going to strike next, and a low-calibre person get their just deserts.

There were, of course, in Nathan's own life everyday small matters which, although they didn't impoverish him, he found irritating. As pleased as Muriel could get over gifts of gems, she was socially ambitious and niggly over aspects of his table manners. Like not breaking a slice of bread into smaller pieces before buttering it. An occasional belch didn't go down well either, despite his maintaining it was very British upper class as it showed all present you enjoyed your meal.

Anyway, if his friends suffered hostility in the form of domestic standards at the hands of their wives, as far as the general treatment he got in his marriage, it really couldn't be better. Even as the express elevator shot upwards past the floors of Midas Towers, he felt an increasing sense of well-being, knowing his current home high up in this spacious apartment had become a safe, tried-and-true oasis where Muriel's voice could be heard.

'Hi honey, how were the prima donnas today?'

In a few moments he would watch a basketball game on TV and sit back with a Martini, shoes off and even sometimes, rare as they might be, the soles of his feet gently massaged by Muriel. OK she read it in a magazine at college that it made husbands happy and admitted ripping the page out. But did actually, these years later, try it exactly four times in five months. And *finis*. But who's counting, when you know that for such wifely ministration feminists would jeeringly have you hung drawn and quartered? Which thought always led to a second Martini and eventually to a third. Then he could, with a glass still in his hand, look down from his high perch in this city and convince himself, especially in a winter blizzard, that for a few hours at least, he was in supreme harmony with the world, free from care and sorrow. A baron of business and numismatically victorious. And if a bitch of a problem suddenly came up, he could resort to his secret office downtown to figure out the remedy. And wear snowshoes to get there.

And when he did have a third Martini, he didn't think of blizzards or snowshoes and they would almost always repair to one of the guest bedrooms. Which did, the way Muriel could occasionally behave, test the bedsprings and distract the mind. Because boy, even with the diversionary amusement he was currently enjoying with Iowa, manufacturing and retailing did sometimes need that kind of horny wild distraction. For in no business on earth was it more difficult to remain numismatically victorious or was the competition faster at ripping you off. But the right amount of commercial hostility can keep you vibrantly alive. And you could in seeking retribution expect to hear, 'Hey Nathan, what are you accusing me of. My own erotically creative genius.'

It was true. Every one of these guys had a wise-guy answer. And you could always count on them being ten centuries ahead of your own plans to rip them off. Plus you better be ready to kick a guy hard when he's down to make damn sure he stays there, with his head well and truly buried in a bushel full of out-of-fashion foundation garments. Although the bottom line was always money, sometimes it was satisfaction enough just how scared shitless you could injunctively make the opposition. Even knowing, terrified as they were, the bastards were going to try to rip you off anyway. As they settled after he sued, Steve, his lawyer, would purse his lips, frown and say, 'But Nathan, wasn't it nice to think that they were for all those months trembling with fear and maybe at least morally examining their conscience.' One took no pleasure in victory, simply relief. And it was only tempting sometimes to ask Steve if he ever examined his conscience at three hundred and seventy-five dollars an hour. But Steve, who had kids at college and was a fencing member of the Game Club, in turn reminded him that as long as people couldn't be relied upon to be honest, he was going to be highly paid. Even though honesty was always the best, fastest and most ruthless way to profit. But reputation counted above all. And those who got to know Nathan Johnson concurred that whatever else he might be, he was a straight shooter and a damn nice guy right down to his non-existent bootstraps.

But he did want, as he said for the sake of survival, to avoid giving a totally wrong impression. Advising his pals, in hearing of their own problems, to not let people get away with ratting and betrayal. Let them know that in due time they were going to be tracked down. That sometimes you had to consider calling in the heavies to squeeze the air out of a few lungs. Of course the pulmonary deflation business wasn't a threat he would ever use himself, although he admitted to knowing a couple of underworld types, who still kept in touch and made him aware of how glad they were he was so successful. Plus always asking him if they could do him any favours. 'Mr Johnson, is there anybody bothering you that maybe we could have a conversation with.'

The lingerie business, no matter how successful, would never get the Johnsons into the *Social Register*, where Muriel astonishingly had recently made hints of hankering to be listed, just as she felt she had now to occupy an even higher apartment in a taller building. She even thought of soliciting to join the Colony Club, not realizing that it could take years of kissing selected asses of members who might, after a couple of years, propose you. And he, Nathan Johnson, already knew how very hard it was to dissuade people from approaching those who really didn't much want to know you. In spite of the fact you'd made your first few million, they still could take comfort and perhaps even a distinct pleasure in keeping you at a galactic distance.

Maybe they, reconsidering a little as you nudged up into your first one hundred million, would target you as a donor at charity dinners. Until that socially all-conquering billion. Even then, on your way, you had to shed a million here and a million there for a dozen good causes to even get invited to tea at the Colony. And maybe not ever be invited again. So he relished being smiled at by such lady members as he launched himself right past that club with his tightly rolled umbrella tap tap on the sidewalk down Park Avenue.

Ah, but he knew the cause was hopeless and reconciled himself on their leisure pursuits to bring them whatever class distinction Muriel craved. The Game Club actually had a fancy-enough country club on Long Island Sound. Could go sailing, play tennis and shoot skeets. But then maybe buy a great big mansion somewhere. Pebbles hitting up under the mudguards of your car as you entered the gates and motored up the tree-lined drive. And there ahead, whoopsie doodle, was your lavishly landscaped English country house. Meanwhile attend more dances and special dinners at the Game Club, which indeed as a building alone was a vast palace into which you could fit a few other socially snooty clubs. And whose founders, dedicated to the manly arts, established it as the first temple of athletic achievement in the city. But he wished the members wouldn't grin so much in their photographs in the club magazine. Although he knew it was de rigueur not to exhibit a downtrodden spirit. But Muriel using his chequebook could at least go mix instead at the big charity balls. While he still could happily retreat to and operate out of his original window-less room down the street from the Flatiron Building, not giving a good goddamn, its slightly shabby furnishings belying the size to which his business had grown and the amount of money he had made. And the logo that was now making him famous:

NATHAN JOHNSON LINGERIE
NEXT TO YOUR SKIN SINCE 1989

And he did donate a chunk of cash to the New York Botanical Garden as their lady fundraiser was so charming.

While not getting anywhere with the *Social Register*, or the Colony or the Union or Knickerbocker clubs and caring less each day, Muriel and he were interested in nature and had become members of the National Geographic Society. Enjoying a pass-port to the world and meeting equally nice people like themselves, members of what he referred to as the doctor and dentist class. In their wanderlust, Nathan, the new mogul, taking a break from lingerie, they flew off to the Galapagos Islands and saw the giant tortoises about which Nathan, never one to get too excitable, was impressed. 'Hey, Muriel, look at the goddamn size of these goddamn things.'

Alas, he couldn't be more profound since Muriel's reply was simply, 'Yeah.' And now getting more venturesome, they next chose an exotic jungle safari where, just as he feared he might be bitten by a deadly puff adder he nearly did step on, he instead got firmly nipped in the ass by a lion cub. And all the while sitting on the portable lavatory during his single most enjoyable time of the day for splendid concentration. The playful little beast straying into the tent out of the jungle and just about to be followed by its mother. Although more a pinch than a bite, the tour guide instantly chose to shoot the mother and the playful creature dead.

What surprised him most about getting back to civilization was his pleasure at seeing Iowa. Who in the interim had taken up ancestor worship and visiting St Bartholomew's Church to listen to the choir. She was detail-specific about the location to convince him that not only had she been there but had reconnoitred the Waldorf Astoria lobby, which he'd recommended she should see as one of New York's great interiors. But she was also feeling homesick for the Midwest, where you could hear the trains crossing the prairie and their whistles at night wailing in the distance. And where the morning dew could be so thick on the grass and the horizon meets the sky in every direction. He was tempted to tell her she'd remained on his mind all throughout his travels and he'd rehearsed so many stories to relate on his return. And now here she was, alive and near. Her breath so sweet. He forgot everything he was going to tell her as he leaned as close as he could. Just to take her muskiness back into his own nostrils. Fill his lungs with her magic elixir. Even her mild little criticisms could make him want to hear them said again.

'Hey, pops, here you are back, a crumpled face in an old crumpled hat. Wait, your face isn't that crumpled. Sometimes disgruntled and that's what I meant to say. Don't worry, the hat looks good on you. Only you need a haircut. But I got to go now. Important shenanigans to attend to.'

His whole being leapt to the suggestion that she could care if he got a haircut. And then crushed he was as she gathered up her things, headed for the door and before closing it, curtsied and at the same time gave a little wave goodbye. She was gone for the weekend. An eternity. And now, even in the considerable air-conditioned comfort of Midas Towers, he did look around him every time he sat on his bathroom throne in case his own cat, called Neutered Snooky, jumped on him. Recalling at the same time the way that poor little lion cub had thumped to the ground as a 30-calibre bullet hit it between the eyes.

At last Iowa was back on Monday and barging unannounced into his office. He told her of the lion adventure. Nodding her head, she agreed he'd had a close shave that might have turned more than a few of his hairs white. He sometimes wondered if Iowa knew what she, an employee, was doing to him with her easy camaraderie as he in return tried to perfect his heel-clicking and bowing to ladies. All encouraging him further in his pursuit of English behaviour. But if he had no more dangerous safaris to tell her about, other big changes had come into his life.

THREE

IT STARTED on the cruise ship. While in his deckchair having his morning beef tea, with a school of dolphins off to starboard, he had seen a Sotherby's ad in the *International Herald Tribune*. He knew previously that this fabled auction house sold anything from wine to watches, but was unaware that they also dealt in property, including an imposing country mansion. Set in its own timbered acres with a large lake. Eight main bedrooms, servants' quarters, nine full and two half baths, all reflecting superb design and craftsmanship. There it was in the photograph, palatial, built of fieldstone, sitting high on a hill above a forest of trees and surrounded by terraces. And the further particulars that most caught his attention were in large capital letters:

FULLY FURNISHED AND READY FOR
GRACIOUS COUNTRY LIVING

And like a shot he pursued further and better particulars of this residence, described as a Tudor example of a battlemented manor house situated in its high position overlooking its forested acres, and decided to see it pronto. It was a weekend and Iowa had gone to Mexico. He provided an excuse to Muriel that he had to be away vetting new store locations in Yonkers. So there he was. Heading off north on the Saw Mill River Parkway, driving far enough upstate to reach towns still blessed with rural ambience. Hawthorne, Pleasantville, Chappaqua and farther north, beyond Mount Kisco, to stay overnight at an inn. Next morning in Westchester a tweedily attired, entertainingly amiable real-estate agent took him in his Cadillac to view Blueberry Hill.

'Sure glad to get you out here on a nice sunny day like this to see it in all its glory, Mr Johnson. The drive is five hundred and sixty-eight yards long and as you can see gently curves out of sight between its tonsured lawns on both sides, pine trees and shrubberies and part of your parkland as it were to give you complete privacy from the public road.'

Nathan caught his breath. For there it sat, a veritable castle. The drive circling round to deliver you to the front door under a stone portico. A dream so many times contemplated. That of becoming a country squire. Even dismounting from one's horse and striding in riding habit into this large marbled entrance hall hung with a massive crystal chandelier. Ceilings fifteen feet high. Marble main staircase, oak-panelled drawing room.

'Call me Hal, Mr Johnson. Beautiful things to look at surround you everywhere. And all standing on eighty-seven and a half spectacular woodland acres. Boating, fishing and swimming. You reach the lake by a long winding drive half a mile away down through the woods. Come on. Climb aboard. We'll drive down in a jiffy and take a peek.'

And seeing the isolated peaceful serenity of it all he didn't even mind if the nineteen-acre pond called the lake held a few snapping turtles.

'There it is, Mr Johnson. Take a favoured look. A pure, spring-fed lake. Healthy exercise on your own forest-enclosed private doorstep. In complete personal seclusion. A lawn down to your diving pier.'

Blueberry Hill was just as Mr Jones claimed it was, a paradise beyond paradise.

'There you are, Mr Johnson. Surrounded by the unspoilt view. And that's where I used to live, under that rooftop you can just about see way out over there. Some of my kin are resting their final rest in the small cemetery you might have noticed on the hillside coming in the front drive. Grew up here as a boy and I know these woods like the back of my hand.'

Mr Jones could become a friend.

'Now if we put it into brief words, Mr Johnson, and I know you're a man of taste, with that smartly rolled umbrella. I put it to you that this majestic edifice with its old-world elegance, museum-quality interior and incomparable fittings of cast bronze makes for the purchaser a permanent lifestyle statement. And we do have some further good news. At a little extra cost that we can discuss, you can acquire an additional one hundred forested acres adjoining the eighty-seven and a half, all of which is part of the unspoilt view.'

'Well, thanks.'

'No problem, Mr Johnson. I used to own that parcel. Left to me by my parents. And the present owner would like to sell at a modest price and I couldn't see it go to a nicer person. You come back here now on your own and have another think and a look-see.'

At the inn, over a couple of Martinis, he did sit and think of the hand-carved finishes to the woodwork, and the custom-fitted granite. And to put it in Mr Jones' enticing words, a celebration of British taste in the grand manner. Nathan did return alone the next day, and the next. A worker called Newt was in attendance. Wow. There was plenty more to see. A whole array of agricultural buildings. A bullpen. A milking parlour. A steward's house. An icehouse. An entire wing for servants. Each time now as he drove along the pebbled drive, spotting the small cemetery upon the hill and heading out the gate of this mansion, he was getting increasingly nervous, firstly that he could go bust and then secondly that someone making their own permanent lifestyle statement and with more robust financial backing would snatch away from his grasp this dream becoming more magical by the minute.

'The owner's instructions, Mr Johnson. To sell. And I always prefer that it's to a nice person. There is of course a bit of mystery about the banker who built this house and lived here as you might imagine an English lord would. Imported the stone from a castle in Scotland where the laird had minions who at dawn in the summer would dry the lawn with towels so His Lordship could enjoy his barefoot walk in the morning.'

Nathan wasn't yet thinking of barefoot walks, but back at the inn he sure was ensnared. This rambling old white clapboard hotel, surrounded by its own lawns and trees and perched on a hill, was the kind of place he could, as a local squire, call in on and shoot the breeze with another squire. But hold it. There might already be among the present guests someone who was interested in buying the property. But he sensed Hal would have said so.

Meanwhile solitary to himself, in the lonely rambling hotel, he was really missing the casual presence of Iowa. But it was an isolated feeling, twiddling his thumbs and taking an after-dinner Armagnac and coffee in the residents' lounge before retiring. Then in his room he spoke to Muriel for half an hour on the phone with the subterfuge that he'd found a perfect lingerie outlet and location for maybe two or even three new stores in an upmarket area of Putnam County.

'Haven't you already got enough on your plate, Nathan.'

'Honey, when on the plate you already got plenty of potato, why not also a truffle or two.'

That remark about a truffle was supposed to make him sound like a hotshot instead of the plodding stick-in-the-mud that he mostly felt he was. These nights he'd stopped having dreams of hippos, rhinos, water buffalo, elephants and leeches, and instead dreamt of leaving things like briefcases crammed with leases and other important documents on trains and planes, which last night had changed to being on a jammed-full bus and needing to get off. Unable to find out how to signal the driver to stop at the next stop. The crowded bus continuing farther and farther past his destination while he hysterically pulled on cords and pushed buttons. Struggling in his dream, shouting out complaint. The driver, a girl, stopped the bus and fought her way back through the packed passengers to remonstrate. Then, to his utter astonishment, suddenly told him that if he got off so would she and they could go swimming together. And that voice sounded just like Iowa's.

'Hey pops, come on, let's you and me plough some waves and do a few flip turns.'

The dream made him realize he was in a simmering panic over the purchase of this fabulous mansion, Blueberry Hill. Next morning he parked his gleamingly polished Daimler in British racing green out front of the mansion he intended to buy, with Hal Jones waiting to close the deal.

'Here's the descriptive inventory of the appraised contents, Mr Johnson, including the magic clock you can see through and can't see what force turns the hands. All of which are available. Along with Newt, the caretaker, who's been here many a year, trustworthy as they come. I can say there's been a little bit of a recent bull's rush for this property, which may not be everybody's cup of tea, as you see by its size as we stand here, but it sure is nearly beyond describing for its sumptuousness. My client wants someone who'll love the place as much as she did, before her husband so tragically died. Including contents, seven and a half million. What about that?'

'Five million seven hundred and fifty thousand.'

'No can do. And as I've said, in the past few days and from Thursday's ad in the *New York Times*, there's been more than just some nosy interest. What do you say, Mr Johnson. I'll give you a few minutes to mull things over. Take another look around while I go make a couple of calls and I'll give you a shout.'

Nathan Johnson, now a squire, heading up the grand staircase to the marble-floored landing. Facing a great mirror in which one could survey oneself and one's English voice of authority could echo beyond the vista of the front hall below. But Christ almighty, seven and a half million. Could start the business all over again and open a load of new lingerie stores. Or even sell out of lingerie and retire to Palm Beach. Could also go broke and end up renting someone's garage to live in. Mulling things over, he remembered something Iowa mentioned when they spoke about her English accent.

'Pops, before an asteroid hits us on the head, you winced just that little bit when I said that taboo word, which I'm not going to say again unless it's with my perfected English accent.'

And the word was 'cunt'. And he was shocked. And here he was, miles north of New York City, thinking of his nearly lowliest employee. And while on the verge of taking a step so big that he could fall into an abyss as deep as the Grand Canyon. One thing had to be said about Hal, he sure knew how to screw down the victim in a deal with non-rust screws. Locking Nathan into the most important secret he had ever kept from Muriel in their lives together. Her birthday coming up. He'd already made enough excuses why he was away in Westchester and he did nearly blurt out a hint why, but she interrupted because she was always instantly in a hurry to do anything she thought beneficial to her looks, health and, last but not least, her brain.

'Nathan, I'm in a rush. I have an exercise session, an appointment with my shrink, then a facial and lunch with Claudia at the Essex House.'

Claudia, her best friend, had just taken her recently divorced husband to the cleaners, practically landing him in a rooming house with not even one of his early-Georgian mahogany library armchairs to sit on. And talking about chairs, Muriel might not think highly of some of the furnishings being thrown in with the sale. That they were not her style. Indeed even he, not too much worried about such things, thought they could be considered a little garish for a building of such grandeur. Still the whole allotment and variety could be the perfect surprise for Muriel. According to the appraisal, though, every item of furniture was priced expensive. Plus maybe, if Muriel turns up her nose at them, not that easy to sell off. Especially the shelves of books in the library, a few of which he examined. But he might keep the two copies of the *Social Register*, in which the owners were listed with their address at Blueberry Hill.

There the name was, along with a litany of abbreviating letters listing the many clubs to which they belonged. The Newport Reading Room and Princeton graduate, after their name. And he had to translate Bgt. Cda. Dar. Mds. Myf. Nrm. Nscd., which were spelled out in an index. The last initials standing for The National Society of Colonial Dames. And what was the Newport Reading Room? Maybe a lounge full of sophisticated society magazines. Of course he could have Njl. after his name, which could stand for Nathan Johnson Lingerie. Just as the Newport Reading Room, who knows, could be full of pornography. And even though they themselves hadn't made it into the *Social Register*, a mansion of such significance made him an aspiring member of the landed gentry, plus any wife had to think it was a pretty good birthday present. And quoting ole Hal, 'Now Mr Johnson, isn't it fantastic, the terraces alone. Just to stand out here, the breeze on your face and gazing out on the primal unspoilt miles. What the hell more does a guy want than his own personal paradise kingdom.'

'Well Hal, I guess you're right. If you can afford it. And that's exactly what I'm beginning to have to consider.'

No need to listen to ole Hal any longer. Nathan's mind was fully made up subject to price. He was now remembering that on his ramblings round the mansion there were even glass jars of preserved peaches left on a larder shelf. Also stocks of hay and straw in the barn. Buy equipment. Get a tractor. Sow lettuce, potatoes, tomatoes and spinach. Farm a bit. Why not. Of course you hear it said that there are plenty of ways to break your ass but if you're really in a hurry, there is no faster way of doing it than on a farm. The children, see more of them. And meet their friends. They'd all have a real ball, if they don't break their asses first. They could help dig up the potatoes. Pull the weeds up from around the roses. Get stabbed by thorns. Teach them the meaning of life. Could hold picnics by the lake and fireworks for the Fourth of July. Orchestrated events.

'Watch this one, kids, the golden cascade firebomb, keep back, keep back. Now did you see that, I told you it was really something.'

'Hey, but Mr Johnson, it blew your fly open.' Exactly what one would expect to happen when there's always some smartass kid kibitzing.

Hal at every turn seems to have some new blandishment to offer. 'Mr Johnson, I can truly say that you'll find here a real tranquillity. Big old owl with a five-foot wing span lives out there in the trees. On most of this land only Indians have ever trod with their bows and arrows, over all of which you'll be the sole lord and master.'

Nathan Johnson taking one deep sigh before he did his damndest to knock off a few hundred thousand. Or even a million. The only defence against Hal was to behave just like him. Hal was a real charmer. No doubt about it. Might even suggest giving him a Nathan Johnson Lingerie franchise if he ever wanted a change from the real-estate business. His persuasiveness could sell burlap underwear to Fifth Avenue dowagers.

'And if ever you have an inclination, we can introduce you to a few good ole folk to play bridge with, plus the stables you've got here for horses and ponies, to go riding with. A bit of foxhunting. And a few of us play polo around these parts. That's right, those are polo mallets there sticking up in the umbrella stand.'

Standing in the stone-paved entrance hall at the foot of the flying main marble staircase and just beneath the chandelier, that if it fell on you you'd never thereafter need a house to live in or toes to worry about. Hal pointing his finger could sure change the subject fast. From snapping turtles to polo mallets. Two choices now. To break your ass. On a tractor or on a polo pony. But then, dead in your coffin in this joint would make a damn good place for a state funeral. And no doubt about it, there was no beating Hal. Affably charming as he is, he is aware he's got a fish on a hook and exactly how to reel him in.

'Ah, Mr Johnson, you deserve Blueberry Hill, you really do. And who knows, in a business way this is all potentially big development one day. We may not in our lifetimes see it that way yet, but consider what you leave your heirs. The house may be a corporate headquarters. We've had that kind of enquiry. So, what about a simple six and three-quarter million.'

'Hal. Six million.'

'Well, thank you. I think we could be getting there. And I guess if I were to be philosophical about it I'd have to say it matters a lot where you live. Yessiree. And with the kind of people around you who have a sense of the elegance and gracious style in which they also live, worth every penny of six and a half million.'

'Hal. Six million two hundred and fifty thousand.'

'Six million three hundred and seventy-five, and you've got a deal Mr Johnson. Is that a nod I perceive of, yes.'

'Yes, Hal, it is.'

'Done. Congratulations Mr Johnson. I see you have your chequebook out. So now why don't we just mosey on down this way along the hall and over this fine carpet of yours and down these couple of steps where you can sit on your own chair in comfort right over there and be at your own desk where I can lay out the contracts of sale with which I believe you are already entirely acquainted. Scribble in a few numbers. And you can take procedures on their way, and in your wife Muriel's name as I understand. Nice to do business with you, Mr Johnson.'

'Ditto, Hal.'

Just to stand up again from behind this desk, the stunning reality seems unreal. He, Nathan Johnson, owned this. Everything. The carpet. The massive chandelier. The books on the shelves. The pebbles on the drive. The lawns. The forest. And he nearly wondered at one point if he finally agreed the price just to shut up ole Hal for a minute. Then finding writing the cheque more than a little bit disquieting, a deposit of six hundred and thirty-seven thousand five hundred smackeroos. Locking him into finally having to sign the biggest negotiable instrument he'd ever written. A little scribble of numbers on a small piece of paper light as a feather you hand over in exchange for a massive mansion, its contents, land, a million trees, a whole heap of barns and a lake. A final resting place free of charge to lower your coffin into. And for certain you also owned at least one big goddamn long black snake.

Hal stood there grinning ear to ear, the cheque in his wallet, the wallet placed inside his jacket and given a pat. His contract put in his briefcase, the briefcase snapped closed and the lock combination twirled. And as one might have guessed Hal had yet more to say and Nathan was listening eagerly enough as it seemed useful advice might be needed soon to set up and live like a squire. He was anxious too to be able at the appropriate time to show

Muriel he knew plenty enough about farming. Meanwhile to live with his thoughts and hold the big secret from Muriel for a little bit longer than the time being. When finally upon her birthday, sweeping in on the pebbled drive, he could say, honey there it is, it's all yours. And he and Hal stepped up a couple of marble steps out of the drawing room and proceeded to the front hall. Under the chandelier and opening the front door to stand outside again. Hal wanting to reassure him of his bargain and a real cheap way to keep cool in summer and warm in winter.

'When it's too cold, cutting plenty of wood a year ahead you'd keep yourself ready for Armageddon or if in wintertime you ran out of oil, you'd keep warm enough with that big ole Austrian ceramic stove in the hall. Belonged to an Austrian arch-duke, whoever he was. Of course we should be thankful it never gets as bad here as it might out in Montana or Wisconsin where you could be tunnelling to nowhere out of your house in a snow-drift in November. And by the way, we do have something of a trespasser interceptor so to speak. Three Irish wolfhounds available, but we'll leave that for the moment.'

Holy cow, here Nathan was contemplating the utter freedom of nature and right at that moment wondering how and where he could get peacocks to have them strutting around on the lawn on a summer's day. But also now to be aware that he had available a pack of Irish wolfhounds to defend his land and to break free and tear the peacocks to ribbons on the lawn. While twenty million marauders were waiting to invade his privacy.

'Now, Mr Johnson, no worry, just a couple of growls from these giant dogs will sure save you having to go shooting anybody. But if you don't want any of these city-slicker-type hunting folk invading your privacy and making you and your butler ... Don't laugh. I know a butler for you. Serving your coffee, while you duck bullets in your drawing room. So it's up to you to let them know they're not welcome and post signs.'

'I guess straight off the bat I sure don't want to get sued for hounds chewing folk up or having to shoot somebody, Hal.'

'There's reasonable force and deadly force. Now a bird-watcher or hiker, they're different. In some parts of these great United States you can sue them for civil trespass even if the lands are not posted. Always nice to enjoy more than the *usufruct* of your property. And be the title owner of the soil extending not only downward to the centre of the earth but upwards into the sky into the celestial infinity. *Usque ad coelum*, as the lawyers say.'

God. Here Nathan was running a dozen operations over the eastern United States and ole Hal had him dizzy with *usufruct*, Latin lingo and massive Irish wolfhounds plus a whole mansion of furnishings and an estate of regal splendour plus a withering crossfire of Hal's good-natured semantics galore. Even in Latin and with British overtones no less. And all down to his cavalry twill pants for which one reserves the much more appropriate word trousers. A lecture in conveyancing. But truth is you'd buy anything that Hal was selling, he's that kind of guy.

'Oh Mr Johnson. The keys, the keys. I almost forgot. Just some of them of course. This big fellow is the main one to the front door. Newt the handy man will look after everything. Once more, congratulations. I couldn't see Blueberry Hill go to a better owner.'

Nathan realized he was exhausted. A battery of impressions, clouds of dreams. Was he overcommitted? Spread too thin? Buying his wife a paradise for a birthday present. He sure could do with another few hours in rural peace to help calm the nerves. To rush back now cityward, might be tempted in his excitement to blurt out everything to Muriel instead of waiting for her birthday. Better to get on the phone, check out with Reginald, one's still-trusted accountant, who is damn sure there's an embezzlement in progress in the biggest of the two Queens stores. Amazing how quickly one gets back to troubles from bliss. Meanwhile all is mighty friendly here in this country hostelry.

Sitting in the bar with his thoughts, Hal sure was curious at first as for whom Nathan was buying Blueberry Hill. Was it his daughter, his aunt, or his girlfriend. And until he mentioned the word 'wife', like a gentleman, Hal didn't question further. With the whole purchase price held in escrow, at least he didn't have to worry any longer about another buyer. Just relax and read the local village newspaper. Weddings and funerals. A barn dance next Saturday night. Hot diggity dog. The bartender says, Rightio sir, when you order another bourbon and branch water. Ruin his palate for the wine, which is bound to be something special. Then clearly hear echoing conversation. Which in catching the first few words makes more than a few hairs stand up on the back of his neck.

'Yeah, John, hear Blueberry Hill could have found a buyer. Same old story. Old husband throws a seven and young beautiful wife sells. Just like, and you remember that old geezer, the rich city slicker some years ago who forked out over a couple of million for that other big old mansion, Gentle Pasture or some kind of name like that, married that beauty-contest winner, Miss America or Miss Chicago or something like that. She just got out of prison for good behaviour. She came up behind the old geezer in front of his fire one evening just as he was sitting there in his chair reading *The Wall Street Journal*, and he had some kind of tape machine on at the time he was dictating into. And without looking around he must of heard somebody coming because he said, "Hi honey, is that you?" She said, "Yeah. It's me." And whammo bammo, she flattened the poor old fart senseless with a polo mallet, right at the moment the grandfather clock in the hall was tolling six o'clock in the evening. She didn't know her every sound was being recorded on the old guy's tape machine, which somehow got tangled up in proceedings. You could hear her say clear as crystal, as she grunted, dragging him along, "This goddamn wizened old piece of ancient baggage is sure goddamn heavy." She threw him down the cellar stairs. Claimed he fell and it was an accident. Burned up the polo mallet in the fireplace. Guess, depending upon how much insurance you're carrying on your life, more than a few wives are still murdering husbands these days. Stories like that make you thankful you're a happily divorced man.'

Holy cow. Bring on the bourbon. Have another drink. Lower it straight down. Is there no limit to what one human being is capable of doing to another? How is it in life that whatever you plan or imagine and dwell on to dream is always going to be exactly not the case. One's downfall signalled by dropping and losing a driving glove, which he briefly did reconnoitring at Blueberry Hill. Augers ill if you don't bother to retrace your steps to look for it. And he did. And found it. Hal said he'd introduce you to a few good ole folk around these parts. Play bridge and a bit of polo. The polo mallets right there in the umbrella stand. He never mentioned concerning the brains that got belted out of some poor old bastard who by the sound of it was a defenceless elderly gentleman taking his ease in a big old mansion viewing his asset portfolio in front of his evening fire glowing within a magnificent chimney piece, which must have been just like Blueberry Hill. In any event it called for another drink.

'Rightio sir, coming right up.'

The now-familiar waiter hands over the evening's menu with another drink.

'There you go.'

It will be his second or third. And Christ he must not have a fourth. After which Muriel says he's not worth a damn in bed. Tonight it's not going to matter and is going to be a private celebration with a bottle of booming burgundy and his usual steak, spinach, baked potato and salad in the dining room. Then instead of making any goddamn calls about embezzlements in Queens, go watch and listen to the glad faces on television till he can't stand them anymore. And thank god are forgettable in an instant.

Everyone trying to say something truthfully memorable. Or even worse, trying to be funny. And even worse than that. As Iowa said in one of her less shattering off-the-cuff remarks, 'Hey, pops. The civilized world's sense of humour is being eliminated by canned laughter. I mean it would be better give us the pure laughter and leave the screen blank. But it's amusing watching things that aren't funny at least when you know the perpetrators are desperate to be.'

Nathan Johnson, squire, in his bedroom ready for bed. Hoping not to have a nightmare of polo mallets flattening anybody senseless. And in order to invigorate with a moment of fresh air, after a solemnly delicious dinner, opening up the window. Voices of a choir in the church across the road singing. Just when you look for and need optimism. It almost unbelievably comes. A soul-soothing sound of reassurance after this most fateful day. Holds at bay paranoia when it seeps into one's consciousness to sap one's confidence. Which Iowa said she needed. And got. When she entered the great doors of St Bartholomew's Church to listen to the choir. She said the words she heard sung in a hymn were wonderful. Love so amazing. Love so divine. And she realized that but for a little boy who sat next to her in school and died, she'd never again been in love. 'Pops, because I guess I felt, in case the next person I loved I became dead.'

And now trying to sleep, think of dying. Hypochondria always attacking at such times. Chronic crut of the foot. Shrinkage of the gonads. Or lightning strikes of pain up or down the alimentary tract. The obstinacy of the human spirit keeping you awake to what you imagine is a disaster coming. Two stores in Queens. How much money has been embezzled? On top of a mansion and an estate will he be able to afford a tiara for Muriel to wear at big dinner parties. And Newt. Reminder that he now had to hire a staff. And wolfhounds. Boy, do they eat. While here he was already thinking of Muriel in a haute-couture ballgown descending the grand staircase of Blueberry Hill. Waiting for her in the front hall in his tuxedo and speaking in the best British accent he can muster, 'I say, my dear, you do look ravishing.'

And that's what he'd say so long as she hadn't kept him waiting, spending an hour or so at her dressing table. A massive one already waiting in what might become her bedroom with brightly flowered wallpaper and pink shades on the bedside lamps. The two of them proceeding to the drawing room for champagne. Christ. He'll need a hell of a lot of servants. Pop. That was the cork that the butler pulled out. Hal said in passing he knew of one. A major-domo formerly in the employ of a duke, who could eliminate household concerns for a wife. And who knows Muriel may hate the place as being too big and gloomy. Then in his dreaming sleep he did have a nightmare in which a cottonmouth moccasin was coiled waiting to strike. Woke up as its fat dark grey head with its fangs were about to sink into his leg. He took it as a signal it was time to go and paid his bill.

'Hope you enjoyed your stay, Mr Johnson.'

'Yes, I did, thank you.'

'See you again soon, I hope.'

'Yes, you will.'

And he wasted no time. The Daimler was, at fifty miles an hour, gliding out along this meandering road south and back to New York City. The sky growing grey with clouds in the fading daylight. Worry creeps in where happiness suddenly fears to tread. So why not end his days in a place where he might even be buried? Which, thinking of death, reminds Nathan he's insured for a tidy sum. This is no time to get paranoid. Thinking someone is tiptoeing up behind him with a polo mallet. Plus Muriel and the children already bequeathed, practically own everything. So no one will starve after he's gone.

Now driving through this nice little town of Armonk, curtains of rain pouring down. Replenishing the land upon which everything on earth comes. And goes. And the countryside has got to be a hell of a lot more relaxing for the mind than a dry-goods business like lingerie. Enjoy the real scent of a rose instead of an artificial fume of perfume. Instead of inventory nightmares, have the sun shining down on your honest sweat when you were out toiling in the open making hay. Also, as folklore has it, making hay makes you horny. Come in from the fields and creep up behind Muriel as she is bent over the cooking range in the kitchen. Let her have it from behind just as she was baking his favourite blueberry pie from all the different varieties of blueberries. But as she cries out so loud, such a canter with Muriel only possible without a nosy staff around. Anyway, no shortage of blueberries. They were growing all over the place.

The big engine of the Daimler purring in near silence leaving behind the town of Armonk and now along by the reservoir and past the great dam holding back most of the water that once flowed mightily in the Bronx river and all the way into Long Island Sound. Nervous now. Fast within striking distance of the city. He reminded and assured himself that he hadn't bought a disaster having seen Blueberry Hill several times and climbed all over it in the company of Hal. And it had to be said, so far he was a delightful and elegant real-estate representative. Also had the place checked by a surveyor. Which took him long enough. And except for a bit of roof repair, got an OK report. But with all furnishings deal thrown in, didn't get the price down much. And in borrowing from the bank, one could be confident one was doing the right thing. Because it was just only days ago he held up a photograph of Blueberry Hill across the bank president's desk, and at the sight of which Mr King smiled.

Whole thing happened so fast with such few words, maps or drawings it made you even more nervous when a banker says, 'Sure, go ahead.' Mr King smiling indulgently, calling for a new gold-embossed chequebook and even suggested a bit extra for contingency.

'Well, Mr Johnson, provided something big doesn't suddenly go wrong with the roof of Blueberry Hill, there is no good reason why you shouldn't dine in your tuxedo and reach out into the pleasure grab bag of life and see what you might come up with. And you'd find few living things in this world more beautiful than Arab horses. And your trading accounts say you can afford one or two.'

Nice, in the present rainstorm, to be reminded while driving past Woodlawn Cemetery up on a Bronx hillside, that even in the turmoil of fashion changing, lingerie will always remain in demand and something few women can resist. At least so long as it keeps more than a few guys drooling at the mouth and paying her ladyship's bills. Not the nice way to look at things, but an inescapable erotic fact that gets Nathan special treatment at the bank. And the likes of Mr King nodding his head sagely and to give Muriel his regards. Of course he didn't volunteer any of his own fantasy thoughts to Mr King like if dining evenings in a tux at Blueberry Hill gets too boring then maybe he could also pretend to be one of the hicks in the sticks in dirt-soiled dungarees hanging out on the porch of the general store. But the more he fantasized about it, Blueberry Hill could be the smartest thing he ever did. How about a lingerie fashion show in Blueberry Hill's sumptuously panelled rooms? A fanfare of bugles. As Iowa, the girl from Iowa, comes out gently shifting the pitch of her hips and strutting in her wonderful way under the majesty of the fifteen-foot high ceilings. Gasps from the audience.

'Now, look at that stunningly beautiful girl.'

Hope Muriel when he holds the fashion show doesn't, when she sees Iowa, throw a fit of jealousy, take a polo mallet from the umbrella stand and let him have a swipe of it on the noggin. Then drag him to where she can dump him down from the top of the cellar stairs. Which, come to think of it, he couldn't remember where they were at Blueberry Hill. Or if there were any. And him as a squire, working out such conundrums. Wake up out of all these speculations. He'd driven all the way back to Midas Towers.

The kibitzing Irish boys in the lobby seemed glad to have him back. Salutes from their peaked caps as they rush out to carry in his luggage. Taking the car and driving it around the block into the basement garage. Only a flurry of snow had fallen and they were already sweeping the sidewalk. And with two umbrellas making sure a snowflake didn't land on him. Rise up pronto in the mahogany-panelled elevator. Express all the way. And the interior just like a smaller version of the drawing room at Blueberry Hill. And now it feels cramped to step into the apartment.

'Hey honey, I'm back.'

'At last.'

'Well, you know how it is, it's always location, location, location. The setting has got to be right in selling lingerie.'

FOUR

THE RITUAL of getting out of a suit. Find hangers to hang everything up. In the lingerie business you never wear a shirt twice. Or underwear. Jump into a shower. Put on slacks. Silk shirt. Gold cufflinks. Rehearsal for Blueberry Hill. A dressing room where he will hang his crimson velvet smoking jacket. A rack for his loafers. Six pairs. That first came to America as Norwegian slippers. And then swept across the nation because that's what the citizens think they know how to do best. Loaf. Take it easy. Have an Old Fashioned. Or two. Don't let any wild chill wind blow around your soul. Three nice kids gone out in the world in pursuit of their fortunes. Your most loved one left, nearby. Looking her usual pleasant best. So many of his friends' wives could erupt inhumanely ferocious, arm-wagging and shouting over nothing at all. And all you can say to yourself is, 'God, what a lucky guy I am.' Slippers on. Be able to just sit back and quaff down number three Old Fashioned. While just shooting the shit with his wonderful wife. Yes. Why not. Wonderful. Ask her a nice question.

'What have you been doing, Muriel, while I've been away. No new clothes, nothing new I can see in the apartment.'

'I've just been going out to a few art galleries, the Met. The Guggenheim. The Frick. What a mansion that was once upon a time. Had my hair done by the Mario Studios, which by the way you don't seem to have noticed.'

'I noticed. But why don't you go into the best stores like Bergdorf Goodman and spend more money.'

'Nathan, I don't want to spend money for the sake of spending it.'

'If you do, it means you got faith in me. You know how I like it when you spend money.'

'Maybe I wish you weren't making all the money you do in lingerie in the proximity of so many half-naked girls on the make.'

'They aren't on the make. Just trying to make a decent living while they get somewhere in the modelling game.'

'Well, I believe you. The money they make working for you, you'd hardly call a fortune. But meanwhile they're on the make, kiddo. And you better believe it.'

'Even so, honey, forget them. You know I think you're someone to be indulged and adored. And I want you to be the woman who has everything.'

'Nathan, you've had too many Old Fashioneds.'

On his empty stomach, he'd downed a couple more Old Fashioneds watching the astonishing fall of snow fall thicker, the thunder rumble, the lightning flash and the lights go on across the city.

'Nathan, if you look at me like that just one more time in that funny way with that funny expression, I'm going to divorce you.'

'What expression.'

'That kind goofy one old people get, which makes you think they should be in an institution for the severely elderly.'

'I'm just pleasantly relaxed. It's good to be home. And I just knocked back three Old Fashioneds in a row. I'm as pleasantly drunk as a skunk.'

'You knocked back five to be precise, but who's counting. And your face has gone lopsided silly like some cat who just got more cream than was good for it.'

'Holy cow, honey, thanks for the observation, but what say you come over here and kiss some of that cream off the cat.'

'Well seeing as you are just a nice big old horny tomcat, why not.'

Tonight, snug and warm up high in Midas Towers, why wouldn't everything seem a godsend. Peace gathered around you. The rest of the dangerous world down below way out beyond your windows. How much more of the magic of life could you ask for. But now, provided the children weren't around, such repartee as they just had always did start a procession hand in hand towards a guest bedroom. The frisson of clothes thrown off on the way. Flung everywhere as upon this Thursday it was also Ida's day off, visiting relatives in Brooklyn till the morning. The freak weather. Snowflakes swirling in the bursts of high wind outside, Muriel's nakedness silhouetted against the city's illumination. An appetizing sight and even in the dim light a smile could be seen on her face.

'What a feel you are to have close, honey.'

He could never dream up words more original than that since that's what he felt. Inebriated by her musky scent. The faint groan she made. But most of all, her smile. The most warming. Increasing to a broad grin. Nowhere near goofy enough that she should be in an institution. Shaking her breasts as a bird might rustle its feathers. Crossing to the bed to where he lay waiting. 'Wrap up,' as she would say. Keep him warm in her squirming and willing limbs. Even their feet entwined. Lips touching against his ear, and her voice softly sweet.

'I could kill with love. Couldn't I. Couldn't I.'

'You could, honey, you could.'

'And maybe, Nathan, you wouldn't find that the worst way to die.'

'No, maybe I wouldn't.'

So rarely ever using the word, it could be said they were still so in love. They had made a pact beyond their wedding vows never not to be nice to each other. Although Muriel did say unless it was a matter of life and death. And he trusted her that she didn't mean her life and his death. Now here it was, the undreamed-of awaiting them. A splendid estate. A magic mansion that you would expect to find in a storybook. Peaches fattening on trees in an orchard he still had to go find located out in the woods. Get cows mowing summer meadows. And milking, as Hal said, could be done to make butter out of their own golden cream. A cream separator in the milking parlour. Just press the button, pour in the milk. Out comes the cream. Plus press upon this warm body. That he was now locked upon. The same body that would be soon there in their palace. A constant comfort to be embraced at the end of an evening in sleep and to awake to at the start of another day. They could even plan beyond their living lives. Be buried together on their own land in their own cemetery. Their epitaph on their tombstone:

Here lie the bodies of Muriel and Nathan Johnson
FAITHFUL UNTO DEATH AS THEY WERE IN LIFE

Maybe have to think up a little something better than that even though it says it all. Or had he now, owning a castle, gone too sentimentally European. Or was he just plain romantically nuts. Because it wasn't the kind of idea any true red-blooded American woman wanted to normally have to entertain. Hey honey, let's team up together in the same grave. And if we get killed together in the same car, train or airplane crash, let's be buried in a his-and-hers coffin for two. Or would he hear the words you heard everywhere these days, in good old American vernacular, 'Hey fuck you, sonny boy, and get the hell out of here. I need my own space, you get your own goddamn coffin. I've had enough togetherness to last this lifetime and any other goddamn lifetimes to come.'

Anyway, as much as he wanted his mortal remains to rest in peace with those of Muriel, he sometimes couldn't banish the sacrilegious thought stealing into his consciousness from the edge of his brain that he wouldn't mind being buried with Iowa. And, too, amazing to think that it actually made one even able to relish death. If fifty years later her willowy and stately body were placed there to rot beside him. Lying there eternally in peace. Her bones next to his bones. The thought of which could give him solace the rest of the days he lived. He recalled a recent suggestion an employee had imparted: 'Mr Johnson, we've really got to put that girl from the boondocks on the cover of this year's company calendar.'

'Well, give me a while to think about that.'

Pretending he had no favouritism, he had to fake his temporary reluctance. But agreed. Then was astonished when Iowa turned them down, the top sleepwear and swimwear model. Could make any lingerie look a dream to behold. And even when his taste in women could be considered a little eccentric, he could nearly regard himself an expert on female beauty. Which now had come without warning into his life and whom he could use to demonstrate his standing to the world. It galvanized attention to just be seen with her on the street. And very close up Iowa's smile uncovering the most alluring tiniest gap between her front teeth. And if you needed something to be the least critical about, she was just the slightest bit pigeon-toed. But her dark brown hair unforgettably falling to her smoothly faintly tanned shoulders, which looked so much whiter when she wore black lingerie. And for another vision her so uniquely curvaceous body could appear memorably agleam in a skin-clinging bathing suit. For a nickname he thought to call her Idaho.

'Hey, Idaho.'

'Why are you calling me Idaho.'

'Because the last thing you look like is one of the potatoes they grow there.'

With Iowa a frequent presence in his life, he had to remind himself over and over again that he was married. For more than once he had contemplated as to what hope there could be, with him nearly twice her age, to ever really seriously prolong her interest in him. And instead to be sensible enough to say to himself, 'Get rid of that dream.' Like many other models, she was not to be long term in his life. Not that he needed her to enrich it. But maybe he did need. Just occasionally. The forbidden. Her mere nearness was enough to excite and simply enjoy. Finally working up his nerve to the breaking point at the end of a shoot one day, he asked her if she ever wondered what her body did to guys. Some of them actually trembling in their tracks.

'Sure. When sometimes I look at myself naked in the mirror, I can get convulsive laughing myself half-delirious when I think of it. That it's only me. Nobody. A hayseed from the prairie. A cheerleader who flunked home economics in high school. But then I guess I was grateful when I discovered that a nice body can be your passport through a lot of doors in life. Where on the other side you think everything is going to be better. Until of course it isn't. Mostly just people after what you don't want to give them. And you might have been saved all the trouble if instead the doors got slammed in your face.'

'I didn't slam a door in your face.'

'I know.'

'Iowa, you even have the most beautiful Achilles tendons I have ever seen.'

'Hey, pops, you know where exactly to strike, don't you. If a girl knows she has a beautiful face. Tell her she's got great strong-looking legs. I know, aren't these tendons something. I wouldn't want to snap one streaking up the ladder of success. Where at the moment I'm safe in Nowheresville. I don't mean working for you is Nowheresville. Here's one for you. What starts and goes on and never needs to stop.'

'I don't know, Iowa.'

'Hey, dummy, it's counting of course.'

'Wow. I'm glad at least I've learned that today.'

'No problem, fox.'

'Why are you calling me fox?'

'That's how sometimes you behave. Wily-like. As if you didn't know that I know what you're thinking.'

FIVE

AND IT WAS an afternoon of a chill rainy day only a couple of weeks later, that, reclusive in his private secret office where he was surveying maps and plans of Blueberry Hill, the shock of a knock came on the door. Was his toilet leaking again? And no excuse. He'd have to let the janitor know he was there. He'd have to open the door. And there she stood.

'Iowa. What on earth are you doing here.'

She swept into the room. 'I know. I'm sorry. I shouldn't be. I'm on my way to acting class. But I wanted to ask you a question.'

She stood there shrugging her shoulders. Wearing a stunningly tailored tweed hacking jacket and with a half-closed dripping umbrella hooked over her arm. She had what looked like a script and a fat tome pressed up to her breast. Not a hint of her astonishing body to be discerned beneath a black cashmere sweater. But as always there was more than a hint of what was for him a delicious fantasy for the eye.

'Pops, I'm wearing my horsey pre-convent outfit. Because if I don't ever get to Hollywood and become a star, I'm going to become a nun.'

'And what's the question you wanted to ask me.'

'Fox, it sounds a little nuts. What's worse, having all your life in front of you. Or having it all behind.'

'I'm just a bit past the halfway point and I haven't got the full answer yet.'

'If life's a lesson, teacher, how do you know when to stop learning.'

How the hell did she ever find out where his private secret office was. Her head tilted over her left shoulder, her beautiful left knee propped forward from beneath the plaid skirt she wore. Flat shoes and green collegiate knee socks. Her parked umbrella rolling off raindrops on my rug. She was so full of familiarity. One might have thought, if one had a civilized chance to think, that she'd become downright impudent.

'Hey pops, and not to pry, but it looks like you live here. A kitchenette. Coffee percolator. A pot and a pan. Pretty fancy stereo equipment. Refrigerator. This little box with a cake I brought as a present should go in there.'

'I'm not living here. Only pretending to be.'

'Is that a couch you sleep on. Oh my god, you don't have to answer that. I should go.'

'Please don't.'

'But pops. I see you lift weights.'

'Occasionally.'

'OK. Now before I call you Tarzan and before I join a convent, I'll tell you why I'm here. It's sort of an emergency. I need a promotion and raise in salary and to give up my necessary moonlighting as a singing waitress accumulating my hundred-dollar tips late at night but losing too much sleep. It's too easy for too many in this city to make hay out of me and leave me without any left for myself. The trouble with the big tips, pops, is that they're always followed by the guy's phone number and the information about the impressive station he enjoys in life and wants to share with someone forever. If I don't telephone him, he's back again pretending he isn't waiting for an answer why I haven't telephoned. Because I should be aware that the big opportunity to get to know him better is going to flash by. So before I get political as a member of the youth who against all odds grew up honest, what about me becoming your lingerie designer specialist?'

'No problem.'

'Oh.'

'I said, no problem.'

'Hey, let me go on saying *oh*. *Oh, oh, oh*. I'm trying out my English accent for acting class. See that tome there on your desk. It's on foreign dialects. And underneath it is a script for a movie. And a play script. The latter I may be auditioning for. But I had a long spiel to tell you why you should take advantage of my creative flair.'

'Sit down. Please. There's a chair. Shoot.'

'Gee, pops, I don't want to sound like a complicated scientist.'

'Why not. You're already a philosopher.'

'God, I'm anything but. So OK, here we go. In my lingerie research investigating the beauty of symmetry, I've been reading about the science of pattern analysis, you know, shapes in multidimensional space, things like arabesques of intersecting arcs, motifs becoming smaller towards a limiting circle and circles touching circles. Stuff like the curvature in the filigree shells of diatoms.'

'Holy cow, Iowa. That's fantastic. Really fantastic.'

Of course as she sat there, queen of all she surveyed, he couldn't understand a word of her spiel on symmetry. Except that it didn't sound like it could help in designing brassieres. But standing stupidly nearby he knew he would agree to anything she said. And in order to intrude a departure from scientific discussion, some crazy notion made him bend over and grab up the seventy-five pound weight on the floor. Straining all the tendons and muscles in his arms, back and shoulders to the limit, he two-handedly pressed the weight up to hold it over his head.

'Fox, you're strong.'

'Since you're calling me Tarzan and before I start calling you Einstein I thought it best to attempt a demonstration of something droll. And since I've hopefully got this weight over my head had I not, my dear, in considering your scientific suggestion, had I not better call you Jane Einstein?'

Having busted his gut practising to be a farmer and now parading as Tarzan to impress this wonderful creature, it hadn't escaped Nathan's attention that he was demonstrating what a stupid nut he was. But Iowa, by her expression at his exhibition of strength, seemed actually touched if not awed. While he instantly began feeling a sense of redness growing in his face as he kept straining to keep the weight up. Until he couldn't. The barbell came down like an actual ton of bricks sending up a cloud of dust rising from the long, uncleaned carpet on the floor. Luckily Iowa had been keeping her distance while he jumped back as the barbell landed, standing waiting in horror that it might go through the floor as a weight previously had done and knocked plaster off onto the cutting table of the one-man tailoring establishment on the floor below who no doubt thought this was a repeat and had already run shouting for the janitor.

'I'm so sorry, pops, I can't stop laughing. You poor man. You're not ruptured or hurt, are you.'

'No, my dear, just mortified at being a show-off.'

Here he was alone with Iowa. Brave enough now to call her 'my dear'. Having fun with her making an utter fool of himself. He was now looking at contentment beyond contentment in the presence of this beautiful creature who was suggesting a repeat weightlifting performance.

'Let's see if you can do it again, lift the weight and make sure your back's OK'

'My back, I think, isn't OK. Feels like it's broke. But for you, I'll gladly break it again.'

'Oh, I say, you're an incurable romantic. Like me. But sometimes it leaves me that I'm laughing till midnight and crying till dawn.'

He wanted to believe it, especially said with her English accent. But he could already discern Iowa's cheeks filling with air ready to explode like a bomb with more laughter. As he pretended the weight landed on his toe and hopped on one foot, in need of her urgent physically-close attention. But he felt employer–employee discretion was required to temper matters. A practice he got plenty into dealing with the jealousy and resentment shown Iowa by his other models. And complicated by the bias he had in favour of Iowa, the youngest and most beautiful.

'Pops, you're in good shape. Got a wrinkle here and one there but you're distinguished-looking and I know you weren't trying, but that's the first time I've ever known you to be funny. Making-believe it fell on your toe. Can't you tell by my bashful and slightly evil childish laugh that I'm only halfway kidding and saying whatever comes into my head? Look at me asking for a raise in salary.'

'Well, Iowa, you've got one. I'm doubling your salary. And you certainly have an enquiring brain under that bountiful brown hair of yours. But it's sometimes difficult for me to tell when you're kidding.'

'That's what absurdity is for, to be able to tell the truth, sneaking it in between the lies, and not getting lost in the too-deeply serious. In this the town that has it all, it's necessary. And I guess I just want to get a little unserious taste of every kind of life as it goes flying by. This is a pretty expensive leather chair. Is it OK if I sit down a second.'

'But of course, please do.'

'Hear that British manner. How did such a smart guy like you ever get into such a dumb business.'

'I think, Iowa, you mean how did such a dumb guy ever get into such a smart business.'

'I do sometimes get it assways backwards when I'm trying to become unkidding serious, tempted to say things like, Shouldn't this place, under the city by-laws, be condemned for human habitation. Sorry I said that. But hey, look at you. That's champagne. A bucket, glasses. My god, all those wooden crates. See why I call you fox. Pops, you're not a secret lush are you. No, of course you're not. Lush is a New York word I just picked up.'

'I'm just a champagne-lover, Iowa.'

'Heidsieck, Roederer.'

'And Iowa, you can join me any time you like in tasting them.'

'Oh my god. I'm looking at my watch. I'm going to miss my acting class.'

'Miss it.'

'Fox, I have already and will be severely admonished.'

'I'm sure they'll excuse a brief absence.'

'But I don't want more gloom to face. Especially as I had a nightmare dream last night of diving into a deep pool of thick red human blood full of guts. Sorry. I know that sounds awful. But having a dream like that slows me down in wanting to get a taste of every kind of life that goes flying by, rather than make a meal of old customs and tradition.'

'That's why I'm chilling this bottle.'

'And you seemed to be away so much recently, that's how I finally worked up my nerve to see if you could be bored in your lair. You see, fox, I like all those little English touches you pay attention to. Even while you're battling in what must be the most cut-throat business where all the courtesy and civility in someone's behaviour is a sham prelude to getting kicked in the balls.'

'Iowa, you do know a lot about this business. Here, your glass of Heidsieck.'

'I guess I can miss or go late to one acting class. Anyway, wow. This tastes good. That's why I appreciate the beautiful cloth in your suits. The real bone buttons. And now look at that cravat. The vest. Whoops excuse me. I mean the waistcoat. How am I doing, brandishing my own kind of courtesy, civility and honour. I'm even practising my aristocratic accent. I say, look here you ruddy bounder, or is it brigade or cad or you low form of lowlife you. Or, damn it sir, you spiv, the swirling rococo plasterwork culturally screwing up your bloody ceiling is rather pretentious and rather fragrantly over the top. How am I doing, pops. Do I deserve my raise. Pish pother and all that.'

'Iowa, I'd prefer you called me fox. But as you seem to do in whatever you do, you're doing fine. And you more than deserve your raise. But the word I think you mean is "flagrantly". And the previous word you might mean is "brigand", not "brigade". Also just one or two usages may be slightly out of date. The word "spiv" might be a bit old-fashioned.'

'No wonder the British have something I hear about that they call the season going on over there with everyone prancing around in big hats, talking like they're hot shit, if you'll pardon my French. While we're talking and drinking champagne, let's get into the chocolate cake I brought you to have with tea. You see, I anticipated. You've got all the stuff there.'

He watched in amazement her elegant skilful pair of hands. Pushing back the sleeves of her cashmere sweater. A bracelet falling down on her slender wrist. He got hungrier and thirstier filling the champagne glasses as he watched her taking the cake out of its box. Her eye spotting the other tea ingredients as she spoke back over her shoulder. Have you got this. Have you got that. Until there it was. Tea. As she sat back in her chair, swigged her champagne and put in his hand a wedge of chocolate cake and handed over a cup and saucer full of golden tea.

'I guess, pops, a clash of tastes. And maybe making tea rates as being old-fashioned. But I'm learning what is not old-fashioned, my dear chap, is British class distinction, which is built into the English accent and tonal pitch. Keeps up that phoney front that hints at everything they want people to know about them. You don't have to tell everyone you meet in the first sentence how much money you make or have. Although boy, that's exactly what the English want to know and pretend they don't. Out west social life is a bit more basic. It's how many steers you've got kicking up dust in the distance or how many tons of grain do your silos hold.'

'And provided, Iowa, that such assets are not mortgaged.'

'Touché, pops. Now that's what I'm trying to get. That accent that comes out of the arrangement of the words. God, what a snobbish conversation we're having. Down with the lower class. Further up and higher with the upper class. Fox, I like it.'

'One day, Iowa, at the height of the London season, maybe you would also like to take tea at Fortnum & Mason. And in pleasant addition might like to be seen smoking a cheroot and sipping champagne on a banquette in the foyer of Claridge's while the Hungarian ensemble serenade you with "The Teddy Bears' Picnic" or your own favourite piece of music.'

'Hey, really. I'd like that. No kidding. Just like what seems is going on here. Because when I followed you to discover where you went on your long walks and saw you go into this ramshackle building, I thought this is where the guy cooks the books.'

'Let me meanwhile fill up your glass. And get back to the London season. You could also then attend Ascot racing and Henley rowing wearing a big hat. Then Wimbledon for tennis. Who knows, if you like, one day perhaps I could perhaps even take you there.'

'That's one perhaps after another. But what an utterly ripping suggestion.'

'Yes, ripping is the word. Then perhaps there's no perhaps. Nor am I kidding.'

'Hey, fox. You're married.'

'Happily married people travel.'

'Not without a psychological ball and chain around at least one of their ankles.'

'The pleasant company one finds oneself in helps you carry it.'

'Fox, are you propositioning me. OK don't answer that. I'm not complaining. Here, have another piece of cake. And this goes down in my book as the longest, most revealing talk we've ever had. And so I'm getting I guess a huge salary raise, can even quit my once-a-week cocktail waitressing at night and buy a car. And now before I skedaddle to my acting class, I think that with another bit of British usage, it's time after my two cups of tea I request to use your loo, my dear chap.'

And so arrived the moment of her presence he most dreaded. As she stepped around the piles of newspapers, hoping she wouldn't bump into and crash one of the teetering stacks to the floor. And for her to see, instead of his being a country squire, the dreary chaos in the most private area of his life. This unpredictable human being having right now, even as he treads on dangerous ground, become a predictable pleasure in his daily existence. And planning that she should be there more and more. Able to watch her close up in all her beauty. Not least of which were her remarks. Her demolition of sanctimony.

'Pops, this is bedlam in here. I know my shower curtain falls down if you turn on the lights in my bathroom, but crumb buns, you've got tiles hanging loose off the wall. And less said about your taste in towels the better. And you have all the travel reminders stuck up on the back of the door of the dates to go to London, Paris and Milan. But it's what I like about you. All so casual without pretence.'

'Thank you.'

'You're welcome. I maybe mean you're not a real snob. But maybe you're just a little bit pretentious. Ah, but you're a real gentleman. God, haven't I got a nerve. Giving you backhanded insults followed by compliments. Anyway, allow me a week or two and I could clean up the place. Get the cobwebs off your old air-conditioner. Wipe the dust off that portrait of George Washington on the wall. And hey, this book. I like this. *Life in the English Country House*. With the picture of these people on the cover sitting under a temple.'

'I'm looking for inspiration. When one doesn't want to hear of the outside world anymore, one thinks of building a big mausoleum to be interred in.'

'Does one then think of sculpting a pair of bloomers and a brassiere over the bronze door.'

'Well, why not, Iowa. Why not. Make a mockery of my life.'

'OK why not. But you don't, according to little old me, deserve it. And while we're on an emotional subject, like what do people do in their secret spare time; do you want to know how I found you here. You'd just gone around a corner on to Broadway and I followed you because of that yellow rose you gave me. Are you more shocked than surprised.'

'Surprised. Knowing that you have a lot of better things to do.'

'Well, I really did. But couldn't resist seeing where you were going on one of those sudden mysterious afternoon disappearances of yours. First time I followed you a block. Then two blocks.

You seemed like some little lost person wondering where to go. But then I thought, aha, a few more blocks and that's where he's shacked up with the bimbo. And she of course attired head to toe in Nathan Johnson lingerie. Hey no, don't look alarmed. Sorry, pops, it's the champagne talking. You're a nice married guy. I didn't really follow you. Yes I did. All the way to the Flatiron Building. Then you turned the corner and then halfway down the street I saw you disappear into this building. I knew no bimbo worth her bazumas and in her right financial mind was going to park herself anywhere like here.'

'I beg your pardon.'

'Pardon my aspersion. I mean a girl needs a little glamour. But then came the really big mystery. Next time when I got another attack of curiosity and took the afternoon off and followed you, you just kept going. I thought, now this is really where we find the bimbo. But then you walked way past the Flatiron Building. Block after block nonstop downtown. I got an attack of conscience. No, I'll be honest. I got tired. I stopped following. I decided I had to be satisfied to just keep wondering where you were going when you disappeared. I'm just a curious girl. That's all.'

'Iowa, I'm devastatingly flattered you'd follow me. But I was in fact probably only going for a ride on the Staten Island Ferry. And I walk there.'

'Sixty or maybe seventy blocks all the way down Broadway.'

'Yes, if I'm finding things really bleak, that's what I do. And I occasionally take a bus or a taxi if I want to get there in a hurry.'

'I never knew you ever got so bleak to take a ferry ride. Here, let me pour the bottle and have some more tea and another slice of lemon in your cup.'

'Just the champagne, please.'

'A ferry ride. Fox, I'm going to cry.'

'You look back at a disappearing New York skyline, where all day you've been fighting the greedy, the chisellers and cheats in a sea of turpitude. And as you step off onto Staten Island, a different land, and not even leave the pier, you feel strangely you have left all your bleakness behind.'

'Gosh.'

'But it's on the ferry's return journey that something really happens. Even though you're returning to the tip of Manhattan you've only just left, it's like setting off to approach a new world, across a sea towards its buildings rising triumphant in the sky that now inspires you. In the breeze you stand there on the ferry's bow. The island of Manhattan gets nearer. There it is. The city that sits on top of the world. Towers soaring. Then as your troubles seep back into your mind, you can, by just holding up the palm of your hand in front of your eyes, blot it all away. Into a sort of insignificance. Until of course the ferry is again squealing along the greasy pilings. The clank of chains and gates opening. Reminding you that you have arrived back where these massive buildings, which rear into the sky, have also stuck their foundations down deep into the bedrock of Manhattan Island. Where once the Indians roamed, hunting deer with bows and arrows, sitting round a campfire over roasting legs of venison. Makes you think to yourself that maybe all you need to survive is a bow and arrow.'

'Oh pops, that's lovely, the impression you paint of New York. I've heard people try to say impressive things about this city but it's always been a statistic recited to make you feel you're just a hayseed. And never anything that reminds you that New York can be really beautiful and was once ancient and old like a forest.'

'At the moment, over the rim of a glass of champagne, such sedate ceremony does sentimentalize the mind. But in fact I may have on a few occasions said less beautiful things about New York.'

'Can I say something that I really mean? It sort of seems now I've only just met you. That no matter what happens to us as we go our separate ways in life, which might even happen in the next month or two, I want to always know you. And I'm sorry. I didn't mean to pry into your private life like this. My curiosity and my need for a raise sort of got the better of me. I guess if you just hadn't got mixed up in lingerie you'd have been a poet.'

'More likely a bank robber. But I wouldn't have been that bad with a bow and arrow. Way up in the Adirondacks we hunted as kids in the woods. Anyway, it doesn't take too long to be reminded that maybe it's time to go for a ride on the ferry again.'

'And you know, pops, now I can go back to my apartment to do my sit-ups, practise my phonetics, cook my spinach and broccoli and while eating not have to wonder where the fuck that Nathan guy is really going. But hey, would you mind. No you wouldn't, would you. But maybe your wife would.'

'Mind what.'

'If I went once with you. On the ferry.'

'I wouldn't mind. I'd much enjoy it.'

'But I wouldn't want to impose on your bleakness.'

'I can't think of anything more wonderful than your coming with me.'

'Now you've got tears in your eyes. Does that mean I won't have to wait too long till you all get bleak again? I'm feeling a little tipsy on this champagne.'

'Happily there's more from where that came from. Top you up.'

'And fox, what I haven't told you. No. Maybe it's too private. I won't tell you. But I promise I would never make you be bleak. And you know, here's a funny thing I will tell you. What I would like is for you to take me for granted. And I'd like you to take it as a compliment. Like I was just some kind of baggage hanging around in your life that you just took along. Now I've said too much.'

Iowa suddenly jumps up. Swallows her wine and puts her tea-cup back on her saucer.

'Iowa, don't go. Fill your glass. This bottle is not quite as chilled as it should be.'

'I sometimes do really get scared, pops. Of what may happen to me when none of these things I dream of will ever come true.'

'Iowa, they'll happen.'

'Sometimes makes me feel I'm on a wagon train like my ancestors. Heading west. Bundles of sagebrush blowing across the prairie. Rocking chairs on the porch. If you had a porch. Rattlesnakes hissing under it. Quarter Horses out in the corral. Like me sometimes, they can gallop from a standing start. They have a cow sense. Helps you rope a steer. Pick-up trucks parked in the yard. It's all just territory I return to in my dreams. Like a history book describing Abraham Lincoln with his axe building rail fences. And now. I'm here and it's now. The world. Bio and cyber error and terror along with a fatal venereal disease coming down the pike. Or when a massive asteroid hits us. The winter of winters descending. Back to the primordial slime. But then why not let us be more cheerful than careful. No matter whatever else or other life there may be out in the cosmos, and so long as women are around, nothing will outlast lingerie.'

'Iowa, you are a constant mystifying surprise. You can ride a horse.'

'I reckon so, pardner. From the age of about three. Oh god, pops. These premonitions come flying into my brain. I'd hate to ever have to go to your funeral. Whoops. Hey, what am I saying. I mean what I'm saying is, I don't want you to die. Like suddenly drop dead. In a stress death. Like so many guys not even in their prime yet are doing. I mean you're older, but not that old. I better shut up before I begin to sound even more foolish. And please. One day soon take me on the ferry. Now, look at the time. Missed my acting class by a mile. But gee, this is the nicest conversation I've ever had with you. And thank you again for my raise.'

Iowa lunged forward. Throwing her arms around him. Her moist soft lips landing full on his mouth. Just as she had once before kissed him on the cheek. Embraced by her arms he now found his hands sinking into the unbelievably pliable flesh of her buttocks. With a whisper. She gently pushed his hand down and away. But he knew that if he'd kept his hand there she might relent. Especially as he was dreaming of taking her, months hence, on the Venice–Simplon Orient Express. And even applying for their admission to the Royal Enclosure at Ascot. Dreams ending with her smile back over her shoulder as the door of this, his sanctum, closed. She saw his sadness. Her words struck home.

'Bleak heart, don't be bleak.'

But bleak he was. Left where he had at last now shared this scruffy sanctum with somebody he wanted never to leave. And by the creaking sounds of the freight elevator, she was gone. Abandoning him to the loneliest loneliness.

SIX

ALL THE legal matters for Blueberry Hill were complete. Hal said he could find an employee or two. Could find a maid, and even a butler was a possibility. Then a major computer catastrophe in the uptown office. He lost sight of Iowa. Missing her when another new store opened in Philadelphia and Iowa was enlisted to drum up publicity. Which she did in any number of newspapers in a few semi-clad full-length photographs. And her face on a magazine cover. But just her staying away three days seemed like a century. Especially when, on her return to New York, he did not see her for a further four days. Rumour of her getting a part in an off-Broadway play. Haunted too now by the vision of her running off with one of her pursuing boyfriends. Or that she'd quit. And there was no kidding about it. A snippet of gossip about something like a palace being built for her out in the jungle some-where in Mexico.

Ensconced in gloom he had to say to himself more than a few times, 'Bleak heart don't be bleak.' But then when it seemed an eternity later and he least expected it, footsteps came on the stairs. Stopped outside his secret office door. A gentle knock. He almost dare not open it. He'd even thought of giving her a key. But there she was about to give the door a kick. Her face flushed, catching her breath. Pushing past him. Her arms stacked full. Electric kettle, teapot, cups, saucers, spoons, dishes. Even a wrench. A cake. Unloading the lot on his desk.

'Sorry pops, for barging in like this. The elevator was stuck so I had to climb the stairs. It's nearly four o'clock. When you weren't around uptown I thought, Hey, what's that old guy doing. Isn't it time we had tea again. Brought a wrench to fix your dripping faucet. That kind of sound is ticking away your life. And you know I sort of missed walking past that old Flatiron Building. And my sincere apologies for being absent without leave. Hope you didn't mind. And only missed me. I had to go to Mexico. So I hope while I was gone not too many Nathan Johnson brassieres have been giving customers cross-eyed nipples.'

Christ almighty, what right did he have to mind? She could get her fees raised ten times on any catwalk in the world she chose to saunter along. Even if she'd gone to live in a spacesuit on the moon. But here she was. Again the unbelievable. In the flesh. Ready to have tea. But then at the same time gently rejecting his overture of an attempt to kiss her on the lips, reducing it to a peck on each cheek. She heated the pot before putting the tea leaves in. Pouring the water from the kettle just before it came to the boil.

'Hey Mr Nathan Johnson, old fox, first let me say you've cleaned this place up a bit. And by the way, there's something funny there about your door, pops. The clink and clank.'

[65]

'Yes, there is. It's heavy bulletproof steel made to look like wood and open up like a door.'

Nevertheless, before her amiable conversation would detour his attention, she also at the same time led him on a little bit. Fluttering her eyelids as she poured tea and concocted more crazy ideas. The contrast to Muriel with her aloofly selfish day chockfull of appointments and hours on the telephone. And it was amazing how fast after a few words in his secret lair, Iowa could, as it pleased her, forget that he was married. Alluding to a togetherness they might explore across the world.

Some big change had come in her life. Just as one even bigger change seemed ready to dawn in his. She also had other ambitions and long-term plans. To mix among the sophisticated classes. Plus didn't mind searching around for further stuff to look at in his office hideout. He had yet to discover Iowa's racial origin except that such a girl so different was bound to combine all the best things in women that he had ever known. With just an associational part of her lineage being revealed. 'The only little distinction I can find in my background is an ancestor who was a pall-bearer at Ludwig van Beethoven's funeral.'

He told her this news was wonderful and she reached out to touch him on the knee. This girl as slender as silk, who seemed strong as steel. She liked being nice to you and to see you having a good time. But when as a joke he asked her more questions about the Indian porridge and said that maybe she could cook some for him in her apartment, it was the first time that a fear overcame her face. That he was married and she wished he wasn't, but as he was, she wasn't going to help him cheat on his wife. 'My character as a person doesn't allow it.'

Nor it seemed, according to her lecture, could he have anything to do with her sexually because, despite her risqué chatter, her gratification depended upon lifelong true love. And he in turn told her that she thought exactly as he did. Their conversation descending into the profoundly banal. Believing in eternal devotion to one's spouse. And then she bent over double laughing.

'Jesus, I should be crying. Our lives in a whirlwind changing fast. And I have exactly two options rearing their troubled heads in front of me. If I stick to my principles and wait to marry the spouse I love and he is unfaithful, what's going to happen to me. If I tell him to fuck off, I may never have faith in or meet anybody else. Then without children I grow old as my spirit moans, please give me another chance. In lonely death get dumped in the grave and ravaged by worms. Or like a dead steer on the prairie eaten by the buzzards. Maybe that's why it's better to die young and get scorched to ashes in the incinerator. Somebody just sweeps or lets the wind blow the dust and memory of you away.'

He was tempted to tell her that with all her beauty and her vitality, it would always give her a life that would keep the grave far, far away. Indeed only a sentence later she was saying she really loved her new car and only wished now she could find somewhere cheap and safe to park it other than on the street. Plus, although she never saw his apartment, she wanted someday to live somewhere way up high the way he did in Midas Towers. Or failing that, on Fifth Avenue between 60th and 69th Streets where she could, in a hop skip, and jump, jog in Central Park.

The time Iowa spent with him now always seemed swifter gone. He felt he knew for certain that the option was the palace in Mexico and needless to say the guy would be at least pretending he was rich. Of course Iowa with her feelings about space and the outdoors would go out of her mind if she knew he not only enjoyed living high up in the sky but was now one of the landed gentry. With his own palace up in Westchester County. A palace in a paradise with a garage for eleven cars. And day was dawning. Soon, soon. Muriel. Her birthday. And how to persuade her to take a drive into Westchester? But here and now with Iowa and maybe to see much less if not no more of her he suddenly asked her, with her faraway expression, what was she thinking about. And a smile appeared on her face.

'Pops, I'm thinking about crabgrass. And that I hoped it was there still growing on those bastards' lawn who with a shotgun blew up my dog Gesundheit. And I'm glad to think of what the decumbent stems of the crabgrass must still be doing to their lawn. Infests everything. And those bastards sprayed dangerous poisons all over the place to kill the grass and then shot and killed Gesundheit just for crapping on it. And pops, before I go, let me say something personal to you, OK.'

'OK.'

'You know when you think no one's looking at you, your face can seem harassed and a little haunted. But when I see you, I'd think that's just the way I feel sometimes, wanting to be a great actress.'

The things she could say to you. And she did fix his dripping tap. Tidied newspapers. Puffed up the pillows on his chair. But he knew as his life was moving to Westchester that something serious also was happening in her life. And he was totally tolerant of her ambitions to become a movie star and great actress. But he worried. What if she only became a starlet? And if she totally failed she could come back and he could at least raise her salary yet again.

SEVEN

THE DAYS were now flying by rapidly in anticipation. Blueberry Hill to be taken full possession of. Even the thought of bringing Iowa just to stand on the terraces and view the woods as far as the eye could see. He wanted to ask her as they sipped their lapsang souchong behind his bulletproof steel door as to how many more toilet bowls and shower stalls than three did she want if the sky was the limit. In his own life in Midas Towers, where he rated four toilet bowls, he had along with Blueberry Hill reached a crest not even yet socially registered. Plus if he were unfortunate enough to meet someone with sixteen or seventeen toilet bowls, he could then tabulate in his score his extra four in Midas Towers. And the one in his private secret office, decrepit seat and all.

Iowa, taking yet another leave of absence, again on a trip to Mexico. But his new country home. He drove up yet again just to wander in the woods. Newt, from whom he'd borrowed snake boots, advised that if taking the previous owner's wolfhounds for a walk he got lost, to say to the wolfhounds, 'Go home.' And then follow them. He did get lost and did say 'Go home' and did follow the wolfhounds back. Indifferent dogs. Making it a long goddamn walk through every kind of terrain. Including that favoured by snakes. But he made use of delays, stopping on the way where he thought vistas could be bulldozed. Right through the rocky outcroppings in the woods. Extend an old, seemingly disused bridle path. Find places to frame a distant statue or a stone edifice. But as anxious as he was to reveal and discuss his intending landscape triumphs, he still had to keep these schemes from Muriel tightly under his hat.

And when he was back in the city, lying next to his beloved, having just jumped on her, he remembered in his pre-Blueberry Hill days not that long ago when he'd wander along Madison Avenue and realize that he was getting increasingly rich, thinking it was time to let a few of his competitive pals know, by maybe buying a farm and a horse or two, out in the sylvan beauty of New Jersey where super celebrities were rumoured to foxhunt. In fact it said so in newspapers and magazines. And strolling on this fancy midtown avenue he would stop to stare in the window of an elegant little store where they sold foxhunting and horse-riding artefacts. He would stand there in front of the store window trying to work up his nerve to go in and start buying whips, boots, jodhpurs, but far too shy to be discovered as merely a novice who didn't yet really know what a pastern or a stock was and whose riding was confined to Central Park. Or worse, as he discussed the flexibility of whips, they could end up thinking he was a sadist and enquire of him, 'For hunting, sir, or are you intending for domestic use.'

'Nathan, you haven't said a word in the last twenty minutes.'

'Well, honey I was thinking why don't you tomorrow just go over and mosey around Tiffany's. Buy something nice you might need for yourself.'

'What do I need.'

'Come on, a few trinkets. I don't want to sound crass, but jewellery tells the world and shows everybody just how much a guy thinks of a woman and how much she is worth to her husband.'

'Am I worth a lot to you, Nathan?'

'You bet. You're every bit as beautiful as when I first met you. You and the kids, you're my whole world. It's what I do everything for. Everything I have is yours. I arranged that both you and the kids own eighty-five percent of everything in the business. All in your individual names. I'm organizing another five percent to be added. Like this apartment one hundred percent is in your name. And you know honey, I've just kind of been thinking that maybe our life hasn't been all that bad. You know, the struggle. When I was selling lingerie out of a cardboard box. When we lived over there on the worst side of the West Side, just married in our very first apartment all cramped up in two back rooms breathing other people's smells, and cigarette smoke seeping through the walls. Listening to their lousy music, arguments and coughs and staring out the window into somebody else's two back rooms. Us with only half a kitchen and one bathroom where there wasn't even enough room to take a crap. But just room enough for maybe a couple of thousand cockroaches.'

'Nathan, please shut up.'

'I was just also thinking should we get dressed and go out somewhere for dinner. Like to La Grenouille. To give it its phonetic meaning, the great yes.'

'I don't mind going out to dinner, but please don't ruin my appetite by bringing up that apartment.'

And as he was taking on his next new giant status step upwards in his life it felt good to remember the tougher old days without ceramic pots to piss in and to count up the fifteen he had. Plus now as he and Muriel lay luxuriating in each other's company, stretched out and nearly asleep in bed, the city's sounds muted below, he could enjoy his reverie, ignoring the red light for a ringing phone which was flashing on the bedside table. In his present state of languish, why the fuck be distracted from bliss by a telephone? Just do as you're doing. Nothing. Except waiting till the flashing stops. Or do as you intend doing, laying a loving hand on your wife. Till, holy cow, it seems now like an eternity has passed with the phone light continuing to blink.

'Gee honey I'll just slip into my den to take this call. Someone's in a real persistent mood.'

'Well if it's one of the kids, they've already had this month's allowance, plus next month's, and I'm going to go to sleep.'

It reminded him of being out in distant towns visiting a store and then coming back to his hotel at night and it always lifted the loneliness a little and made missing Muriel less if he found the message-light flashing. But Muriel was safely next to him, and as she did when she was fucked, she turned on her side and was already, with eyes shut and fists clenched and breathing deep, fast asleep. Must be now a full two minutes and the telephone light is still flashing. And maybe something has happened to one of the kids. Get to the den. This hall still needs a few pictures on the wall. A Charles Addams or an Edward Gorey or two. Whose each drawn line touched on the sombreness as well as whimsicality of

[71]

life. And still through his mind, even in his naked embrace with his wife, ran the visions of Iowa. Where was she at that moment? What was she doing? As he now sat down in his creaking leather chair. And picked up the phone and let the outside world get back in to disturb the idyllic peace. To hear a voice known well. For mostly nuisance news.

'Mr Johnson, this is Jerry in Queens. We got a problem here. We've just arrived about ten minutes ago at the store. We called an ambulance and the police and they are on their way.'

'What's wrong.'

'It's Mr Goodwin. We found him. Hanging.'

As you sit up, catch your breath. It feels like a Mack truck slamming into your chest. To instantly know, without being told, what it was all about. Embezzlement. The inventory team. Three fast-counting guys. Descending. Goodwin was the manager of Nathan's biggest outlet, which included another opened a few miles away. Both stores were doing boffo business in what he always felt were desolate spots off the main drag of Queens Boulevard. And now his mind, trying to obliterate that word, hanging, and he was holding his breath against this news of death. He had never bothered to acquaint Muriel with all the apartment houses in Queens, where plenty of happy lingerie customers populated these townships. With their bucolic names, Sunnyside, Woodside, Kew Gardens, Forest Hills. Goodwin lived elsewhere in Flatbush, in Brooklyn. And these places had to have some kind of vibrant life. Where people weren't hanging themselves.

'Mr Johnson. Are you there.'

'Yeah, Jerry, I'm here.'

'We were counting the sleepwear garments and found him tied by his neck with thongs from one of the racks. He's been taken to Queens Hospital. And no doubt the morgue. It looks like it's going to be bad news in the books. I'll try the best I can to take care of everything. But Mr Johnson, maybe I don't want to do this job anymore. In fact when this gets wrapped up, I'm quitting. Ted and Jim know a good guy who'll take my place. Hell, I can't go on with this. I'm sorry.'

The fourth embezzlement in nine months. The first two in Dayton, Ohio. The third in Cincinnati where Mr Goodwin was manager a year ago and where the present manager had already been charged by the police and fled to Mexico. Seems a country that attracts a lot of people. But it was almost as if he'd prefer the losses, provided they weren't too great and built into over-heads, to be treated as petty pilfering. For if there was anything he disliked, it was sneaking in at night to take surprise inventories. But even though it was a part of the business he detested, he knew that what Reginald said was true.

'Nathan, human nature being what it is, you can never eradi-cate fraud, which sadly inspires some of the best brains to invent ever more cunning methods to cheat. Even people you invite to dinner might disappear with a fancy ashtray.'

It also meant always checking up on even the most trusted employee, usually the manager. Especially the ones who seemed to enjoy their work most. But who somehow also personally felt they were doing all the drudgery, grind and hustle, while the boss was sizing up all the tits and asses of the models. With all the money flowing by, why shouldn't they be grabbing a bit more than they got in their pay cheque? The ingenious schemes took time to track down, maybe a month or two going by, until his three-man team descended without warning to tabulate the stock through the night till dawn. The guilty, at least, were never sure when they might be caught. And the causes of the problem always seemed similar. First and foremost a woman. Or as the Brits so aptly say, a bit of fluff. With more than a bit of cleavage. Then more expensive cars and apartments. Sometimes gambling came into it. And even cosmetic surgery. But not everybody hanged themselves. Whenever he felt taking an inventory was not worth the human misery it sometimes brought, he was again always corrected by Reginald.

'Nathan, as we know, lingerie is a dream business for theft. No trouble to walk out the door of a store twice a day with a thousand dollars' worth of lingerie shoved up under the armpits. With the flimsiness of some garments, how are you going to tell a girl is wearing five pairs of something. And if you're going to be forgiving and kind to the guys and girls in the families of the guys and girls who gypped you, you're going to need to take inventories more than ever. But we won't go so far as to say it was a sad day when these delicate rayon, nylon and gossamer fabrics were invented.'

And in the deep silence of thinking about inventories, he had also been thinking how good life was. All could be ruined, though. The joy ahead of giving your wife a present on her birthday she'll never forget. That both of you had sort of climbed up to Parnassus, and holy cow, so high that he could now think of himself as a squire in the most wondrous dream of all. Over which he would rule. A Garden of Eden. Then why in the very middle of joy, do you get handed a death? That could start an avalanche of disaster. Needing again so soon to gird your loins and fight. Weathering these traumas brought by life. First lesson he learned was it was best to get out under the sky. Go somewhere on your own two feet. As he'd done in past desperations. Walk it off. Mile by mile on the street. But don't get mugged. See thousands of other passing living anonymous beings whose faces hide worse sorrows and worries than your own. But first. Tonight. Get back to the bedroom. Drapes drawn. Muriel, turning over and suddenly awake out of what he thought was her post-fucking deep sleep, was going to ask questions.

'A little problem cropped up over a deal in Queens.'

'For a little problem, you sound pretty tense.'

'Sometimes too many little problems happen all at once. And all over the place. Hey, you don't have to turn on the light.'

'Why? What's wrong? Nathan, you look white as a sheet. Do you feel all right? Has something happened?'

'I'm all right. I guess feeling so good I suddenly felt maybe it was time something was going to go wrong. Always a worry these new locations because they take you away from other things you've got to watch.'

'Well, I'll be glad to go up to look so you don't have to.'

'If you want to. But maybe we could leave it till the end of next week. Then we'll both go. Your birthday. Sure, you come up with me and we'll look together. Then have a wonderful birthday dinner in a great inn up there. But right now I've got an urgent meeting.'

'With whom?'

'Honey, I got a lot on my mind. I'll tell you about it when I get back.'

Amazing how women pick up on things and then suggest for the first time to go somewhere on business with you. And on his mind was bad publicity. Which if it came, could make front-page news all over Queens and Brooklyn from Jackson Heights to Canarsie. And if that could be avoided at least Muriel would never find out. Keeping things from her was always a wise precaution because she could go ape hysterical and it was, as she railed at you, like claws tearing out your guts and leaving you feeling like an abandoned husk that the simplest breeze could waft away out to no man's land where the haunting echo of your voice could be heard crying, 'Help me. Help me.'

As he groped for clothes to wear, any thoughts about anything were better than those of suicide and now an inevitable funeral. Concentrate the mind on an improved degree of safety and those wolfhounds at Blueberry Hill going for the throat of some hoodlum rapist or pillager. A hound could end up being more friendly to you than a wife. Especially after his recent dreams in which a bloody polo mallet or smoking gun were held in a wife's hands.

[75]

'Nathan, do me a favour. If it's late, sleep in one of the guest rooms when you get back.'

'Sure thing, Muriel.'

On his way down in the Midas Towers elevator, he was glad that life had dealt him a decent card in marriage. But to continue being a wonderful husband it was essential to keep everything quiet, especially with Muriel. She should not know about Blueberry Hill or the suicide. She met Mr Goodwin once and said what a nice man he was. Nor should he mention a whole gang of pony-sized Irish wolfhounds that could start growling at potentially traitorous visitors like Muriel's relatives could be. Especially her sister. The kind who sue you because a big hound licks their hand and the fear of being bitten causes them acute mental anguish. While you wouldn't mind seeing a hound bite one of their asses off.

It was never easy to sit chewing your own piece of steak when you thought one of Muriel's relatives was going to choke on theirs and you were going to end up having to face the court awards sought by their lawyers. Maybe you'd start thinking it would have been better to have yourself snuck up on from behind and whacked senseless with a polo mallet and put out of your paranoid misery. And if one was to be honest with oneself, one did not always view Muriel through rose-tinted spectacles. Which she could splatter opaque especially when she once pronounced, 'Hey Nathan, you know, even when I know we're not, I sometimes think with you in the garment business we're full-blown nobodies.'

'Well honey, I'm not glad you said that. But if you know something that can make us full-blown somebodies more than money can, I'm ready to be enlightened.'

Strange the thoughts you get descending to the lobby of Midas Towers, where you know the Irish kibitzers are always waiting ready to kibitz. Although he was a fucking awful philosopher, his answer to Muriel kind of quietened her. Somehow she thought that he hadn't quite achieved the big time. Like her receiving invitations to exclusive New York charity dinners. But now with the present catastrophe of suicide, he would have been perhaps better off staying in his abode, retreating to his den to pour himself a drink and stare out over the city where the citizens still scurried down below. But even descending on this luxurious elevator or sitting back up there sipping a tumbler of Armagnac, his past little miseries and struggles would come back to haunt him and justify catching someone in one of his stores committing criminal behaviour. How in their early cockroach days, when he was still selling lingerie out of a cardboard box, he remembered the time he came home to Muriel with a black eye. 'Where did you get that, Nathan?'

He got that black eye being shooed and shoved off a porch and chased down the street by a nightclub-bouncer husband shouting, 'Pervert!' The wife ready to buy a thong when the big hulking bouncer, wearing yellow braces over a red silk shirt, appeared from out of nowhere. He seemed like an outright pervert himself, was so incensed he socked Nathan. In the left eye. And then, growling like a monster possessed, jumped forward to take another swing and stepped on a kid's toy, a squawking duck with wheels. His feet sailed upwards and he crashed on his ass, toppling down his front steps. The desperate thing was, Nathan was on the verge of a sale, the first in two days.

Nathan headed like a bat out of hell for his car. Then, returning to the miserable little apartment, the children either sick or crying, he wondered whether he could ever work up his nerve enough again to get his face slapped, or a fist in the eye. Worrying even more about making the next dime and noticing the hair beginning to grow sparse above his temples and a fleck or two of grey around the ears. Or worse, get arrested as he once was by the police. To hear Muriel threaten him just at the moment he was about to put his hands up to his face and sob out the words that he

[77]

couldn't take it anymore. And he did sob out the words and put his hands up to his face. 'You better take it, buster, and get back out there and get somewhere in this world or else I'm going to leave you.'

And here he was crossing this elegantly expensive lobby of Midas Towers where the kibitzers were dancing their total attendance on the dowager who lived above him. She had an ancestor involved with the Comstock Lode, the largest precious-ore find in history. And Nathan, amid luxury, felt again as if he were in the midst of the desperate doldrums of the past. Knowing your wife could any second hire a cut-price lawyer out of the ten thousand available in the Manhattan *Yellow Pages* and with a divorce slam you into eternal bankruptcy. Amazing how even after the cleansing feel of success and freedom from debt in your life, the reality of utter despair can still come back so strong.

So much for being out on the road selling. And now here he was back on the street. With tyres squealing, police racing by. Bus engines with their low growl of smooth power. As he sidestepped through the crowds. Past the windows of some of the most glamorous stores in the world. So rich they don't have to have the lurking worry about who's going to embezzle and hang themselves or jump out a window. Just when you thought you had reached a time when you were going through life nice and easy. Shock and surprise. And still looming up in one's mind, Iowa. How dare he want to talk to her. Further transgressing upon their employer–employee relationship for the comfort he could take from her dizzy remarks. 'Life is like always reaching for something stuck in a tight spot, pops, and the more you reach to pull it out, the further you push it in tighter.'

He entered a bar. The sort of joint he'd never go into. Even if thirsty for a glass of water. Bartender didn't know what Armagnac was and then had to look everywhere for it. He'd passed the bar a hundred times before with the distinct feeling that it was to be avoided but it held a fascination for that very reason. Maybe because it was a suitable joint to be in when a bombshell drops into your life, explodes and breaks your head. When only hours ago, you were sitting on top of the world purring in pleasure and prosperity. Goodwin. What a name for a catastrophe. Threatening all that you ever worked for and don't want to lose. Bringing back all the ignominy of your struggle. Up from the wrong side of the tracks.

And this memory over his Armagnac was at least buoying up his soul. Reminding the spirit of all the travails it had already tolerated, undergone and overcome. That nothing now should stand in the way of his taking up squirehood. What was surmounting all was someone's death and even though it may have been through dishonesty, three children left fatherless. Yet Goodwin might have also been diligent and worked hard. Becoming a good salesman. So he could, in his later years, have counted on a little luxurious longevity. Just as Nathan had done. Why should he allow himself to be scared shitless? The head of a company with over two hundred employees that any day he chose could go public and sell shares worth many multimillions of dollars. And he could, lotus-eating, keep all that. Provided news of a suicide in the Nathan Johnson empire with a headline like *Hung by Thongs* doesn't get press coverage over at least half the United States.

He knew that no boat sails peacefully in a storm. That an unpredictable wave could swamp your bow. That a whole range of lingerie could be wiped out overnight just by someone else's fashion innovation swiped from Milan or Paris. He also knew what it was like to take inventory. Flying half the country from Cincinnati to Milwaukee to Brooklyn. Finding the cheapest places to stay in America, being bemused by the modest prices and saunas to be found in some of Milwaukee's hotels. Then, with his master keys, secretly arriving at a store three hours after closing. Spending as much time as it would take during the night to count and tabulate stock. Box after box, rack after rack and drawer after drawer. Returning to the hotel exhausted. Sleeping for three hours. Remaining just long enough in a place to count the stock and catch another plane. And there are some doors and drawers you shut behind you in your life, which you don't want ever to reopen. Or think of again. Then you hear someone's voice somewhere. Uttering from the soul. Silently crying, 'Please, please. Give me a break. It's all I ask for.' And it was all he asked for. When once, the first time, Muriel said, 'That's right, buster, you heard me. Get somewhere soon or I'm gone.'

Although her words were meant to be facetious and were said before they had children, it always did, in response to any criticism, stir deep down in his guts. And even now at this moment when he had yet to reveal to her the pinnacle of pinnacles, a veritable palace in paradise. But then you can never forget the reality of someone who could simply leave you in the lurch. Walk out the door. And never thinking twice. Knowing that she could, with her looks, find a millionaire in a hurry at any bar of any fancy hotel. Maybe not a multimillionaire, but at least a car salesman posing to be one and on an expense account. But who could, in those long-ago days, outspend him in an hour and in an amount that he might end up living on for a month. He knew enough now not to rush out to Queens, needing more than anything to be alone in the city that never sleeps and where commerce never stops. Iowa's words sounding in his ear. 'Pops, you never know how people are going to react until the chips are down.'

But time to leave. No rich men in this bar. For sure. Only one drunken woman loudly announcing she used to be in cabaret, till a taxicab broke both her legs. And after spending all the money she got for the injury, she was living on welfare. Nathan bought her a drink. Her spiel enough to make him go out again on the street. Pass among more strangers. Who remind you in their namelessness that even now with your millions of dollars the best person to help you is still yourself and do it pronto while you can. Yet if such a person can be found who would come to your rescue, there is nothing that can fill you more with hope. Just the faint touch of a loving hand laid upon yours in encouragement. The simple pressure of an arm around your shoulder. A whispering against your ear. As once happened long ago in a reassuring haunted interspace in his life. In Atlantic City. When a beautiful hand was laid upon his. When he said, 'I'm not going to be able to say goodbye.'

And her voice said, 'After five days, with another five days to go, our love could last a lifetime, straighten up and fly right. Because I really want it to. And please say you don't mind.'

And for those who might behave thus and tell you so, thank your damn lucky stars. And he did, criss-crossing the nearly deserted side streets and returning to Midas Towers. To sleep the rest of the night away in one of the guest rooms.

EIGHT

WAITING. Scanning the newspapers. And not yet any news of the hanging. Could spread disaster across Westchester before the Johnsons even move there. And the bank call in their loan. But it was bound to come. Forcing Nathan once again to get dressed in his best. A purple silk cravat. Get out. He had a secret reason. Her name was Iowa. Nathan Langriesh Johnson. Get out. No need to look at a watch or a clock in the city that's always alive. Clench your fists again to fight all adversity. Swing your umbrella again. Up and over your head. In the meantime don't bang your head on a cupboard door. Or trip over a chair leg. Or spill a pot of hot coffee in your lap. Take hope and follow that bright spot in the sky, don't shrink back. Be a meteorite and come out of orbit and smash to smithereens all adversity.

Putting one foot in front of the other down the street. Knowing it is the only way to rid the mind of demons. In fact, swing the umbrella around in every fucking way. And speaking of fucking, switch back for a moment to the bright side of life. Muriel is going to get a fucking thrill when she gets a load of Blueberry Hill. Feeling better even as he descended in the elevator of Midas Towers. Without the Comstock lady and her chihuahua, to whom you have to nod or maybe even talk to. What's it like now for Goodwin's widowed wife, whom he'd met twice and to whom a visit had to be paid and who wasn't that bad to look at? A sad situation with three children. But he was reassured stepping out to a welcoming warmth of the lobby.

'Mr Johnson. Nobody rang down, but do you want your car brought around?'

'No, just going for a walk.'

And it was amazing. The unseasonable weather. But now on the street, how the chill was so welcome. The difference to come back from the rolling wooded hills of the countryside into the city and have hundreds of cars going by in every direction. Plus any human fumes, faint as they may be. Feeling for nearly the first time he could remember wanting to be away and out of New York. Yet having to remind himself that the only cure he had ever known for depression, when suddenly nothing seemed right after something had descended drastically wrong and even seemed worse than when everything had been going perfect, was just to walk these streets again and again.

Now raindrops began to fall, big ones. Triumphantly he put up the umbrella, useful one day in a month. Then to the telephone at the corner. Call Iowa. Something he'd never done before with one of his models. Having to drum up courage. Especially to call a magic human being.

And no wonder he was stage-struck at a public telephone scared of tapping out Iowa's number. One two one two seven six two three four eight seven. Which could produce the miracle of the voice he so much wanted to hear again. Tempted to say that he was desperately delighted her tits had triumphed. Her honesty, always refreshing, could sometimes be frightening. But ding-a-ling. No answer on her phone. Be suddenly grateful that she wasn't home because having the excuse to tell her of the suicide and if invited, he would have compromised his marriage and gone to her apartment. Down that street he'd made familiar.

Walk on. Hang on to your courage at all costs. He reached a cross-town street where they sell gems and jewellery. Black hats and beards. You know they're carrying a million or more dollars in diamonds wrapped in cotton wool or a handkerchief to bring to or from Antwerp. A crowd ahead out on the roadway. Confront someone else's problem to make you forget awhile your own. Voices shouting as they surround a tow truck ready to lift up an illegally parked car and take it away. Inside the car, clinging with both hands on the steering wheel, a boy, refusing to get out, tears streaming down his face. And a diamond merchant on the side-walk offers an explanation.

'See that. You think they'd take away these big limozines that park and wait all over the place for criminals. But no, he's just a kid in an old junker. No money to pay a fine and get his car back if it's towed away. Poor kid, he was on his way to drive to Bayonne, New Jersey, to take his girlfriend out. So what do these towaway guys do. They ignore the limozine of the criminals and they take this poor kid's car. It's a fucking disgrace, I call it.'

The crowd closing in. The tow-truck operator shoved and pushed. Shouting to the driver in the tow truck to call the cops. Someone grabbing the winch. The tow-truck driver looking out at the crowd. And then suddenly nodding assent, yelling, 'OK, OK, for Chrissakes.' He jumps out, releasing the boy's car. Members of the assemblage holding back passing traffic. Windows opened now both sides of the street. Clapping and cheering up in the gallery. Nathan shouting 'Bravo.' People in doorways raising fists in victory. A standing ovation from the entire street. Like curtain calls to a great ballerina. Even Police Lieutenant Gallagher witnessing it all. Smiling his approval. The crowd now helping to stop traffic and making way for the kid raising his hand in thanks, as he pulls out on the road and disappears in a polluting cloud of exhaust. And the diamond merchant on the sidewalk turns to Nathan, now with tears in his eyes.

'He's fast on his way to Bayonne. You know, the great city of New York has a parable for you around every street corner. Once in a while something happens that you got to thank god that this is America where you can praise the human spirit.'

Nathan Johnson picking up his footsteps, passing onwards through this teeming city. An incident of justice and fairness. Which can change everything and let the heart be brazen again. Eased of its sense of doom. Brought courage back into his veins. But then also brought even more trepidation at the thought of when he finally reveals to Muriel that Blueberry Hill cost borrowed millions. And then a strange desire to telephone Iowa again. She might have gone out to the store. Walk and wait awhile and think of Iowa. A conversation with her replays in Nathan's mind. He told Iowa of his hardships and dilemmas. She in turn told of her own sadnesses, in her short disjointed revelations, tears welling in her eyes.

'Hey, pops, did I ever tell you, no I didn't tell you. That I was so broke I had to sell my blood to feed my dog Gesundheit. It was just before they blew him up. So I know what it's like to be truly down when your most precious principles are finally at stake. But if they ever come along threatening to arrest you for being engaged in vice, lingerie is just about the best bribe to give a married policeman, or even an unmarried one. But it's people like you who set a good example. And how you let people know that is by your nice manners and tailoring. By the way, those guys Janáček and Tolstoy knew what they were talking about when they referred to love and life.'

What strange words to hear. That's what she would do. Cover centuries and subjects with just a smattering of words. And he'd have to look it all up in the encyclopaedia. Made one wonder just how much Iowa also knew about the seamier side of New York life. And here he was, nearly loitering on a New York street wondering how to discharge his worry. And whether to call Iowa again. Iowa, who only smiled in appreciation at his umbrella while his own dear Muriel most recently, in rather unnecessarily strong language, cast an unfair aspersion.

'Nathan, people are going to think you're one of those English paranoid old-fart eccentrics hanging out in their castles and fucking their servants.'

Meanwhile hold his own head high. Try to be patient and not always jump to the worst conclusions. As he'd been doing over the Goodwin suicide. Meanwhile an ethereal message born in the air urged him to stop at another telephone. Knowing no one will answer. And yet. Someone might. Try again. Plug in a coin. Take no chances. Read it in case it's counterfeit. Says liberty. In god we trust. And so did he as he tapped out her number. Ring. Ring. No answer. Wait. And oh my god it does. It answers. A voice.

'*Allo.*'

'Hello, may I please speak to Iowa?'

'*Elle est absente pour le moment.*'

'This is Nathan Johnson, will you tell her I called *s'il vous plait.*'

'Oh. Hey. Hi. Sorry, I didn't recognize your voice. I always answer in French until I know who's calling. The delay answering the phone was I was in the shower.'

'I'm sorry if I'm calling at an inconvenient time.'

'Hey, old fox, you don't have to say that. And apologize. Gosh, this is the historic first time I've ever heard your voice over the telephone. And you don't sound too cheerful.'

'Well, I'm not exactly. Can you come for a drink?'

'Oh gosh, I can't. Oh gosh. Oh golly. Oh gosh. Gee. Are you really inviting me?'

'Yes.'

'Hey, your voice. Are you in trouble or something?'

'I can't tell you on the phone.'

'Look. OK. I tell you what. Next to that big oak room. The bar at the Plaza. No, that's too busy and noisy. The Pierre Hotel. Just diagonally across the corner. On Fifth. Go in the Fifth Avenue entrance. Take a seat in that oval room with the high ceiling. Don't worry if it looks too empty. It's my favourite hangout. No one bothers me if I sit sedately on my own. I call it the throne room. I can't stay long, but I'll be there in less than an hour. Oh gosh, by the sound of you, I'll try to make that much less than an hour. See you.'

Nathan Johnson staring at the phone still in his hands. The whole world changed in seconds. Less than an hour to live hanging on to an emotional cliff side with the tips of your fingers. Even though less than an hour is a lifetime to wait. No trouble about knowing where the Pierre was. He had once been in that very room. And she was able to tell by his voice how he felt. It brought the sudden splendour of relief. Her words so confident. Another human being who's among these millions and to whom you're not a stranger. Yet how could someone so much younger, hayseed recently in her hair, now seem such a total social superior. Already familiar with a sanctum in the city. An almost secret rendezvous. And her last words in his ear before she hung up. 'Old fox, did you ever run naked along a beach with great mountainously curling grey-green waves smashing in foam on the seashore. You don't have to answer that. But that's what I was thinking when you called.'

Iowa could with her intellectual ju-jitsu send his mind spinning in circles. While she's standing in the centre contentedly smiling. She was always balm to soothe the spirit. Which he now felt enfold him strolling farther along Fifth Avenue. Bastion of wealth. Knowing within the hour there will be someone to talk to, savvy and sympathetic. Before she modelled in lingerie, she tried to be a plain Jane and worked two weeks as a salesgirl. Once having to rush away out of a changing room when a woman tried to grab and kiss her. Which he could understand, once having put his hands almost accidentally upon her ass. But everything that could happen in life happened in the lingerie trade. As Iowa, shockingly endearing, understood.

'Pops, you just are as you are. A guy hawking lingerie. That's why I love you.'

Stopping on Fifth Avenue and turning. Retracing his now purposeful footsteps uptown in the direction of the Pierre Hotel. Sedate stately edifice rising high in the sky. Popular with an elegantly discreet clientele. And in less than a matter of brief minutes, it would be made, at least for him, stylishly sacred by Iowa. The prospect of seeing her. To snatch a few minutes of her time. Disperses all gloom. Let the whole goddamn staff in Brooklyn, Cincinnati and Atlantic City go hang themselves. Oh god. He didn't mean that. Maybe he meant take the whole inventory out a back or side door of every store, pile it in a truck. Take it all by the quickest way across Brooklyn's Maspeth, Bushwick, and Brownsville and by boat out to a lonely somewhere like Canarsie Island in Jamaica Bay. Dump buckets of gasoline on the pile. Light a match. Step back from the heat. Watch female vanity go up in smoke and all lingerie explode, forever gone in flame.

He stopped at a store and bought a present for Iowa. A CD of Beethoven's *Ode to Joy* in memory of her ancestor who, if he was, as he was, a pall-bearer at the composer's funeral, deserves to be so commemorated. Then to step back out on the street, that small packet in his pocket like a little treasure.

Nathan waiting for the lights to change and cross the very centre of geographical wealth of this city. Fifty-Seventh Street and Fifth Avenue. Counting the minutes and now seconds away. And what if she doesn't turn up? Although the emotions have a way of exaggerating both pleasure and hurt in equal measure, for him it would mean centuries of pain. Listening to her voice reassuring him as she did after a shoot one day when he was bitterly complaining over a design theft, which had just come to his attention in a magazine.

'Hey, pops, you mustn't worry, I have it all figured. I want to see you get somewhere. I mean not that you're not already a big success. Just getting your designs stolen and pirated worldwide in minutes if not seconds is proof. Isn't all this illegal imitation, fashion fraud and copyright counterfeiting a global industry and a sign you've really made it. In fact there are whispers that you're fast becoming the best-known lingerie label in the country and even beginning to corner the market in basic cotton underwear. Cheer up.'

And he did cheer up. Even if computers keep computing faster, so a design seen in Paris one day is, before even eighteen hours have passed, on sale in a garment bargain basement in the Bronx. And there's no point asking yourself what kind of greedy sneaky people do the thieving. Or wondering why they don't invent their own styling or merchandise planning, instead of imitating or stealing someone else's ideas, or worse yours. Or even Iowa's.

'Hey old fox, what about having an exotic perfume counter in the lingerie outlets. But as well as women's, selling men's aftershave lotions, perfumes and scents. Plus, employing among female salespersons, the odd gentleman who prefers gentlemen, but avoiding hiring ladies who prefer ladies. OK, I can see by the look on your face you think I'm going to suggest sex toys next. But boy, some of those things they've got going now for women's satisfaction are state of the art. Oh hey, you're blushing. I know I'm talking a mile out of my orbit. And all the while you so patiently listen.'

'Yes, I listen. And could listen forever.'

Iowa always left him thinking about what she'd said and in her wake creating an even bigger mystery than she was before. Increasingly over these past few weeks missing her acting classes for a tea-drinking ceremony in his private sanctum. Even brought a fruitcake she'd baked. A piece dropped on his foot could break a toe. She still seemed for all her worldliness so young, so unbeaten, so untouched. Even innocent. Still imagining an odd golden hayseed could fall from her hair. And he did give a fuck about all the good things she had inside herself. But had to admit he, nearly twice her age, was also guilty and did more than anything want to touch her marvellous smooth skin. Kiss her eyes. Wrap his arms around the soft warmth of her in a hug.

Nathan folds up his umbrella. Shakes off the rain. A smiling nod of greeting from the doorman. Turn now at last into the revolving door of this hotel. Head along this hallway. Come to the steps up. Turn left. Into this vaulted high-ceilinged oval room. Sombre privacy. Sit at a table by the wall. Faced his back away from the entry so that he can't count the minutes away and tell that she hasn't come. The exquisitely polite waiter. Delighted to see a customer seeking such solitude.

'Sir, we have champagne by the bottle or by the glass. Should you like a glass or a bottle of Louis Roederer?'

'Ah in that case a bottle please.'

'Very good, sir.'

Why be a piker at a time like this when everything that can be done must be done if it can help to buoy the spirit? Will she come as she said she would? With an hour now long elapsed. A boss at the dramatic mercy of an employee. A hand. Her hand, silver ring on a finger, has just reached itself over his shoulder and been placed on top of his hand. The weight of the world in her palm. Lifts.

'Sorry I'm a little late. Thought it would be a hop, skip and jump across the park in the chariot and we got caught in traffic. Then I got caught on my cell phone. A guy proposing marriage said if I don't accept he's committing suicide tonight. I know. Let him. It's his refrain. But Jesus, pops, even as a threat I don't want anyone killing themselves. I can't stay long. Now let me ask how are you. You don't have to answer. But you look as if you've seen a ghost. I know you're smiling, but I know you're sad. Why?'

'Iowa, you look lovely. You will I hope, as you've already got one, have a glass of wine.'

'I will, you spendthrift. It's champagne. And by the bouquet, very good.'

'I didn't think you were going to come.'

'Of course I was going to come. Just in case the end of the world was on the way. Heading roaring down the pike and sweeping us all away. But pops, you're not going to drown. So get that grim look off your face.'

'Well, I might drown.'

'Hey, come on. You look fit and full of fight. You've got a hold on at least a little part of this city. Maybe not by the tail or if you have, then not as much of tail as you might like, but the tail. So what's the joy destroyer. We're winning. Always remember you've got me. You'll not ever be swept away without friends if I have anything to do with it. But you've still never taken me on a ride on the Staten Island Ferry like you promised. And before it's too late. Let's do it. And you know, pops, if I were sizing you up, I'd say you were a prospect to join the power elite.'

'One thing I know for sure, Iowa, is I'm not ever going to be a member.'

'But such guys must be customers. Lingerie for their wives and girlfriends. Or for their boyfriends.'

'Iowa, all I am is just an ordinary guy. With maybe a few exotic tastes. Not powerful. Not made of money. Nor would I even remotely approach being, as you are, so splendidly possessed of and endowed with intelligence and talents, which, after all, are the supreme riches. A beautiful body in which resides an even more beautiful soul.'

'Fox, you sure know what to say to me, don't you. It's wonderful, like this champagne. Makes it taste even better. Here's a toast.'

'A toast, Iowa. To your being here. Especially as here you are, for a flashing-by few minutes, and so exquisitely adorned in an evening gown in which I've never seen you before.'

'That's because you see me undressed all the time. Oh pops, what kind of shit are we stirring up in a great big pot? But god, that's what I like about you. If you're pushed, you can even be a bit romantic. Plus you care and you're kind. Yes that's right, don't shrug, you care and you're kind.'

'I'd prefer to be that instead of sounding more like some pompous professor. And Iowa, it's you who makes one care and makes one kind.'

'Hey fox, you're telling me things you've never told me before. And so maybe it's time to tell you something. You know what finally and fully impressed me about you? No. That's not true. I was already impressed by your nice eyes that really looked at you. But I'll tell you more about that over a future glass of champagne. God, I'm going to sound like a stalker. But it was when I first went following you. Down to your old dusty joint by the Flatiron Building. Saw you stop and buy some oriental mildly erotic junk laid out on the sidewalk, for which you paid a dollar each for this poor kid's stuff, which nobody I can imagine would ever think of buying. Except maybe me. And I knew your bad taste could never be that bad, but that you were doing the poor kid a favour. Then god, later when I knew you weren't visiting a hidden mistress, to actually see that you've got the artwork tacked up on the wall in your bathroom. And now here we are, impervious for a moment to a suffering world, the pair of us do-gooders, titillating our palates, smashing back champagne. Pops, I adore you and you're such an old sentimental worried-looking sourpuss sometimes. But hey, come on. You haven't told me yet. What's the trouble?'

Nathan, just sitting there looking at her across the table. This miracle vision so full of promise and life. The last thing in the world one wanted to mention was his trouble. And unnerving now, having given Iowa the impression of his humanity by buying the kid's oriental pictures when all he was trying to do was to get something to cover holes in his bathroom wall. But it was true, he did feel a caring concern for the homeless. And now in the midst of her wonderful company, even reluctant to say anything about what had happened.

'Come on, pops, tell me, before I've got to go. What's wrong?'

'A suicide in one of our Queens stores.'

'That's sad.'

'Mr Goodwin. They were doing a stocktaking. And just the sort of story that might get in the newspapers. Ruining a family and children's lives. Not to mention business. Hung himself in the middle of a lingerie rack.'

'That's really sad. A nice guy. I met him. Asked me out on a date. Don't let it get you down.'

'It usually means larceny.'

'Oh poor pops. Hey come on. Bleak heart, bleak heart, don't be bleak. I wish I wasn't going where I have to go, having to be in such a hurry. I'm now really late. Everything is going to be all right. Wish I didn't have this date tonight, so I could just share a little bit of this sorrow with you. Why don't I come see you at your downtown hideout tomorrow. We'll discuss it. There's a lot happening that maybe I better tell you about. There's a little kiss.

For the time being, on the brow. To keep you brave. Not that you need it, OK. But remember, even if you have to die, you need a little energy to do it. So bleak heart, don't be bleak.'

'I'll try not to. And Iowa, I nearly forgot. A present. A CD of Beethoven's *Ode to Joy*. In memory of your impressive ancestor.'

'Oh aren't you a sweetie pie. Thank you, thank you. Now don't worry, fox. Ignore this unreadable mask I sometimes wear on my face. Underneath it says I love you and that I'll see you tomorrow. Everything is going to be all right.'

She pecked him a thanks on the brow. Leaving him in a way even sadder. Not knowing where she was going. But as the British say, chuffed as well. Enormous comfort coming from her parting words. Young as she is, she behaves like such an anciently wise mother. Whose children will be brilliant gems. Pretension beyond pretension, wishing they could be his children as well. She was like a lightning strike. Earthed and was gone. Even such trite words as he was thinking he knew would be inadequate to describe the hollow emptiness she left behind.

In this room. A sanctum from the rest of New York, Nathan Langriesh Johnson standing. Standing so, so alone. A nod and smile from the waiter as if in sympathy that the substantiality of her presence and the miracle of her being had vanished. Move now slowly. Ignore the usual tendency to parsimony, leave a large banknote on the table. But now hurry to step down the hallway of the Pierre just in time to watch, at a discreet distance, Iowa depart.

Step forlorn now out on Fifth Avenue just as the heavily pouring rain starts to flood along the street gutters. Under his umbrella Nathan took his time. Ignore the whole goddamn world. Walk the short distance down to Central Park South. A safe journey. Then head back to Midas Towers. Wanting to tell Iowa that though he might not have a ton of money in the bank, he was loyal and could be at least utterly trusted and depended upon if she ever needed him. But the case, in truth, was more likely he needed her. Which alas, with the world at her feet, would leave him squeezed out to infinity.

And the sorrow he wore on his face when she left him at the Pierre must have been so woeful as she swept away in her white satin evening gown. Having almost carelessly also said the words, 'I love you.' Said more than once now. And which he wanted to believe.

NINE

ANY SECOND NOW it would be Muriel's birthday. Hoping for a clear sunny day for the trip and the surprise of Blueberry Hill. But just lie low. Also counting days gone by with nothing in the newspaper over Goodwin's suicide and his funeral delayed with an autopsy. But one thing was certain. He could contend with suicide and sabotage in business better than with the dilemma of love into which he had unawares fallen. Even the acute competition of an enemy once sending a woman into one of the stores with fleas in a jar to release the bugs to jump upon customers. The same lady, making a fast getaway, tripping at the store entrance. Then suing, claiming to have twisted her spine and thrown a bunch of discs out of place. No need to search very far to find a lawyer with enough criminal inspiration to take a bite out of you bigger than those from ten million fleas.

New Yorkers nearly kill themselves trying to be different. The recent trend in the city's better apartments was purity of space, especially among the arrivistes. And which purity was taking New York by storm. While the cream of society were knocking the shit out of their apartments to make them look lived-in. But if Nathan left a newspaper badly folded or, god forbid, an empty beer can anywhere in the apartment, or moved one of Muriel's sacred trinkets two inches out of place on a shelf, he was instantly reminded of the matter. And it was one of the rare times her nagging got the better of him. As who doesn't dream back to good old college fraternity days, putting your feet up on window sills. Driving him to complain, 'Hey Muriel. It's not as if I'm leaving fifty leaking beer cans dripping over the carpet.'

He was as astonished as he was nearly pleased when, later that same evening, there was to be a candlelit dinner in the dining room of Midas Towers. But he should have been warned. As he came to the kitchen door to see what Ida the maid had cooked, Muriel said it was a surprise. And as he turned to leave, she poured a pot full of hot spaghetti over his head.

There was no doubt Muriel took tidiness seriously. Had she ever seen his hideout downtown or even learn he still had it there, she would have blown a gasket. The reality of Muriel and spaghetti dripping down his skull propels the mind to pleasanter thoughts — of Iowa and how she reacted to a lack of tidiness at the hideaway. 'Jeepers creepers, pops, the dust is so thick on this stack of papers, and on this nice shiny magazine, I can write my name with my finger. And before it all gets wiped away, I'm going to draw a big heart. But hey gee, look at this, stuck between the newspapers. You played baseball. Would this be your glove?'

'Yes.'

'This brings a new phase to our relationship. I used to play. Here, catch. Did you know that married women are always anticipating their husband's death, either in the context of love or hate, either wanting to keep or get rid of them?'

Iowa always had something inspiring ready to slam into the intellectual solar plexus. Instead of a bowl of spaghetti on the head, she threw him a crystal ball she picked off his desk, which thank god he caught before it hit him. Then she stood back and, noticing under more newspapers another leather finger protruding, pulled out the well-worn third baseman's mitt he'd used on his high school and college baseball teams before he was kicked out and sent to be disciplined in military school. He was aware that any accumulated junk or shabbiness was something people always noticed. The total social devastation of a conspicuous hole in the heel of your sock. A rip or tear or button missing off your coat. Or that the haute-couture label you tried to sew on your clothes was hanging by a thread. The very tenet that the socially conscious lived by, not to be out of style. Which Muriel never was.

'Nathan, when are all your days away up in Westchester going to end?'

'Tomorrow. And you're coming up with me to have a look-see?'

However, Muriel had an even more embarrassing question. She asked was he opening stores in Iowa because he shouted that state's name five times in his sleep.

'It's a state I've really been thinking about a lot. The name Iowa is from a tribal Indian name. You know the American Indians had their own style. Plus out there on those prairie plains they grow a lot of corn. Decent people.'

'That sounds ridiculous. Decent people grow corn everywhere. Iowa is most famous for hogs. What makes you so sure they're ready for slinky lingerie.'

It just goes to show. Best to say nothing when that opportunity of silence exists. It was damn lucky that suddenly it was Muriel's birthday. With a bombshell distraction. The plan, long hatched, was ready for execution. Muriel's gift of a tiara already couched in purple satin in its sky-blue box. And costing the price of a couple of good racehorses and making his hand nearly tremble writing the cheque. He trusted Ida, their horny maid, to pick out Muriel's favourite ballgown and all necessary accessories. He packed his tuxedo and all appurtenances right down to a purple silk handkerchief. A lobby boy brought down a few other household oddments to the basement garage and locked them in the trunk of the car.

Good ole Hal, ever cheerfully up there in Westchester, would be helpful. Already organized with everything ready whenever they wanted to show up. Newt would have the front gates open. A cook, a maid and even a butler found and the latter soon to be hired. Plus Nathan, with such news encouraging him, went totally extravagant. Ordering from the wine merchant on Madison Avenue anything he saw. 'I'll take a case of the Château d'Yquem.' Or, in the matter of champagne, two cases of Louis Roederer. All now reposing in Blueberry Hill's wine cellar. Along with big booming burgundies, noble clarets and the slightly lower-rank musky-scented Sauternes, the cost of which nearly made him wonder what his palate had driven him to. The main bedroom to be festooned with flowers.

So jumping out of bed that historic departure morning, he ran to the window, caught a glimpse of Central Park, and, like a gorilla, pounded his chest and announced to Muriel.

'Come on, honeybunch, it's time, let's get going on our outing. Check out these Westchester sites. And then afterwards go and have a nice dinner in a nice inn.'

'I'd love it if instead you'd become a member of one of those nice clubs right in the neighbourhood and we wouldn't have to go all the way up to Westchester for a nice dinner.'

'Sure thing. No problem. One day damn soon. I'm telling you. It's all going to happen.'

OK, the city was hysterical with its social climbing. But one did not want to further explore the complications of snooty clubland. Who needs clubs anyway with so many good restaurants around? Plus he was about to formally become pasha of his own absolute domain and be as exclusive as you can get. One goddamn member in good standing. Two members, actually, counting Muriel.

'Nathan why are you getting so formally dressed?'

'Just for a change.'

'Do we really have to go up to Westchester today? The weather's so nice. And why don't we go eat at La Grenouille later?'

Jesus Christ, here he was on one of most momentous occasions of his entire life and Muriel wants to stay in town and flex her social muscles locally. Something she did enough of, frequenting the places where the general public were not permitted. She loved the big time. Rubbing elbows as close as she could get to high society. She read magazines featuring the celebrity cliques, along with the pronouncements of the idolized fashion editors. And she grabbed any chance to wear one of her ballgowns. And here tonight was a chance. She even donated money to the New York Botanical Garden and the Bronx Zoo so that she would be invited to their functions. But she would never, although she thought she might, be asked to join the Colony Club nestled so discreetly in its elegance on Park Avenue. Her club was and probably would remain where she ice-skated three times a week on that quiet sunken oasis in Rockefeller Plaza. And open to the public.

What a stubborn bitch she could occasionally be! Only at last relenting when I said that folk up in Westchester where we were going fox-hunted on horseback and played polo all over the place. Some had even made deep personal relationships with Hollywood celebrities. And were many of them socially registered.

'Well, all right, Nathan, I'll cancel the auction, my facial, my mud treatment, my aromatherapy and my new guru at eleven, and even lunch with Cecilia, who's just kicked her husband out and whom I haven't seen for three whole months. She's a member of our society.'

'What society?'

'Oh you know. Our club.'

'I don't know your club.'

'The Determined Society of Devious Dames, we call it. The members have just been alerted to a new kind of blow job. You wrap the guy's testicles in silver foil and hum through the covering. And so, why not, we'll drive up and see what the hicks are doing in the sticks with their women in their slinky lingerie.'

In the course of getting her to Westchester, Nathan was going nuts with the stress. With such emotive distraction and now having to drive straight. Certainly, for the moment with a hard-on, temporarily glad Muriel was trying to be risqué. All he's trying to do is to give his wife a birthday present of a tiara worth a few million dollars and delivered by an armoured truck and awaiting inside a palace. And to steer himself away from the fast-growing irresistible temptation of a girl called Iowa.

Now here he was on the eve of Muriel's birthday. Exerting the discipline of placing aside present troubles out in Queens, and also realizing, shocked, that he didn't have time to get Muriel a few other baubles from Tiffany's for which he had already laid all meticulous plans. God, how women love presents and the peace and quiet it brings if they're even approaching being priceless. But it was amazing she didn't even seem to notice anything these days except what he was shouting in his dreams.

'How's everything in Atlantic City, Nathan?'

'I don't know, why do you ask.'

'In your sleep last night you were shouting, "Let's walk on the boardwalk in the rain!"'

In spite of the day dawning so bright and sunny, somehow he was growing in pessimism. Christ, what's wrong with taking a stroll on the boardwalk? It was romantic to walk in the rain. But Muriel's unanswerable silence said it all. Plus her thinking he'd forgotten her birthday and sulking as they finally set out for Blueberry Hill. A clear sky. Crispness in the air. That feeling of freedom Nathan got leaving the city behind. Encountering the grandeur as you look across the massive flow of the Hudson river.

The majestic stone cliffs of the Palisades. And left behind, cold and white, the spires of Manhattan Island. He'd told Muriel to wear tweeds, presuming she had such in one of her vast closets. But didn't mention thick stockings to ward off Lyme Disease. Because, who knows, one might even go for a stroll in the woods to work up an appetite before dinner. And she caught him up short. Just as he should have known.

'What. Stroll in the woods. And get Lyme Disease.'

'Holy cow, Muriel, what an exaggerated attitude.'

'Oh yeah. That's what you think. All you have to do is brush up against a weed or something.'

And so it was, birthday and all, off to more than a little bit of a wrong start. That pang of pessimism in the pit of his stomach. My god, what had he done? A farm, stables and paddocks for horses. Woods where Indian trails were still evident. And if he took up Hal's suggestion, polo ponies gambolling around the joint. A milking parlour for cows, a bullpen for bulls. Heads of other equines sticking out of stable half-doors. Tractors. Ploughs. Hay barns. Holy Christ. At least two, three, or four maids, plus a cook and a butler. His name already revealed as Boris.

Where the hell was he going to get lessons on how to behave with Boris? And the added salaries would increase his overheads, as would paying for fire, storm, earthquake and employee insurance. Not to mention taxes. No wonder people got obsessed with trying to make billions. Maybe Hal could counsel him on how to deal with moving to the country and spending lots of isolated time there. Anyway, he'd be starting a new life. Free of the discomfort that the close proximity of people can cause. As Muriel now made evident sitting beside him in the car.

'My God, I'm glad we're out of the Bronx but some of these other poky little places are really for the birds. Just look at them.'

Now. Get ready. Muriel, you're really going to see some poky little place. But at least in her tweeds Muriel and, as it turned out, also in thick stockings, could avoid Lyme Disease. But his stress factor was accelerating, heart beating faster, travelling now towards the Kensico Dam along the Bronx River Parkway. Distracting himself as they went along, calculating how much water the massive dam held. Anxious now to arrive at Blueberry Hill. Conscious too of how long a bored and miffed Muriel was going to tolerate the ride, or that she might attack him for having forgotten her birthday. But who now suddenly ventured an opinion of the passing sights. 'There's an awful lot of woods up here in this neck, as they say.'

She, he knew, was trying to be funny, already convinced now and getting increasingly uptight, thinking he had forgotten her birthday. Even though she preferred not to be a year older. The final biological scrapheap getting closer makes you take such days more seriously. Her sulking was diminished, however, upon Muriel's sight of the sun-dappled surface of the water in the Kensico Reservoir. She even evinced a bit of interest in the town of Armonk as they passed through. And frowned just a little as they headed off on the more rural Old Post Road. But flashing through his mind was still Iowa. Can't stop the thoughts. Of someone humming through the foil around your testicles. And how much difference it could make as to who was doing the humming. A bloody hell of a lot, was his uninitiated conclusion.

'Not far now, Muriel. See these big estates. The kind of customers I'm looking for. Owned by men who don't give a fuck how big a woman's lingerie bills are.'

'Well, that's not my concern. I don't see one single human being. Never mind a woman.'

'Don't worry, they're there in their big palaces with acres of closet space.'

Hold back one's trepidations. Not even a mile now to go. The wonderful thrill of ownership. To realize that familiar landscape passing on the right was now actually his land. But it's Muriel's, her birthday present. Another few hundred yards. This is it. The moment of truth. Tonsured lawns and ornamental trees. And a palace set within all the sylvan splendour.

The gates wide open just as Hal had promised. And Newt would be on his rounds. He began to laugh as he turned in. Christ, if this is social climbing, and even though it's damn expensive, it sure is becoming a hell of a lot of fun. Even in spite of it being goddamn endlessly unpredictable. And if, with the palpations in his chest, he didn't have a heart attack. Muriel, waking up fast as she realizes that this blue-pebbled drive is not the public road.

'Hey Nathan, where are you going?'

Prolong the mystery. Muriel turning to look at him. Fully awake from the boredom of her country-touring trance. 'Did you hear me Nathan. I'm speaking to you. Where the hell are you going?'

'In here.'

'You can't. Can't you see it's someone's private drive?'

'Oh god. Hey, maybe I made a mistake. There was no sign. I thought this was a shortcut someone told me about.'

'Come on, Nathan. Oh god. They could have dogs or call the police. Nathan, do you hear what I'm saying. You could have already set the security system off. We could be criminals. My god. There's the house. Could be a Mafia don of dons or something. Let's get the hell out of here before somebody sees us.'

'Aw shucks, Muriel. This is a democracy. Country of the free and home of the brave.'

'All the more goddamn reason somebody brave could come out of the house and shoot the shit out of us.'

'Muriel, a decent citizen makes an honest mistake and a decent citizen lets you turn around. Anyway, maybe nobody lives here.'

'How do you know?'

'There are no cars parked. People who live in a place like this at least have a few Ferraris hanging around. Honey, just hold it a minute. See. What did I tell you. Look. A big circle to turn around. Plus, it's beautiful. Some people have everything, don't they. And if someone comes out, we'll just say we're lost and ask directions to Armonk. You know lost people go and knock on someone's door to ask the way. It's civilized.'

'Like hell it's civilized. Nathan, are you completely nuts. Don't go any closer. It's suicidal.'

'I'll just knock a light tap or two on their door. Nobody's going to mind in broad daylight. Otherwise I'm lost. A simple straightforward question. Which way is it to Armonk? Or to somewhere bigger like Mount Kisco.'

'They especially shoot at cars like the one we're driving. Oh my god, that's barking. Guard dogs. Up there on the balcony. Look at them! Killer monster dogs. Good god. Come on. Let's go. Let's seriously get the fucking hell out of here.'

'You are, honey, looking at Blueberry Hill. It's yours. Happy birthday. I love you.'

'Nathan, I know you like being funny, but this time you're out of your fucking blueberry mind. I also know you like blueberries for breakfast, but before we get shot or devoured by those goddamn giant dogs, you get us the hell out of here.'

'Don't have to, honey. This is where we live. The dogs are safe up there, they can't get off that balcony. They're pedigree.'

'Fuck pedigrees. Nathan, the joke's over. If you don't move this car this instant and drive straight the fucking hell out of here, I'm going to divorce you. I mean it.'

'Honey, it's ours. This is our house. Those are our dogs barking. And I'm telling you, you're absolutely safe.'

'All right Nathan. Take it easy now. I'll drive. Everything's going to be fine. Just give me a second or two to think. I've left my cell phone at home. Maybe now it's a place, if you don't mind, where I'm going to have ask for help. And risk my life knocking on the door to call an ambulance.'

'What for?'

'To take you back to New York and Bellevue.'

'Oh Christ, Bellevue. How can I convince you? Is my tone of voice wrong? If you don't mind, Muriel, I prefer you call my doctor rather than Romney. I don't want one of your gynaecologist's astronomical bills to land on my doorstep just now. That will really send me nuts. But you don't give a guy a chance who's trying to do something nice on your birthday.'

'OK, Nathan, OK. Of course you can do something nice. Just stay calm. But if you don't mind, I'll just take the keys of the car with me. Sit tight while I go knock on their door.'

'There's a button you push to ring the bell.'

'Change seats now, while I go tell them it's an emergency.'

'Oh Jesus Christ! Here. These are the keys to the house. You're looking at them, right here in my hand. Take them. You don't have to ring the bell. Go in and call Dr Romney. I'll admit he's a brilliant gynaecologist. And a damn good-looking guy as well. And knows everything there is to know. And charges accordingly. But I haven't got a feminist disease. Yet. And my heart's still ticking. There's a telephone on a table in the front hall just near the staircase. You listening now, Muriel?'

'No need to get angry. These are the keys, are they? I'm listening.'

'Yes. And you're safe from the dogs on the balcony. Tell the good Dr Romney that I'm severely under the illusion that I bought a house and you think I've gone bonzo ape. But don't forget to tell him we have the keys to the front door and that the telephone you're calling from, if you check recent listings with information, is in our name.'

'Oh my god. What. Oh my god. What is this? These are the keys?'

'That's right, honey. I've just told you. Those are the keys. I bought this place.'

'The whole place. What we're looking at?'

'Yes.'

'You bought this? This place. I don't believe it. You mean you really bought it? It's a palace or something. You mean this whole place, going back all the way out to the road?'

'That's right. I bought it. Lock, stock and barrel.'

'If this is true, you should be put away. You really are crazy.'

'Well maybe I am. But I still seem able to pay all the bills, and in particular the price paid for this place bought in your name. I guess you'd have to call it, if not a palace, then a castle. It's yours. All the furniture inside. That big spruce tree. That wall. The drive. The woods. Everything you see. Lock, lovely stock and wonderful barrel. Happy birthday, darling.'

Muriel steps out of the car. Swaying unsteadily, her feet crunching the gravel. Gently closing the car door. Moves towards the house. Seems to wobble a second. Stops again. She must be counting the windows. From behind, her beautiful hair still makes her look like a college co-ed. Women have minds like calculators, weighing every option up. Amazing how stimulating a situation like this can get. And the filthy stinking dirty thoughts a guy can have. Even if it's the same old body. Knock Muriel over on the pebbles of the drive and fuck her right there. But now she's coming back to the car. Maybe she's gone bonzo ape nuts. Her face wreathed with a different kind of worry. And different kind of suspicion.

'Nathan, I'm scared speechless. OK, maybe you're all right. The keys open the door. These are the real keys and all. And I don't have to call Dr Romney. But the place is massive. Who's going to wash and iron the curtains? Mow the lawn? If it's got curtains, there must be a hundred for the windows.'

'Honey, the house has no neighbours, so you don't need any curtains.'

'I guess there are gardens to grow stuff.'

'Eighty-eight acres.'

'Oh my god.'

'Muriel, relax.'

'Don't keep telling me to relax. I'm sorry, but I've got to say it. I can't relax. Over maybe the biggest mistake in human history.'

'Living on an estate like this attracts people's curiosity. That's why you need a lot of land and trees around you. You don't want someone close by, focusing binoculars on you.'

'No, but we might be focusing on them for a little neighbour-liness. Some ethnic undesirable coming at us without warning out of those woods.'

'Nobody is coming at us out of the woods. Anyway, ethnic undesirables wear masks these days, Muriel, so they can't be recognized.'

'Don't try and be funny. And the dogs. Whose are they?'

'Irish wolfhounds, they keep trespassers at bay.'

'You mean they're our dogs.'

'Yes.'

'They're going to eat the cat for breakfast.'

'Hey come on honey, relax. This is a place that could last for the rest of your entire life. And of course, not wanting to be too selfish, my life as well. Would I give you a bum steer. It's your birthday present. Give me back the keys. I'll show you. And if you'll pardon my French, I'll open the fucking door and carry you over the threshold.'

Muriel, all goggle-eyed, was light enough to lift and get inside. She stood in the entrance hall under the massive crystal chande-lier and, slowly turning around in circles, surveyed the hall and entrances to other rooms, especially the long corridor that led down steps into the large panelled drawing room. Running short of words. 'My, my, my.' She looked as if she didn't know whether to laugh or cry. Or indeed fly. Plus getting increasingly inquisi-tive, but also putting her hand up to her throat as if to feel for a rope that might have recently encircled it.

'But whose furniture is all this, Nathan? And all the paintings?'

'Ours. I bought the joint lock, stock and barrel. Maybe a few more locks, stocks and barrels than I bargained for. I didn't even know about the swimming pool in the sub-basement. But I did, in fact, know about the ice house. Come on, wait till you see the highly civilized drawing room.'

'Nathan, I haven't even digested the front hall yet.'

He switched on the light and the crystals in the chandelier sparkled. The shock getting to Muriel. Not wanting to look at him in case both of them were nuts. All the timing now beginning to work like clockwork unless Newt had forgotten to put the tiara box on the large drawing room table. That tiara cost more than a few baubles might. With its shamrock motif made of pearls and diamonds fashioned for a British peeress by Garrard, jewellers to Queen Victoria, and described by the auctioneers as a priceless relic of an exotic era. They weren't kidding: he'd be paying for it for another five years to come. But a faithful wife, even though temporarily knocked out of her usual superior composure, had to be priceless too. And had left enough composure to follow me along the hall to the drawing room.

'Nathan, I'm speechless. But who the hell is going to dust all this?'

'There's staff to do it. Everything is going to be all right. Be careful down these steps.'

The car in front taken to the back entrance to be unloaded. The staff instructed to otherwise keep a low profile and remain in the servants' wing until dinner was served. The new maid, Suzie, that Hal hired guaranteed she would have Muriel's clothes laid out in her bedroom. Her bath drawn. A whole row of bath salts in gleaming glass bottles to choose from. A white-gloved Boris, the butler, previously worked for titled folk living in one of the great stately homes in England, made himself specially available and was now busy in the butler's pantry chilling the champagne. The cook, called Mary, from rural Ireland, preparing dinner. And now followed by his tried, trusted and true life companion and wife, did he proceed through this unfolding dream. As she looked up. Looked down and looked around.

'But this is like something you'd see in a movie. A palace.'

'You betcha.'

'And Nathan, forgive me for asking, but before I see anymore what did this cost?'

'Forgive me for not telling you, but it cost a bunch and that figure is going to remain top secret. '

'But you could nearly fit our whole apartment into this hallway. How could you have bought all this. The upkeep. Even with a staff to do it, if we could get enough of them, which nobody can. How can we afford it?'

'No problem. I can afford anything for you. Vetting new lingerie outlets to open. Even up in this neck of the woods. Mount Kisco. Chappaqua. And what the hell. That's what we are. Rich. Let's face it. What's the whole purpose of getting rich. Or at least modestly rich.'

'For a start, not getting overwhelmingly modestly poor in a hurry with a place like this. And I'm still wondering who the hell, with Bergdorf Goodman available, is going to start buying their lingerie up here in the sticks? And so this is what you were doing.'

'He who hesitates is lost.'

'He who hesitates and thinks twice might avoid getting his financial ass broken. And go bust. What are you holding there, Nathan?'

'Honey, it's a box. For you to open. Before I drop it.'

Muriel's interest instantly caught by the sky-blue heraldically embossed jewellery box. Lifting off the lid. Drawing in her breath as she opens the leather encasement. There, nestled in the soft purple satin, a tiara fit for a queen who had indeed worn it, according to the auctioneer's catalogue, at some of Europe's most elegant gatherings.

'Oh my god, this is lovely. Lovely.'

'Another happy birthday, honey. It's for you to wear descending the grand staircase out in the hall. Try it on.'

'It's almost too beautiful to wear. A symbol. As if it crowns the culmination of our life together.'

'It is a symbol. It is.'

'Oh Nathan, I'm sorry. I really am. You must forgive me. I was, honestly, really worried. I thought for a moment you'd just tipped over the edge. I'm relieved. All we've got to worry about now is a white elephant we've taken on. My god, what will it cost to heat this place in winter?'

'Don't worry about the heat. Between us we're going to generate plenty. What do you say.'

'What do I say. For starters, I've just remembered I've left something slow-cooking from last night in the oven back in New York, left for Ida and a friend she was having over from Brooklyn while we were out. I better telephone.'

'No problem. I already told Ida we wouldn't be back. Dinner's here. Being prepared. Go up to your dressing room. Big enough to play basketball in. That's right, we brought a few of your clothes. Get ready for dinner. We're having a little champagne.'

'Nathan, I'm just too happy to even take this tiara off. I'm sorry for my behaviour. But you knew, didn't you, that this is the kind of house that I've always dreamt of and any woman would kill for. But please. Even with dogs the size of those, please tell me again if and before I see anymore, that this is really ours, because I still can't believe it.'

'Believe it. I bought it. And the deeds duly deposited in a deposit box in the bank in your name.'

'Nathan, I simply have not got words to say it again. But this is the happiest day of my life. If all these funny doors can be locked, and nobody is going to see us, let's have a fuck right here and now. Put that gorgeous table to use. I'll bend over it.'

'Well ma'am, I couldn't be more delighted at your suggestion. But Newt's still got the keys, and I fear the joint is not fully staffed yet, one more maid to come, so we'd better get to the privacy of the bedroom and lock the door there.'

They did. And wow. Muriel stuck her legs straight up in the air and held onto her ankles with her hands. He couldn't believe the loony behaviour, but he wasn't complaining. One minute heading in a straitjacket to the nuthouse in an ambulance, and the next screwing one's wife on this fantastically beautiful soft rug. Knocked over a few vases on Muriel's dressing table with the effort. They continued with another fuck on a couple of well-placed pillows on the parquet floor of the enormous dressing room. And then, even as Nathan was running out of steam, engripped on a golden chaise longue. Knocking over more things with flailing feet. What is it with women that makes them so suddenly easily available? An elderly rabbi had an answer to that question. He said, 'Don't ask.'

Anyway he didn't ask. For this was for sure a new existence. To be in their own dining room tonight. Steaks and burgundy on the menu. Hal again, good ole boy, came up with the Irish cook, Mary. And to top it all, and taking up his duty this very day, Boris. Already spotted in the butler's pantry preparing an after-dinner choice of Sauternes, Armagnac, coffee and chocolates to produce tranquil sleep on first night at Blueberry Hill. You wonder sometimes what life could really be like when bliss strikes without warning. And future living seems to be all about being afloat as you paddle gently on through the clouds of contentment. You say, 'Jesus Christ, maybe I've got it right at last.'

'Nathan, Nathan. This is. This truly and really is. The happiest day of my life.'

Nathan was nearly tempted to accompany Muriel and get in the tub with her. Instead he proceeded what seemed a mile farther on down the hall into his own bedroom and bathroom. And never did a bow tie get tied so perfectly on a silk shirt from London's Turnbull & Asser in Jermyn Street. In his full kit and rarely-worn tuxedo, he awaited in the hall under the crystal chandelier at the bottom of the main staircase. Down which Muriel descended. Muriel in her favourite ballgown she'd worn to the New York Botanical Garden event, which set him back more than a few thousand bucks. But, he thought, worth every penny.

'You're breathtaking, Muriel and I'm speechless.'

Arm in arm, they walked down the hall towards the drawing room, his leather heels marking echoing steps on the marble. Three steps down through the archway and there, waiting, was Boris in his pinstriped trousers, with a smile and bow for Muriel and a gentle understanding nod of his head for the master.

'Good evening, madam, good evening, sir.'

What splendid words. God bless the British for teaching servants how to behave. But Mary, the cook, didn't seemed to have Boris' finesse. Dinner delayed. And a distant smell of smoke. Plus a crash of crystal and crockery coming from the pantry and kitchen beyond. Which, when all the interconnecting doors were open at once, included hearing a few slurs uttered against the English. And in answer, a comment unbecoming to the Irish. Otherwise everything was going swell.

'Madam, sir. Dinner is served.'

And so proceeding from the first sip of champagne through to the elixir of Château d'Yquem with peach trifle and cream and onto the last taste of Armagnac, one floated through one of the most magically blissful evenings of one's life. For once Muriel, across the rather distant stretch of the dining-room table, just feasting her eyes on him with admiration. No marriage could now have ever been better cemented.

TEN

NATHAN HADN'T once thought of Iowa. Much too involved now with Boris, no longer serving the duke in his castle but now buttling in Westchester USA for commoners, but upwardly mobile commoners. Boris carefully sizing up his employers. Indoctrinating his two new pupils in the art of elegant existence. And on the lookout for a pack of hounds, just in case the squire of Blueberry Hill wanted to do a bit of fox hunting. Probably in memory of the duke, who sat on a few hundred thousand acres of Leicestershire and had recently died.

And outside these concerns there remained other niggling worries. Investigations now going on over Goodwin, further delaying his funeral. Could it have been murder? But the days speeding by, Nathan getting more countrified by the minute. And his spirit not doing too damn bad. Smiling welcome at one's butler's every appearance. Laying out Nathan's changes of clothes. Shoe trees in his shoes. Learning more of and from him on each occasion. *The New York Times* collected from the village by Newt and the pages freshly ironed and presented upon a reading board that could be propped up on either of one's knees. However, Boris' relationship with Muriel, to put it mildly, was less than smooth. Any moment he expected to hear Muriel's argumentative refrain, 'Let me tell you something, buster.' Especially as once when in passing at the half-open door of the butler's pantry one could just see Muriel and overhear her saying to Boris, 'Of course I know it's no problem, but what are you ironing the newspapers for?'

'Ironing does make the newspaper so much easier to hold, read and turn the pages.'

'It seems a lot of attention to something so minor.'

'Not so minor, ma'am, as a crease in the paper can produce an intolerable degree of annoyance and impatience as then the master of the house is compelled to stretch the crease apart in order to accurately decipher the text.'

'What do you mean, master of the house? I own this house and everything in it.'

'Very good, madam.'

'And don't call me madam.'

'Very good, ma'am.'

Nathan was learning. Servants close at hand have all the time in the world to size you up. The first apprehensive tremor to come through one was the fear that the word 'duchess' might be used to Muriel, for Boris was fond of reminiscing about the duke to him. Then there was employee liability. A tray dropped on the stairs, a foot slipped in the grease. Someone's spine dislocated and ass broken in thirty-six different places. And the ensuing gloom of courtrooms. Until he realized Boris was merely trying his best, letting go with both barrels and painting with a full brush, simply to reduce the amount of smoke coming out of the nostrils of Mount Etna. Hoping that perhaps one of his replies would shut up the owner and would-be lady of the manor. As it most certainly, surprisingly, did, Muriel preferring the quiet life she was fast becoming accustomed to, turning on her heel and barging out the pantry door.

Of course, when the honeymoon at Blueberry Hill was well and truly over, Muriel's first words of rebuttal were, 'That eunuch bastard, fire him.'

It did cross one's mind that ole Boris did seem rather sexually neutralized but sure didn't come any cheaper as a result. His salary was astro. Plus a car. Brand new. He also expected in due course that if not a groom of the chambers, then an extra maid under his supervision. And was himself expecting to have attention danced upon him. Taking up at the head of table in the servants' dining room. The words scullery maid were also used. Reginald, who was administrating costs and writing the cheques, was called upon to see what he could do. 'Nathan, no problem. We could franchise Nathan Johnson Lingerie in the morning. You wouldn't know what to do with the money.'

He did, in fact, secretly know. And that Iowa, already gone from his employ as it turned out, might figure in such a dream. But also knew he shouldn't panic about her disappearance or what was as yet only casually a financially running-away horse. Although the direction it was galloping in was totally unpredictable. He was also finding out fast that the staff had an almost unbelievable appetite for exotic food and wines and in definite preference to good healthy staples like carrots, potatoes, cabbage, even peaches and cider that the farm could offer. Muriel, despite outbursts of complaint, saw the sense of keeping on Boris as he inspected her tray when she had breakfast in bed and she was enjoying no end the ceremonial evenings when they dressed for dinner. Boris popping open champagne in the drawing room and Muriel doing strengthening exercises for her neck, in order to wear her tiara more often. There was no doubt they were having odd little disagreements, but awaiting Boris's most splendidly intoned words made up for it all: 'Sir, ma'am, dinner is served.'

Nathan hadn't once tried to be in touch with Iowa, but was finally notified of Goodwin's funeral. Meanwhile, vanity was making him do sit-ups these days as well as preparing for pick-and-shovel work out on the farm. Also contributing to his keeping in good shape were the many footsteps it took navigating the house. One thing was for certain, that even before he included his walks outdoors, he was knocking off three to five miles indoors every day. Ole Boris got enough exercise, too, waltzing dawn to midnight around this place. All that he attended upon at Blueberry Hill was orchestrated to perfection. Which he imparted to Mary, the cook, and Bertha, the maid and tray-dropper. And so came breakfast, lunch, tea time. Dinner a real ceremony right down to pudding, as Boris called dessert.

It was now almost as if one had to find what he could do to keep Boris busy looking after him. Meanwhile, listening to Casals playing the cello. Muriel off to bed. The master of the house staring at the fire, popping back one health-preserving tipple of pot-still whiskey after another. The wilderness out the window in every direction an inspiration to have another dram. Watching dancing in the flames. A dream. Iowa, whom he could never have. But now at least he did have an ultra-grateful wife. Who on the terrace, to birdsong in the background, told him so after he'd smashed back jolts of Boris' recommended pot still.

It was two people still in love. Followed by days of contentment. Reginald overseeing the opening of five new lingerie boutiques in Iowa, Illinois and Indiana, while Nathan went on excursions in this wonderful abode, wandering from room to room and taking in the rural scene out the various windows. With life flashing by in a series of balmy sunny days and in the midst of the present formality and frivolity with Muriel, he was not finding it difficult to actually get as drunk, not only as a skunk, but also as a lord. Or maybe only as inebriated as a baronet. And even devoid of a smoking jacket, holed up alone in the library puffing away on a Bolívar like a coal-burning locomotive pulling a mile-long freight train, he felt himself to be at least a member of the landed gentry. Thinking, as he considered Iowa that she alone remained the only chink of temptation in his armour of marital faithfulness. Wanting to tell her about things he found in the bookshelves of Blueberry Hill. And indeed helpful in his present social dilemma. Being full of stories of the breeding habits of the European aristocracy. Wham. Bam. Thank you ma'am. Put your tiara back on. A lot of which couplings seemed to relate almost exclusively to the acquisition of land. Either by fucking for it or, if not, then murdering for it. And illegitimacy everywhere. Boris throwing further light on matters. 'Sir, it was occasionally His Grace's interest to finger through such pages, laughing with such gusto that his monocle would pop out of his eye socket. Which latter, if sir does not object, I should like to wear. His Grace always furious should I do so.'

'Feel free, Boris.'

'Thank you, sir.'

'Forgive me, Boris, but how, out of interest, did you aspire to buttling, if I may enquire?'

'You may, sir, of course enquire. I served first as a young man as the steward's-room boy for Lord Farranistick in Wales. Then when joining the duke's household in England was put in charge of the wine until I began to suffer from the deuced inflammatory rheumatism brought on by the chill of the castle cellars. Then as a footman, I finally did in my due diligence to that capacity, achieve to serve His Grace as butler. My familiarity with guns came when there was a gamekeeper short when I occasionally helped as a loader. Although I miss the sport, I do rather enjoy the drier air and comfort here at Blueberry Hill. His Grace was most understanding when my rheumatics unfortunately had me take my leave to seek a generally drier climate and, of course, central heating. Of course, life here in America took a degree of getting used to.'

This sure was adaptation time. Boris and Nathan were in the same boat. His graduation to the stately home, paying due diligence as squire. And wouldn't you know that Muriel had now seriously taken up horseback riding, Newt commandeered as groom. Little chats with Boris becoming Nathan's social life. Especially as he couldn't, it seemed, provide him with enough to do in his dancing attendance upon one. Whereas the duke never left him with a spare moment. Boris made it clear that His Grace was about as high as you could get in the titled aristocracy without kicking someone off his or her throne. He diplomatically never let one feel that one need worry about not being titled or even being an upstart up from the hoi polloi. But of course in the present reality of Blueberry Hill, and far down in the bowels of this palace, thundered the roar of a massive oil-consuming furnace to help keep ole Boris' rheumatism at bay.

When, right at the right time after dinner and after powdering her nose, Muriel approached down the hall, smiling. Making for one of life's memorable moments and when one knew for sure she was happy and really liking it here. Falling back into her chair and issuing a great sigh. 'Oh god, Nathan. Is it safe to say something?'

'Sure, honey.'

'Can this, the life we're enjoying, honestly last? Last month's accounts made Reginald whistle.'

'As I said, no problem. Even if Reginald whistles. Only if women no longer want to wear lingerie will a lack of money be a problem.'

'And I guess, Nathan, women wouldn't be women would they, without lingerie.'

'No, they wouldn't, honey.'

'Oh Nathan. I'm in paradise. Really in paradise. I love it. I love it. I really love it here. Forever and forever.'

Muriel, after her two refills of Château d'Yquem, turning to blow him a kiss as she went off to bed. She loved it here. Forever. And forever. Left in the silence Nathan sat and stared at the walls and mahogany panelling. What a joint to find yourself in. And suddenly with the grandfather clock tolling out in the hall, it was midnight. And he then felt an overwhelming urge to go out and stand under the sky. Wandering out the front door. Standing there under the porte cochère. On this bright moonlit night. Climb the gentle grass hill to the cemetery. Cross the drive. His footsteps crunching the gravel spread out before this palace. For no other word could befit it better. Taking deep breaths of this fresh country air. The tip tops of the tombstones peeking above the stone walls ahead, seen in the lucent light.

Open the rusted creaking gate. Walk past the old American names. In themselves epitaphs. First settlers of these lands where once only Indians roamed. And no one yet called Nathan. And as he turned and walked back past through the graves, there it was, a small statue separated away on its plinth on its own little site. And chiselled in the tombstone, an inscription that made one catch one's breath:

CHARLOTTE GRAY
BUT SEVENTEEN YEARS OLD
WHEN HER BEAUTY AND JOY
WERE ETERNALLY TAKEN AWAY

Returning down the gentle incline, a sorrow welled up. Stepping over a hole, an entrance to a woodchuck's apartment. Too chill for snakes in the grass. And looming ahead in the moonlight, this great stone edifice. To spend the rest of his life there. Learn to love this massive monument of stone. Its windows the eyes of a great rearing ghost looking into the future. Until that time would come when he'd lie buried nearby. In another form of eternity. With Muriel, his love. Even though perhaps he also felt some of that love now for another. It was merely a love he dreamt in a dream and would pass with the realities of life slowly but surely blotting it away. But the love he had here and now was certain. Durable. Like the maple trees. Whose bark he could touch and look up into its branches. And to which he needed never say goodbye.

ELEVEN

NATHAN WAS enjoying these gentle pleasant days, repairing to the library. Perusing the incredible stacks of ancient geographical magazines long abandoned there. And on each visit more discovered. Tomes on this and tomes on that. A tome on *The Morality of Marriage*. Containing essays on 'The Status and Destiny of Women'. Then discovering a tiny book, tucked away, *The Knickerbocker Club 1979*. A list of socially awe-inspiring names between the sky-blue covers with not a single member named Nathan to be found among them. He thought, Don't give up, keep looking. But he gave up. But wouldn't you know he'd soon learn something new about Boris? Who could, referring to another clime entirely, quote verbatim the rules in the Royal Enclosure at Ascot. No brown shoes for men, no bare legs or shoulders for women. And Muriel, further learning from Hal that the duke had sacked Boris for wearing a monocle just as His Grace wore his, on a scarlet ribbon.

Tomorrow was Saturday and with staff except for cook given the day off, he took the opportunity to snoop around his own house, or rather Muriel's. A venture of exploration to find, if not more secret doors and passages, then at least a previously undiscovered room and to make sure it was free of skeletons. Which in fact he did, and which was reserved exclusively for a valet to do ironing and pressing. And already put to use by Boris. Then climbing up a circular stone staircase to look through the vast attics seemed like another haunted world. But from which, through cobwebs, one could survey the wooded countryside far out to the horizon. His eye suddenly catching sight of tiny printed words scratched on a windowpane.

I AM GOING TO KILL YOU

A shiver of fear went through him. Remembering the conversation overheard the evening in the bar of the local hotel before he'd bought Blueberry Hill, as well as a remark Reginald once made: 'Big as this country is and with all its sprawling cities, a lot of people, Nathan, are just like the rats, all trying to find a hole to run to, to hide and more than plenty kill and get killed in the squeeze, and murder is not the rarest of events.'

A local woman had recently shot a bestselling-author boyfriend. And who knows. Could a polo-mallet murder have occurred in this very house? And the woman found not guilty of committing it, and yet her intention scratched on a window pane with her diamond ring. But then no decent country house is worth its history without a murder or two being committed within its precincts. And one never knew how many hundreds with malice aforethought may have been garrotted, bludgeoned, hung, drawn and quartered and knocked off or whacked in His Grace's dungeons over the centuries.

There was no question but that such news became, buried in history, more colourful than ominous, especially with all the beauty surrounding one. And with a break away from lingerie, he was catching the more joyful mood of Blueberry Hill's gradually glowing life. Even in the flashing few moments when down-in-the-dumps contentment could be restored by just looking around one out a window or on a walk. Anyway maybe to survive you don't really need all that much pleasure out of life. Although they say it keeps you healthier. Like walking boardwalks by the sea. As he did once walk. In Atlantic City. So blissfully holding hands with someone not his wife.

But he was astonished at how much he was now enjoying these times in the country. Never a dull moment in proving yourself useful. A job to do in every direction. Including pulling an occasional stray weed out of the front drive. Deep dark earth on his fingers after all his years handling silky lingerie. No farmer. But so what. If his social registering was indeed way down in the ratings, he at least retained his belief in the American ethos of all citizens being as good as each other. With just a bit of bigotry thrown in, in order to keep the social climbing steep enough.

Although Muriel objected to the use of the words 'black tie', it was certainly a tuxedo tonight in honour of his birthday. He took the hounds for a walk through parts of the woods he'd never been through before and where it still felt haunted by the Indians. Awaiting now Boris' expertise acquired in catering to His Grace, the duke's palate. It was even a pleasure catching sight of Boris' graceful strokes in wielding the silver crumb-remover across the table like a great master-painter. Even lacking sufficient smoking jackets, everything in his wardrobe a perfection. Shoes polished to a glistening shine in their shoe trees. He complimented Boris.

'Sir, there was a call for you. A lady wouldn't give her name. Spoke in French and I simply said, *Monsieur est absent pour le moment*. And she rang off.'

He knew it was Iowa. Thrilled she'd called and was still alive and presumably kicking. If he wasn't a snob before becoming as an itinerant lingerie salesman, he was sure learning fast how to become a raving one now. Iowa, in from the Western prairies, would never approve. But she would approve the savouring and tasting of Château d'Yquem. As ole Boris ordered the last of this rarest vintage from the wine merchant, unmindful of the long-term astronomical financial consequences. Which had Reginald giving one of his whistles. The bottles now laid down safely deep in Blueberry Hill's cellars.

'Indeed sir, such Sauternes especially favoured by bon-vivant Russian archdukes for the wine's health-giving qualities.'

A black-tie dinner, celebrating his very own entry into this world. The staff even quaffing a magnum of Louis Roederer in the servants' kitchen. And despite a little hair loss and new grey hairs and a few pounds collected on the midriff, and athlete's foot between the toes, it felt OK becoming forty-nine years old. And boy, Muriel was quite a sight in her white satin evening gown, her tiara and a necklace acquired in a moment of devil-may-care generosity, to wit, a diamond and pearl pendant with chain by Gübelin. And the cost of which shall remain unmentionable. And Boris witnessing as he blew out all the candles on his birthday cake, save two. 'Ah bravo, sir, bravo.'

'Happy birthday, darling Nathan. And thank you for all this.'

'Honey, how can I tell you how welcome you are.'

'And maybe, Nathan, that's why I guess it all makes me so horny and sends your pants out like a tent. Oh Nathan. This is it, isn't it.'

'It sure is, honey. This is it.'

Except it began to rain. In enormous drops. And their two glasses left together on the wall, remained lonely little symbols of this night as they left the terrace. Running. Holding hands. Down the steps, out on the drive and across the lawn into the woods. Rain pelting down. Drenched in the rain. Soaked to the skin. Muriel's voice. 'Right here. Right here. I want it thick and hard. Deep down in me. Plunge it in. In as far, far, far as it will go, go. Into my silky juices.'

He threw her on her back. And ground her into the wet earth of the woods. Thinking Christ, this was no pointless, purposeless fuck, this was the summit of all the things that ever happened between us. Joined to explode. As the sky with lightning and thunder and torrential rain. And like no fuck ever before. And a darkness that by daylight would be brown.

And back they came. Hand in hand. Half-naked in the thundering rain. Hoping that there was no poison ivy where they'd rolled over the breaking twigs. Trying to choose in whose bedchamber to spend the rest of the night. And it was Muriel's. And she did kiss him all over. Horniness begetting horniness. Muriel clinging to him as if she never wanted to let go. Until peace and quiet descended over supine bodies side by side.

TWELVE

THE SAD DAY came, finally. Goodwin's funeral.

'Boris, please lay out clothing suitable to attend a funeral.'

'Very good, sir. And of course, sir, I am very sorry to hear that. And I do hope it's not someone near and dear to you?'

'An employee, Boris.'

Knowing already how it was going to feel. The death of a family. Goodwin's children without a father. Like limping on into darkness. But Nathan's problem now was finding, as he was trying to do, his way somewhere across these Brooklyn streets to the Catholic cemetery of the Holy Cross. Hal on the phone suggesting the Hutchinson River Parkway. 'That's right. The fastest way to get there. Sorry to hear it's a mission of sadness.'

As Nathan reached the cemetery and parked some distance away, he could see into what seemed a hollow where one imagined graves might be cheapest. Under a black cloud of umbrellas, mourners in the rain collected. And now here for once his own trusty umbrella would not draw attention. He was late. A priest already intoning over the grave. Another priest and three nuns. Fake grass covering the hill of soil. Surprisingly more people than expected. A few faces turning as he approached. Uniformed gravediggers waiting. Ladies' high heels sinking into the damp ground. Turning his head to nod acknowledgment to Goodwin's family. His elderly mother and father. His wife and children, two little boys and a big sister.

'Why are they putting Daddy down into the ground?'

Final sobs. And far on another part of the cemetery came the lamenting sound of a bagpipe. A tearful blonde arriving just as the coffin was being lowered. A whisper in the gathering behind him that she was from Cincinnati. Reginald with his attractive wife. A handful of older staff Nathan hadn't seen for many months. And then the thumping of his heartbeat. Almost unbelievable. There she was. Iowa. Looking like one of the nuns. In a flowing black cloak. Her face shielded by a black cloche hat. And yet so *soignée* and elegant. He caught her eye just as a young child's voice was saying, 'Tell Daddy not to stay in heaven and to come home.'

The burial over. Sound of car doors closing. Mourners scattering back over the wet grass. He stayed till the very last of the gathering dispersed, his presence to owe Goodwin at least that dignity. And what do you say about this finish of someone's life? Someone you had no reason to be sorry for? As quickly as decency allowed he gave his condolence to Goodwin's wife, who, with vacant bloodshot eyes, merely seemed to look through one, but made a gestural movement of her head. In the Blueberry Hill library, a *Book of Common Prayer*, the biblical words: 'Man walketh in a vain shadow, he heapeth up riches and cannot tell who shall gather them.' We brought nothing into this world and it is certain we can carry nothing out. And on this very sad day Goodwin went an embezzler to his grave.

Then to step away from death. Walk between the gravestones back towards the road and the parked cars. The tearful blonde from Cincinnati nowhere to be seen. And he did observe Iowa. Only short yards away. The living life of her wonderful body moving amid the gravestones. Walking back towards what could have been that same bulletproof limozine he'd seen her vanish into outside the Pierre. A chauffeur opening the door. Another searing pang of jealousy. That her lissomness and limbs entwined. Yielding to someone else. She must have known he was watching her. Could it really have ever been they were in love? Her just a tiny little bit. And him a whole lot. Able to reach, without having to reach, into each other's brain. To nearly know what each other thinks. All of that. Locked up now to be an everlasting part of his own sad soul.

Then over the wet ground move away. Past the permanent cemetery residents. Escape to the car. Dismally alone drive out the cemetery gates and back across Flatbush. Through the rural openness of Prospect Park. Still with him the vision of Iowa beyond the gravestones. Then on the final way back to Westchester straight as an arrow on Flatbush Avenue, get a flat tyre. Quickly brings you back to normal life. And as the saying doesn't go, 'Have a bad day.' But his, as he dug for equipment, just as quickly turned into a good day. A Good Samaritan stopped to help. A master sergeant in the air force in a flash changing the tyre. Refusing money. 'Don't mention it. You'll do the same for someone one day. That way it goes around the world.'

In bed next morning with a giant glass of freshly squeezed orange juice. He sat up against the pillows, sun streaming in the window out of which the cemetery on the hillside was clearly in sight. And under their respective tureens came sausages, blueberry pancakes flooded in maple syrup, blueberry muffins, sliced fresh pineapple and strong coffee from freshly ground beans from Brazil. A pitcher of farm cream to pour over anything one fancied. The ironed newspapers opened up on his bed reading stand to peruse. The coffee delicious. There should be no worries in life. But some strange foreboding gloom still persisted. And paging through the *Daily News*, with its dramatic front-page pictures and murder headlines, didn't help. When instead it should have made you feel lucky you weren't presently down in the city, a victim of man's inhumanity to man.

'Is there anything else I can get for you, sir?'

'Boris, not a thing.'

Churning over and over in his mind, Nathan's next chore. To visit Goodwin's widow. He tried to figure out how does one console a grieving widow whose husband had embezzled you. And also to tell her that despite her husband's actions, her children would be paid for through college and she, if she remained unmarried, would receive a modest emolument for the rest of her life.

And the dreaded morning dawned all too soon. In the Daimler cruising again to the streets of Brooklyn. To brave the task of expressing one's condolences to Goodwin's widow and to explain the financial arrangements, which would be put in place. And to do so under probably less than eight-foot ceilings. And maybe he would feel the difference from Blueberry Hill and have, like the duke, to make a run for it. Which, anyway, was already on the cards. Especially if he were to gently suggest that her deceased husband's death, if not suicide, was no fault of his. Trying to rob him blind, and was caught. And judging by the audit, had produced a mind-boggling deficit. But as Reginald said, Goodwin was basically a nice guy and perhaps we would never fully know what went wrong. Or if someone tried to murder him. But maybe Nathan would find out more by first calling at the site of the crime in Queens and collecting Goodwin's personal effects and also meeting the new manager Reginald had hired on trial. A recent divorce victim trying to pay his lawyers. Prompting Reginald to comment, 'Nathan, I'm telling you, and I don't want to be pessimistic but so many guys are walking around New York these days shocked, dazed and deeply hurt, and swearing revenge over divorce settlements. It's a miracle the streets are not aflood with tears. Of course the wronged women view them dry-eyed, having already done their crying.'

And now one hoped that this new manager Reginald had hired on trial to replace Goodwin was, as he described, a real get-up-and-go guy. Who from Chattanooga, Tennessee, was actually planning to move and live in Queens. One hoped he would soon find someone similar to Nathan's own spouse as a partner, or better still, as a trusted, cherished wife. To be unselfish, loyal and faithful. As Muriel has been.

Traffic heavy.

Nathan Johnson, lingerie mogul, pulling up in front of his emporium. To park in a space especially reserved. Remember the cliffhanging months it took to put this store in operation. And as it expanded to become and remain one of the largest of his fast-growing chain. And as they say in showbiz circles, doing boffo business out in the wilds of Queens. And when he should be glad to see the place, one is instead dreading treading within. Bringing more of Reginald's words back to mind: 'Nathan, these guys, managing a lot of women, and really taking you for a ride in the case of embezzlement, show their hand by the eager happy way they seem to enjoy their work. Goodwin never gave any sign other than that he was a devoted husband and family man. But he did maintain that the sooner you had a wonderful time the quicker you could have another. Did well out in Cincinnati. Had good ideas on new store fittings. Even designed a line of passion-pink sleepwear that unfortunately bombed. Cincinnati women a little too sophisticated. But maybe the problem came with his staff of six hand-picked salesgirls. Who were too carefully picked.'

Up the slate steps. All the sad reminders of Goodwin's death still haunting his old office. The pictures of his good-looking wife Camilla, his children, little girls Jane and Patricia and son Andy, just being removed by the new manager, Swifty Kelly. Plus a sign on his wall:

So Much To Do
So Little Time
To Do It

Kelly, with his bouffant hairstyle, seemed impressed by the distinguished company Goodwin kept, as seen in his photographs with local celebrities, which collection might have even shown a Mafia face or two. Then as Nathan and Kelly, accompanied by salesgirls Carol and Maureen, briefly checked the storeroom where Goodwin had hanged himself, a grim look flashed across this new manager's face. The rack not only had been removed but discarded with other nearby racks and all sent to a distant dump somewhere. And likely where rub-out victims were also dumped if they weren't more untraceably put through a fish mincer out at sea. And then, ominous and stuck on the underside of a desk drawer, a scribbled note in pencil:

Pal beware
The fox
Is watching
The henhouse

The note produced a shiver down the spine. So Goodwin had an accomplice unaccounted for. Nathan tried to be casual. Asked where the dump was and put the note in his pocket. But no one present seemed to know the dump location except that it was not one for recycling. Then remembering when, as a child in school, a fellow pupil had died and the teacher had put at his empty seat a bowl of flowers every day for a week. But here in Queens there was a spark of gaiety. The new manager, already on first-name terms with the attractive Carol and Maureen, was, in the age-old salesman's tradition, keeping the girls amused. With his little quips as Nathan waited to be handed a large box they were packing: 'Mr Johnson. Here you go. In this is all Mr Goodwin's effects we could find in the office to be given back to his wife. Should I take that sign down too? *So much to do, so little time to do it.* Or leave it there?'

'Leave it there.'

'Sure thing. Girls, take this stuff out to Mr Johnson's car. By the way, nice automobile. And let me say, having heard so much about you, it's nice to meet you in person, Mr Johnson.'

His chariot outside the door was ready and waiting with its six-litre cylinders to start purringly combusting and take him away. An upmarket-looking customer coming in said a sprinkle of rain was falling. Astonishing how, even as the owner of half a dozen boutiques, one still gets a twinge of anticipation as a prospect enters your store. Any one of which, of course, could each have embezzlers galore. And one hoping the new manager is to be trusted completely. Who seems to at least know his way around the trade. Controlling as he would now, four stores in Queens and Brooklyn, the fourth store just added. Opening in three weeks. Two more planned in the Babylon and Patchogue direction of Montauk Point.

'I hope we have just a little time to talk before you go, Mr Johnson?'

'Well, a little time.'

Clearly he wasn't going to escape that easily. God, the hindrances that the world can heap up for you in seconds. Swifty Kelly began his spiel. Unrelenting. And to his immediate annoyance on a shocking subject straight off the bat. Iowa. The new manager only ever having seen her picture in the catalogues and then in newspapers and magazines and already displaying a prurient interest. Insinuating that if you could make it worth his while he'd recruit salesgirls just like her. And before long we'd all hitch a ride on his chariot of success full of Hollywood stars heading for the moon.

'Mr Johnson, I don't want to be crass or rude. Rather I'll be frank. But that girl, you know, gives me the hots. I would have never let such a girl escape. She's got a part and fantastic rave reviews in a play showing in a theatre on Second Avenue. Her enticement could guarantee boffo success with these stores.'

'Mr Kelly, I appreciate your positive enthusiasm, but we seem to be holding our own.'

'My credo, Mr Johnson, is to have increased repeat, repeat, repeat customers. One thing I know about a wife is that none of them likes anything better than getting as a present a box full of assorted erotic lingerie. And to put it crudely, to go off and use her vibrator if she doesn't have someone else to hand.'

'I see. Well, Mr Kelly, and perhaps not to put it as crudely, you're way ahead of us with that idea and news of our model Iowa.'

'It's because I believe in the gospel spoken by Horatio Alger in his stories of poor boys like me, who rose from rags to riches. I sincerely trust that my moral compass set in that orientation will guide me and continue to motivate me in the right direction to ride the Internet crest of the wave of consumer confidence. By the way, isn't that name Iowa a swell name for a girl?'

'One does not doubt that Iowa is a swell name for a girl and that you embody the ethos of being an American. But if you'll forgive me, I'm afraid that while I am in pursuit of that very principle myself I soon must head off to proceed elsewhere.'

'No problem. I'll be so brief you'll think I'm gone. Now, what I'd like to do, as we move out across Long Island, is pursue further sophistication, capitalizing on the stylish standard you've already set in the world of intimate undergarment fashion, but making it slinkier. Or let's say, seductively bolder. The colour purple. Or mauve if you want it that way. Let's face it, the further out you go on the island the more upmarket are your clientele. In fact, as it wonderfully happens, that particular sweetie-pie girl Iowa, who's now sort of the overnight talk of the town, could say it all. From Patchogue to Sag Harbor. The Hamptons in between. She is, let me say it succinctly, she is what you'd call real honest-to-god passion bait. Put on the Internet. Whoopee wow. And since she's quit I'd like it if you could cut me in on a piece of the action if I could get her back in your employ.'

'I beg your pardon, Mr Kelly. As far as I know she still is in our employ.'

'Well, you know. OK. But seeing what the big cosmetic companies do. The new face. The new body. Put her out on the fast-growing World Wide Web, in a Nathan Johnson advertising promotion. Produce a global feast of interest so to speak. Gee, by the way, I hope you don't mind my asking, and no disdain is meant. But what was a girl like that with her top model beauty and poise, plus now a brilliant actress, doing in a business like this?'

'I'm afraid I must beg your pardon again, Mr Kelly. And remind you I've got to go.'

'Sorry, Mr Johnson. No aspersions cast. But you know what I mean. There's modelling underwear. Then there's ten thousand bucks a day doing high-fashion haute couture. And for an actress as well, there's Hollywood.'

'If you must know how she's remained working for Nathan Johnson Lingerie, she has principles.'

'Holy cow. A maverick.'

'Yes Mr Kelly, a maverick. But I'd rather, if you don't mind, if you referred to her as unconventional.'

'OK Mr Johnson I retract my remark. No problem. Unconventional. But what a bombshell. Her smile to be seen glowing naturally. I guess that could include her fantastic legs.'

'I'd rather if you didn't harp on the matter, Mr Kelly.'

'Just trying to maybe personally learn a little more about her.'

'Well in that case, Mr Kelly I might be able to help you. It is known that she descends from an ancestor who was a pall-bearer at Beethoven's funeral.'

'Oh sure! I know the Beethoven guy. Great composer. His fifth or something, they call it. Well like I said, I may not play music but I sure play to win. And I do not disdain the classical. Everybody to their own taste. Iowa sounds like one of the kind of people that I'm attracted to and would be really be happy to be friends with. Like you'd expect her to have significant ancestry. Fits in with how she's got on her way to be an actress. Who could really end up big time. That's how I heard about the job, through an important guy who knew a guy who is building her a palace in Mexico in a jungle kingdom by the ocean. Yeah, a real palace. That's how I know she's not long for this world of lingerie. And Christ, I mean a kingdom. Like thirty thousand acres. Offshore he's got something like a three-hundred-foot yacht equipped with helicopters.'

Before there were any more bombshells or uncouth remarks to come, and if a silent stare can shut somebody up, Nathan's eyes were trying to do just that. Kelly of the bouffant hair shifting his weight and glancing right to left and left to right. And this is what happens to you as a mogul. You get paranoid about your minions, all ready to rear up and take you over. Making you suddenly wonder who the hell they may know or recruit to help them to do it. Or are they merely scheming small time to cheat and chisel. Each one already swearing on a stack of Bibles they can be trusted not to betray you. 'Well Mr Kelly, this little meeting is over. As much as I may find it enlightening, I'm afraid it will have to continue at another time. As I'm on my way on an urgent errand right now.'

As he was released by Swifty Kelly, he thought, Christ I hope he's not going to turn into a crook. Reginald having heard more of the Goodwin story from Sabrina, a lesbian assistant with a beautiful figure who had a crush on Iowa, and who described an evening past closing hours before Goodwin was discovered dead. That she in returning to get a cache of subway tokens she'd left behind, heard a noise in his office and went to investigate. Opening the door. Finding Goodwin with a fifth of bourbon on his desk and pounding his fists, shouting, 'I've got to win, I've got to win. Beat the bastards.' And Reginald, relating the story, said there was nothing unusual about shouting out those words loud and clear here in these United States where selling has always been the ultimate moment of truth.

'And as we both know, Nathan, that's right. Goodwin was a good example. Open-hearted salesman par excellence. Could produce a flow of endless, spellbinding positive thinking such as no one would want to interrupt. Who knows what turned him into an embezzler. And I'm still digging into the damage.'

On hearing Reginald's words Nathan thought that the answer could be found on some of the underworld faces in a couple of pictures Goodwin had in his office. And after the swindle is pulled off, getting laid is, of course, always the next priority. The latter achieved by big-time behaviour. Hey, bring us a couple of more bottles of that Krug. And one has to be careful of being charitable, especially if he had accomplices. A shipment being traced of a thousand or more thongs and brassieres a week previous to his suicide found missing. But OK, maybe the guy just simply let too many pressures build up. Then tried to bury them, aided and abetted by high living and out-for-a-good-time girlfriends. The latter obviously enjoying all the free lingerie they wanted.

It was a relief to be at last encased back in the red leather safety of his racing-green Daimler. And watching now from the windows of the store were the salesgirls, Carol and Maureen. Stop getting upset about Kelly. Leaving Nathan with a new vast emptiness. The irony, of course, is that the guy's actually got smart ideas. And although one followed the principle of giving everyone the benefit of the doubt, and remaining magnanimous to the enthusiasm of a new employee, there was always something about such folk which made you immediately dislike the tie they were wearing and who made one quickly grow with the intention of deciding to fire them faster than instantly. For they can incite a gloom in your spirit. When you needed cheer. Which he'd been taking from Iowa's voice in his brain. 'Bleak heart, don't be bleak.'

As one sped away, finally en route, making a brief zigzag way to Brooklyn. Rain torrential pouring down the windscreen. Forget nipping in the bud the things that could be happening heralding some new conspiracy afoot. Just wait till they happen. Well, the worst that's happening is that he had imagined Flatbush was really going to be flat. And it was. Street after street. Invading the suburban boondocks. His conscience clear and clean. Vander

Veer Park. Crossing Ditmas Avenue. Getting closer now. There they are, in all their little rows of houses. Two right turns, two lefts, and he was there.

The third house past the corner. Sits there looking like every other house. Built of brick the colour of a polo coat. Same windowed porch. But curtains drawn. The type of house he used to skip selling door to door. Sure that such was going to slam in his face. And send you with your samples fast farther away on the street to disappear around the corner in a state of gnawing aloneness, trying to find the courage to go looking for and tackle a more welcoming place. Never dreaming that one day, as a millionaire many times over, you would be again standing in such a street. Where once you heard yourself saying to yourself as you walked away from a slamming door, 'I can't. I can't take it anymore.'

Nathan Johnson, stepping down off the kerb and squeezing between the bumpers of two parked cars. Don't get killed crossing the street. And children can still love a father no matter what he's done. And all one can think of now is one's own lucky life. Free of a swirling turmoil of unhealthful molecules to the body and spirit of the kind that must have brought foment to Goodwin's home. No palace but certainly not a bad house. Pre-Second World War. A sunporch. Step up these steps. Press the bell. The front door opened a crack.

'Mrs Goodwin?'

'Yes.'

'I'm Mr Johnson.'

'Don't worry, I know who you are.'

'I apologize for not warning you. I did several times try to telephone. I know it's a difficult time.'

'Are you trying to find out how much our house is worth? Well, it's worth zilch. And mortgaged to the hilt. There's my car parked right over there. That's right. That red thing. A jalopy. You can take that.'

'I haven't come to find out how much your house is worth. Or to take your car.'

'Well then why have you come, why? To try to fuck me?'

'I have these things here belonging to your husband. Would you mind. Can I come in, please?'

'Come in. While everybody on the block is watching. Shut the door behind you. Join the grief. See what millionaires we are.'

Standing as one stands. In the middle of a darkened living room. Wondering how you could get out again. Away from this woman. Who even in her dowdy clothes managed to look attractive. Mrs Goodwin turning on more lights. Put Goodwin's box of effects on the floor. On the soft crimson carpet it looks like a Christmas present. A large brick fireplace. Plenty of self-help books in a bookcase. Magazines laid out on a coffee table. Mrs Goodwin with the smell of alcohol on her breath. An ice-filled glass next to an expensive brand of scotch. Chivas Regal.

'These are your husband's personal effects from his office. And I simply want to tell you that if there is anything I can do to help, I will. And also to tell you ...'

'And also to tell me what. That John was having an affair. That he spent thousands of dollars on some floozy who took him for what she thought he was worth and what he stole from you. The answer is, I know. He was always having an affair. So don't. Don't tell me anything.'

'I wasn't meaning to tell you anything like that.'

'Oh we know, don't we. You're so successful. So smart. All those stores opening all over the country. A new one nearly every week. Got everything you want. John was going to be just like you. He thought he needed money to improve his image. He wanted to be promoted to vice president of operations and manage Nathan Johnson Lingerie all over the United States. Be a multimillionaire. Well the way things are, you can't send John to prison, can you. But you can send me to the poorhouse.'

'I'm sorry, Mrs Goodwin. I'll go. No one is going to do anything to you. My presence here right now was just to inform you of matters affecting your husband's life insurance pension plan, that all funeral expenses will be met and that whatever has happened, no action of any kind is to be taken regarding your husband, that you can seek our help if it's needed in any way at any time and that your children will be provided for in their education through college paid for by a trust set up by the company. And any mortgage paid off if necessary. I wanted to be the one to convey this to you personally. Sorry to have intruded at such a time. But I thought you'd like to know these facts as soon as possible. Goodbye.'

'Wait! Don't go. Oh Christ don't go, I beg of you don't go. I'm sorry. I appreciate what you just said. I appreciate it, I really do. Don't leave me. John had a girlfriend in Cincinnati sucking him dry. And the blonde bitch had the nerve to come to his funeral. I'm all alone. Have a drink. Nobody's here. Those aren't my kids out there playing in the driveway, mine are at school. I made them go as soon as I could. You want scotch on the rocks? You want a Martini? Or a beer?'

'Thank you very much, but I think I've intruded upon you enough, Mrs Goodwin.'

'Don't leave me. You can fuck me. I know you don't want to, but you can. How's that for commiseration, if that's the right word? I'm still a little beautiful. I'm still a little tiny bit beautiful. I'm only thirty-six years old.'

'I'm sorry, Mrs. Goodwin. But please, I think I must go. You are a very attractive woman. You've been through a lot. But you should you know, if you haven't already, it might help to see your doctor. And at the company's expense. It may take some time but time heals.'

'How the hell do you know. You haven't been through it. Too busy, you and your wife trying to enter Manhattan high society.

And like shit, time heals. And a doctor. I got this. A bottle. What do I need a doctor for. Time kills. That's what it does. John was only thirty-nine. I need a husband. A father for my children. I don't need a struggling life alone on charity out in this burg.'

'Your life, Mrs Goodwin, will not be struggling. And it's not charity. All my employees are dealt with in the same way.'

'I don't care what promises there are. I know. My life will be struggling. What do you know about being left alone. There it is. I even thought I should put it on the wall. Look at it. Framed. His suicide note. A police officer trying to be humane, suggesting I needed protection, made a present of it to me. I framed it so I thought maybe it could help my children understand what happened to their father. Here. It's yours. You take it. Hang it in all your stores, so employees will know about that audit team of yours that comes sweeping down snooping in the night.'

My dearest love,
I only wanted the best for you and the children and I have failed. It is no one's fault but mine. I had no time to warn you. Forgive me for what I have done.
Your loving husband, forever.

'Mrs Goodwin. Thank you. But I don't think that's going to be of any help to me or any of my employees. And it's time for me to go. Your husband's effects left in his office are in this box.'

'What, a gold gift box. Are you trying to be funny?'

'No, I'm not.'

'Well go. Get out.'

Her olive-green cardigan jacket drawn closed. This widow clutching the framed suicide note written in pencil on a torn piece of cardboard found at the feet of Goodwin's crumpled body. And retreating step by step, backwards out into the hall out of this widow's sight, there came a lump in Nathan's throat and tears in his eyes as he remembered the words. *Forgive me for what I have done*. How long did it take to compose them. Try to open the front door. This woman with her bloodshot eyes pressing his arm away. And she drops the frame. The glass crunching underfoot on the floor. Turn the lock. Get the door opened. Get out. Pull the door shut. She tries to hold it open. Leave it go. And she slams it closed. Then opens it again. Her eyes on his back as he goes down the steps. Trip over a kid's tricycle. Reach the sidewalk. And one thing was for sure, that there is nothing worse than hearing the mewl and wracking sobs of a female human being. And a voice shouting out at you, 'You murderer. You murderer.'

Another escape, just like his numerous ones as an itinerant lingerie salesman. Only worse. One had always thought that the other boroughs of New York City like Brooklyn and the Bronx were places where despite your own personal speed of departure, you could retreat to more lenient surrounds to lick your wounds. Plus following a suicide and a funeral, Brooklyn ends up changing your life. Even if only for a few minutes, back again to nearly what it used to be. The grey. The dark. The menacing.

Drive back straight along Flatbush Avenue and briefly through the beauty of the green in the Botanic Garden of Prospect Park. Still living with the description of Goodwin given by Jerry. Found hanged, slumped between black lacy sleepwear garments on a rack. A ligature of thongs lengthened by a length of two twisted bras knotted together. Hanging his body by the neck. A final form of scorn that not even a busy Flatbush Avenue can erase from the mind. And hearing Iowa's voice again, enigmatic but encouraging: 'Fox, my heart panteth after thee. That's Psalm 42, first verse. Like as the heart desireth the waterbrooks, so longeth my soul.'

THIRTEEN

HEADING for this island of Manhattan, the great metropolis that can, unnoticed, devour you alive. Where you exist as a miniscule trace of life. Trying to keep safe the body in which you struggled. And which in the loneliest indignity of all could end up spirited away as another unknown and unclaimed to rest on Hart Island. Which at least, with his own grave and mourners, was an indignity of abandonment Goodwin did not have to suffer. Yearn now at this hour of this day. For more than anything else, to be back in his secret hideaway. To be taking tea with Iowa. That wonderful grin on her mischievous face. Her feelings once, about the dear departed, when he said his favourite place to go was cemeteries. And when his own thoughts were in that direction. 'Gee, fox, get that glum look off your face. Didn't you know it's un-American to like cemeteries. And never giving up on your living dreams in a go-get-'em society like ours. Thoughts are kept away from death by the young in life and I guess no one really gives a good goddamn except to get their grabbing mitts on the moolah and success. Don't laugh. Because that could be a picture of me.'

And he did laugh. Because it was no picture of Iowa. But now he owned a cemetery. With its own history, but none of its occupants as famed as those deceased people in some of the cemeteries of Brooklyn. About whom he could have told Iowa. Names remembered from publicity while they lived. And from whom he somehow took comfort. It helped to know what pitfalls were around still to avoid. These people who went before one in this city, living their own stories. Don't be a bank robber. But if you were, be one like the gentleman criminal Willie (the actor) Sutton. Referred to as the Robin Hood of bank robbers. Laid to rest there in Brooklyn at the age of seventy-nine. Willie, in his disguises, escaped jail numerous times and stole a couple of million. Then there were the Collyer brothers. Removed from their junk-filled world and deposited in a much neater one. Minus their fourteen grand pianos and in their tunnels from room to room through their lair of debris. Then Diamond Jim Brady famed for his prodigious appetite, a friendly guy who wore diamonds bigger than door knobs. Taken from his glamorous existence to die lonely in Atlantic City. Spending his last days staring out over a grey stormy sea. And where in this same seaside town Nathan had lain in darkness. The smell of the salty sea in the air. In a space hidden no one else could hear or ever know of. Unforgettable idyllic days of his life with a too-brief lady love. Sweet nothings whispered to the ocean sounds of the Atlantic waves trembling the shore.

Ahead lights go on in the city's windows. Darkness coming. Travel straight as an arrow across this bridge. And if one kept going you'd end up on the steps of City Hall. Where skulduggery over the years was more than just a rumour and was alleged to brew. Although weathering the storm of office made many mayors great men. At least they were all good, attending crises, speeding through the streets escorted by wailing police sirens. As maybe another's life could be saved. And if you sum up your own life, you are now a winner. Approaching top of the pile. Iowa had begun to call his hideaway the fox's den. Maybe it's time to check in there. Go and try to recover his peace of mind with the sadder strains of Mahler or Beethoven. See if rats have got in and started eating his papers. The cockroaches were in plenty already there. Check how business is doing, on a much maligned and blasphemed Wall Street. An address about which Reginald often had reason to complain and always advised for Nathan Johnson Lingerie to stay a privately owned company.

'Worse than throwing dice loaded against you. Or selling lingerie on a street corner. Corporate conspiracy pauperizing the innocent shareholding public. In spite of a rigmarole of disclosures, endless filings, the SEC coming down on their heads. Even the most celebrated and respected are some of the biggest crooks. They say hi, hey hello, to the little guy. And spend the rest of their hot air instilling in him the faith to bet a bundle on a stock. And bingo, a couple of days later, a few seconds trading, and the poor bastard's life is torn apart. Let me tell you, pal, if you ever go public with Nathan Johnson Lingerie, such guys will have a lot to thank you for.'

And boy, did he know what Reginald was talking about. Certified public accountants being driven out of business by armies of law firms in perpetual attack. Corporate culprits who screwed the little guy were themselves taking off from Newark Airport in their private jets. Wine waiters and bimbos aboard. Fly west to Michigan to hide by a lake to shoot ducks.

Passing back into and upon the island of Manhattan thinking, a suicide. The biggest bad thing that's happened to date in his business life. Plus reliving again and again the funeral. Goodwin's young family. His children, the mystery of life in their eyes. Two little boys holding each other's hand. And the eldest, taller girl behind them. Her hands on their shoulders. The forlorn lost look on their little faces as the coffin slowly lowered in the ground. A wife gaunt and pale. Features expressionless. Tears pressing into one's own eyes at the words of a child's tiny voice. 'Mamma, can I cry now?'

The memory like a dark immovable cloud in the sky. A shadow over the soul. He even prayed. Saying to himself Iowa's words, 'Bleak heart, don't be bleak.' Bow one's head among the mourning employees, shake their offered hands. And it was that moment, staring at the muddy ground of the cemetery. And not knowing what face he had to face next. Or what expression to wear. Nor a word to say to show how sorry he was.

'Mr Johnson, can I say something?'

A pair of black shoes in front of him. As he looked up and over the sea of gravestones there was Jerry, the discoverer of

Goodwin's body in a too-shiny dark suit. White shirt and black tie. The mainstay of the inventory team. His best employee. Started to work for Nathan when he first acquired five stores. And how rarely can you say such word. Trusted. The one person at least about whom you could thankfully and truthfully feel that you would be sad were you not ever going to see them again. And to already know what he was going to say. Coming to say his final goodbye. Tears in his eyes as he shook Nathan's hand.

'Mr Johnson, before I go I'd like to say just one thing. You are a decent man and were a privilege to work for.'

Nodding his head to these words that would always last. A comfort in one's mind. Someone who not only saw who but what you were. Decent. And his own future ahead. He'd already moved to Boston where they wouldn't let Nathan Johnson Lingerie establish a store in the dignified elegance of Charles Street. But where Jerry, not that far away, could work as an assistant concierge in an hotel fabled for its breakfast menu and overlooking the Public Garden. A job for which Nathan gave him a glowing recommendation.

And the thoughts that you can think staring out through a windscreen of a car. Nathan, that he never ever wanted to see another piece of lingerie again. And Iowa. Who once asked if he had a clean conscience. At first he hesitated to reply. Never wanting ever to say anything that might make her hate him or even be disappointed with in him. Because he'd have to say, and did say, no. I haven't got a clean conscience.

'That's all right, fox. You see, now you got a clean conscience. You admit that you don't.'

Now ahead at last a brief glimpse of the green of the park of Madison Square. You get to know this so anonymous city too well. To make you feel at home. Moving in one's own little moveable world. Luckily not far from the Flatiron Building, there's a dingy dark barrenness of a garage he used to know.

Nathan Johnson a pedestrian on the hard sidewalk instead of kicking leaves through his woods. And now reaching this familiar doorway, a burst of dust blowing up in his eyes, he can only think of the thoughts that still follow him as he pays a visit to the hideaway. The door squeaking open. To a place hauntingly empty. Turn on the light. To loneliness. The dust deeper in the fox's den. Now pick up the newspaper on top of the telephone. Because in it was Iowa's first long mention in a headline glowing review. Also about the arrest and instant release of a Mafia don and a disappearance and suspected murder of a hitman. Another fish mincer at work at sea. All too un-nice. And now, what's this? His red message light blinking on the answering machine. One message. Only one person other than Reginald knows the number. In order to convey in secrecy bad urgent news that Muriel shouldn't be told. And it could be a message left here on this machine for months. Press the button. No. wait. Think. Sit down. It's always better to know. The worst. Press the button.

'Pops, you old fox, if you're ever there to hear me. It's me. How are you? And by the way, you've never been in touch even once. So I'm calling you. From the sunny if smoggy climes of California, where as one sidesteps all these hotshot go-getters in this business, who are bumping and barging into you and each other, bullshitting nonstop. And I can't bear to have another slimeball come rolling towards me and trying above all other things to get laid. Stacks of scripts to play a whore or a skimpily-attired horny farm girl. And you'll be pleased to know I'm not calling to ask you for a raise. But because I miss you and your shyness and your gentlemanly ways. But there is pleasant variation in my life between my flash but less frequent visits to Mexico and while I'm at the Beverly Hills Hotel in a palatial suite. I could do with fewer flowers every day. Baskets of fruit. Not all the pears are ripe and more than a few of the other citrus edibles are very over-ripe. Just like the rest of Hollywood, where I'm on my way to dooming my soul to perdition. Having been in three movies back to back already, one just released, another on the way. I'm now reading scripts with a little less nudity and am nearly more than a supporting part in a major blockbuster film. Playing, you guessed it, a lingerie model. From the boondocks.

'I tried a couple of times, perhaps too discreetly, to get to you in your palace to keep you up to date. But in spouting my erratic French to a very polished English voice, that made it worse when he lapsed into what seemed equally unpolished French, I always had to hang up. So I'm trying to penetrate into your secret hangout. Knowing there's little chance of your leaving your mansion. Fox, not having seen you in so long, please, please be in touch. I'm not sure room service isn't making me homesick wanting to feel I'm back on the farm.

'So I may not stay here long. That is, in this hotel. Under my nom de plume. Ask for Elizabeth Fitzdare. Very English-sounding name I found in a book. I'm sad over not seeing you before going away. Just to shoot the shit as we used to do. Please, fox. In that dark dusty den of yours, if you're ever there, please take tea to brighten it up a bit in my memory. How I miss that little ceremonial ritual tea of ours. And there's so much more I want to say and tell you but I'm too shy to blurt out over a telephone. So it must remain silent in my heart. Don't forget me. Promise. And I won't ever forget you. That knocking you hear in the background is room service arriving with my corncobs. And so if any more chill winds of life blow, bleak heart, don't be bleak.'

But he was bleak. And he was lonely. And he was cold. He so much wanted her to warm him. And he did, tears falling, ring the Beverly Hills Hotel. Miss Fitzdare has left us, sir, three weeks ago, and moved to the Hotel Bel-Air. And leaving no forwarding address. Closing his eyes, replaying her words. A cry from the heart. Meaning as much to him as anything else in his world. As much as his children and marriage. Lock the fox's den. Maybe for the last time. Already notices served for his eviction. Excuses and rumours that the landlord is selling or intends to demolish the whole building. Tempting him to buy it. Keep Iowa's voice forever echoing in there.

And now think of death. All those who have already died and left your life, remembering everything she ever said, and, at last and for sure, to know. Iowa is gone. Looking through his tears, driving north along the Bronx River Parkway. The Kensico Dam rearing grey and massive ahead. Which made him think the waters it held could break through and one day come thundering, washing all before it. Right down the Bronx and into the East River that flows into Long Island Sound.

'Bleak heart, if chill winds blow, don't be bleak.'

Echoes again of that voice. But now back at Blueberry Hill, feeling unable to ask Boris to slake his thirst and cheer his spirits with some champagne in the library. But he needn't ask Boris to do a thing. Not even in French. Everything anticipated. A bottle already waiting in the bucket. 'I was, sir, first going to serve tea. Then I thought that this wine might make more welcome your return from the city. Good to have you home, sir.'

'Thank you Boris, glad to be home.'

'And let us place the ice bucket so that in taking replenishment, sir's back need not motion forward from the back of the chair. And I thought that a little bit of wild smoked salmon from the Tay in Scotland would do sir no harm.'

The silvery pale liquid poured. Tasted. Swallowed. The comforting word 'home' used by Boris, who must have sensed his dispirit which, however he might resist, continued to drag him down. But somehow Boris' presence was a cushion of reassurance and calm. Grateful to him now as his fingers enclosed the slender Baccarat stem of the glass. Raised to watch the bubbles galore arising up through this wine better known as Charles Heidsieck. Whispering to himself, 'This one's for you, Iowa. That your dreams continue to come astonishingly true. And that the fruit in your baskets may always be perfectly ripe. And you. May you long reign a princess in Hollywood.'

He smashed back the champagne, which always reminded of the moments when he and Iowa had their drink at the Pierre. Now in the present soothing comfort ensconced in front of these licking flames and listening to Beethoven's Fifth. Making him feel as near as possible to imagining Iowa stepping out of the flames. Reaching back beyond the years in her ancestry. To that pall-bearer who performed that duty at the great composer's funeral. His utter gloom enfolded in this ageless music. To make Iowa's departure bearable rather than utterly sad. Already becoming a star. Shooting out across the sky farther and farther away. Beyond the beyond. And into that utter galactic space that she herself, trying to investigate the universe, wondered about. And now full of her name and her life. But his eyes closed to photographs in gossip columns. Her reviews he wouldn't read. But furious, already finding her ridiculed in a headline over a bikini, before he'd chucked the paper into the library fire:

FORMER LINGERIE MODEL NAMED AFTER
A STATE MAKES IT INTO BIG TIME

But in all these weeks and months that she was the toast of the town at least meant she wasn't in a palace in Mexico in someone else's arms. And now to himself he admitted that although their bodies had never touched, he loved her. He loved her. He did. And does. And she's gone. To live her life in other climes. And leave him back in his own lonely world of pure unadulterated survival and sorrow.

FOURTEEN

MURIEL OUT all day shopping locally in White Plains. Accosting him in the hall as he headed up to his rooms. Asking why hadn't he taken the dogs for a walk to the lake. And that a pipe was reported leaking somewhere. What else is unexpected with ten miles of pipes? And announcing too that there was a local hunt ball to which we weren't even alerted. Never mind invited. As if it were something he needed to know. Like a bit of gossip. That we were socially ostracized in Westchester. Where you learn. If not fast. Then slow. That to social climb. And succeed. Don't try.

'I invited those people I met at the charity ball for cocktails and they sent their regrets.'

'Well clearly, Muriel, they were already otherwise engaged.'

He did now think, who gives a good goddamn about neighbours for cocktails. Or showing off to Muriel's kinfolk. Who were visiting and already throwing their weight around with staff and helping themselves to what they could eat and drink. And he'd prefer walking with the wolfhounds down to the lake in the dark as he'd been recently doing. Out with nature tasting the freedom of the crisp air. Then, flashlight in hand, perspire in a gentle jog back up the hill. In time for his bath drawn. Radox to soak in. And the seven-fifteen drink before dinner. To dress now in his recently acquired light-blue smoking jacket that Boris regarded as de rigueur, especially when dining alone in the library.

'Shall I lay out sir's smoking jacket and slippers for this evening?'

'Do, Boris.'

'There's a claret, sir, I'm decanting, that I think will please you. And some duck pâté with port wine.'

'Wizard.'

'Oh dear, sir. I am most heartily sorry, and you must forgive me, yesterday first thing I was intending to bring you a message, but was sidetracked by another outburst in the kitchens.'

'Pray tell.'

'The young lady, sir, the one who has rung before attempting to speak French. Again she would leave no message nor number. I must admit to rather exceeding my brief for, in the hope I could rustle you up, I tried to keep her on the phone. She has the most beautiful voice. Full of laughter.'

One could not believe the bad timing and shattering shame of it all. Just as he was giving up. The one most cherished. Her voice full of laughter. Telephones. While he drank. On a telephone only sixty or seventy yards away. And exactly while he was thinking of her. He did deserve better luck. How would Boris know she was young. And perhaps too young. For an old sourpuss pops. How is it that he went on and on hopelessly thinking of her. Even as he worried, doomed over a tax audit. Rigmarole disclosures. Endless filings. SEC snooping and sniffing. And you'd be forced to wish you were back selling thongs and G-strings door to door.

And you'd wonder. What was one aspiring to in British life, where swearing and bottle-smashing were highly upper-class pursuits. But why not. It could be an antidote to his undoubtedly ever-increasing paranoia. Waiting for another phone call, while seeking solace in the silence of the library. Hoping she calls before a tree brings down the lines. And Reginald, only a day or two ago, unaware of his fixation, did drop an item of gossip. 'Nathan, here's an item to distract you from property taxes. Remember that girl, Iowa, the sultry willowy bombshell? Big picture of her in the paper. Even a bit of a song and dance I caught on television. Believe it or not, she's a Hollywood actress. Driving an Aston Martin. Escaped, while being chased by paparazzi back and forth from the studio and by helicopter, to some guy's palace in the Mexican jungle. And know what, she's quoted saying she was already thinking of permanent retirement and was happier back making pretty little poses in downmarket lingerie.'

And even as crushingly wounded as he was by her down-market remark. To be even remembered with a little tiny stab in the heart sent a shiver of hope through him. Iowa hadn't changed. She was out there, still the same. In the haunting ether of Hollywood. But it was not the sort of news he wanted to hear. Nor could it lessen the gloom caused by the increased uncheerful loggerheads with Muriel busy with her appointments. Massages, facials, manicures, pedicures. And not amused when he dropped the hint that a tiara, provided it was a big one, was in British aristocratic circles of life, when kept on by a lady following dinner, a sign that she would then be without her clothes. But such observations were received with a smirk. 'Oh, more of that British bullshit from your Boris, is it? With whom you seem to conduct dinner conferences in the library.'

'You seem, Muriel, to regard the simplest molehill of a servant problem, any that involves Boris especially, to be monumental.'

'So tell me what's supposed to be monumental, Nathan?'

'Well, such as the increasing disappearances of exotic comestibles. And I should like to know who of your guest relations wolfed down the pound of pâté from the best delicatessen in New York.' He himself had. Slowly but surely. Because Boris hid it for him.

'Well buster, why don't you head back into your monk hibernation in the library. And figure out who is now piece by surreptitious piece swiping the silverware, I suppose was part of your original lock, stock and barrel junk purchase of Blueberry Hill. And your Boris said that an odd piece was actually real silver. And, by the way, why don't you occasionally go and find out how business is doing?'

'Because, my dear, I spent years building it and now wouldn't mind a little spell of spiritual peace away from female undergarments to enjoy a few fruits of reward.'

'We do, don't we, wax eloquent under your butler's example.'

Christ Almighty. What had he done to deserve this. Business was booming. Life at Blueberry Hill was all nearly getting as bad as taking an inventory of lingerie. But without a team to swoop to nail the perpetrator of vanishing comestibles. But one bowed to Muriel. She was right. He was waxing eloquent under the influence of Boris. And Muriel did smile. And laugh. Weakening his efforts to pretend his continued calm formality. So he laughed, too. They were still in love. And he was aflood with a surge of wanting to take her in his arms and squeeze.

'Well my dear, toodle-oo. I know you must to your guests. Give them my blessings.'

'Like hell I will.'

'Oh dear, said the wrong thing?'

'Keep trying you'll get it right. Ask your Boris.'

BOOK II

FIFTEEN

MURIEL NOW seemed to visit Reginald more often. I guessed to find out how her shares were doing. And I will now tomorrow at last head into town. Climb aboard my faithful chariot. Tonight light a cigar and have vintage port after dinner. Peace to reign. With Mahler and Beethoven. Be able once again in affection to embrace one's wife. Chase her around either of our bedrooms. Here I come honey, watch out. And how many times, you ask yourself, can it be not the worst but instead the best fucking time in your life. The news especially refreshing continuing to come. For just prior to my crossing the front hall and under the biggest chandelier in Westchester, which costs a fortune to keep clean, on the way to the car I stopped to read the fax written out by hand and just arrived from Reginald.

> *Dear Old Pal,*
> *I'm no Shakespeare but nevertheless let me put it all in perspective in my best real scribbled American English to*

you. It may not yet be the advent of pure pubic hair showing through the sheer, see-through thong but there's plenty of other frilly frills showing through and fluttering across the boondocks of these great wonderful United States. And boy do I salute allegiance to the profit for which it stands, one bonanza indivisible free to be enjoyed by all. Forgive me, pal, if I use politically confused jargon loud and clear, for beyond the snow-capped Rockies our sultry chocolate satin slips with pink lace trim are knocking 'em dead. Out here we're in the business now of super-superlative lingerie.

CLOAKS THAT
WHICH YOU
WANT TO CLUTCH

No longer maybe exclusive but available to all. Black is the colour now. Purple here and there. Satin silk is the thread. Kimonos embroidered with dusty pink lilies. Thongs every colour galore. Maybe even in the aforementioned line, retro styles may soon reign of a new unforgettable vintage. From those who want to avoid shop-floor embarrassment, the deluge of hits, visits and orders pour into our new website. You got it, pal. We're out in cyberspace with a vengeance now. Men order via the Internet. And I know it's shameful that I yet haven't had a spare second to come see you luxuriating in your beautiful palace on your beautiful estate, but I promise the first moment that I have I'll be there. I hear a lot about it. Those woods. Beautiful rooms. So now you go good fella, drink a toast of that good champagne of yours that that butler of yours serves. Bon appetite. Toodle-oo. For now.

I cruised down the Bronx River Parkway thinking that maybe a beef herd was the way to go. A deeper sign I guess, that, despite Reginald's message, one was beginning to feel the pressures over expenditures. Cut down on beluga and get the sevruga instead. Farm one's own filet mignon on the hoof, grown off one's own meadows. Cultivate blueberries in a big way. Find out from Hal where the hell they're growing on the place. Sell them baked in cakes and pies. And talking on a variety of subjects, Boris seemed to agree.

But now here, back in New York City. Instead of trees, the sensation of people endlessly passing. In taxis, buses, in cars and on the sidewalk. Bemused, I even stood and watched as my own elegant motor was driven away to be parked back down in the basement of Midas Towers. Then with so much to do one did pleasantly nothing, getting accustomed to the sights and scenes. Not wondering whom to call and where to go. One's gait feeling different, taking steps now on the hard sidewalks around the block and thinking of Iowa. Her face when expressionless, saint-like. With all her beauty to offer the world, and not yet ready for sale.

I walked not untroubled, down in the city. And the strange lurking aftermath of the Goodwin suicide unforgotten. To see if the world could change in my hideaway. Where anyway I shouldn't have to sense the presence of another human being. Or hear Ida the maid in the apartment groaning with her cucumber happily put between her legs.

Alone in my private office, news that Iowa disappeared and left no word. I went into a funk. Spent five of the most bereft days of my life. And except for a daily call to the office with no communication with anyone, I lay on my couch in a semi-coma, listening to Brahms. Dining off pretzels and hot dogs from the seller parked on the corner and a few beers in the bar around the block.

Talk about a change in living. This was it. From paradise to a sombre hideaway. Amazing how in the dumps you begin blaming people. Starting with Muriel's impudent, impertinent relatives who visit Blueberry Hill and won't leave. I am being crushed under their trampling feet. And with so many of them it's hard to know which one of your racial prejudices to let come to the fore.

In the lingerie business with so many to hate you it was easier to be pretty goddamn liberal and understanding in the field of ethnic undesirables when some of them could be your best customers. Still barely speaking to anyone I forced myself out on a couple of mid-afternoon strolls. Detouring on the way into side streets down Broadway past the site of the Broadway Central Hotel, once America's most palatial. To Battery Park and the smell of water. Then the round-trip ferry ride to Staten Island. Which never disappointed. Staring out across to Ellis Island and the Statue of Liberty. Always wondering what lurked in this midnight deep. Thinking too that family togetherness between two people was getting to mean a woman providing her relatives with a long bout of free food and board. Although there were only five of them, it seemed like an army. One winced at the damage to come, as the day of my departure, my own children descending there with their friends as well. Estranged as I seemed to be from them they never stopped asking for money.

DEAR SIRE
    THE WEATHER'S FINE FOR SKIING,
    I NEED THREE THOUSAND, FIVE HUNDRED
DOLLARS TO GO TO ASPEN.

The pit of my despair so deep, and although I again and again denied it vehemently to myself, I guessed, if one were seriously guessing, that I was in love with Iowa. Whatever love meant. It certainly meant thinking about someone all the time. And wanting them to always be there. Without them, and in the city now a week the place becoming meaningless. I was still suffering withdrawal from the spaciousness and luxurious surrounds of Blueberry Hill. Until, on the late afternoon of the eighth day, when I was thinking it was maybe time to at least grab a cab for LaGuardia and go fly to check up on a few stores out of state. Or return to Blueberry Hill, to see if another chandelier had been cleaned or more diamonds stolen. When suddenly it sounded like a key was mysteriously turning in the door lock. Wow. Wake up time in a hurry. The door slowly opening. I thought, Christ, get my gun, give my usual calm warning, 'Take another step and you're a dead man.'

'Oh god, pops, it's me, don't shoot. Let me come in and close the door. My god, nobody seemed to know where you were. Sorry. Am I interrupting?'

'No. Please. Iowa. Please come in.'

'I'm in. Gee, I was worried. Because I was in Hollywood, I haven't been at work and then I didn't know how to tell you I got a part in a play. I had a free ticket to the play for you but I thought when up at the office they didn't know where you were that something awful had happened. I even called on the telephone up at your castle to tell you I got a rave review. I laughed. A guy in a very English accent answers, said he was the butler. "Who's calling, please." Just to be on the right side of discretion I said I was Suzie your chief of research and development in Philadelphia. He said sir was not available. Could he take a message. You must be in your absolute element. Gosh, I didn't mean to upset you. Tears are welling in your eyes. What the hell's happening?'

'Well, at this very moment as I stand here and you, suddenly there, I'm not upset. I'm rejoicing at something wonderful that has just fallen out of heaven.'

'Oh pops. You are a sweetie-pie. And I'm doubly glad I brought you a chocolate cake. So now uninvited, I'm going to sit down right here like a lady and cross my legs just so, in fact in the way nuns get taught in a manual on convent deportment. And tell you just a little bit of so much that has happened to me. Gee, you've been disappeared now for such a long time. And by the look on your face you probably forgot you gave me a key.'

'Yes. That's why I grabbed this gun.'

'Then I only saw you in the distance at Goodwin's funeral. Now living in a castle or is it a palace, I was sure you weren't here.

I really came looking for you. I missed you just like you said you missed me when I had to run off that day.'

'Please Iowa. You're still standing. You haven't sat down yet like a nun.'

'I sure ain't like no nun but I'll take a seat and put these packages down. Oh god, pops, what a funeral. I was at least seventeen at my own father's funeral. Terrible, those little kids. They were so young and mystified. I knew you were worried and saddened. I guess now I'm trying to think of something encouraging to say. Like sometimes they try to hint it's boom time in *The Wall Street Journal* headlines. I guess that's when they think an investor crisis might be on the way when the so-called panic selling sets in and wipes away the value and big smart boys dive in to start buying. So I bought a few shares myself. And like everybody is, trying to buck the downturn occasioned by the fickle behaviour of consumers. See, I know all the jargon they use to dupe the public. Oh pops, under the rich man's yoke, I guess it's all about the ten or so million people this city's got craving attention whose total mass of life undergoes tragic constant removal with everyone trying to avoid being one of the removed. Tails between their legs, back to Kansas City, Missouri, or even to Norfolk, Virginia. But I'm only kidding.'

'Those are not kidding words, Iowa.'

'Well I guess I'm just preaching the opposite to the bullshit you get used to overhearing from the guys always trying to impress you with their big deals. But I guess I don't know my ass from my elbow about the market. Or about this big city. At an age when I should know better about everything and don't know a thing about anything. But gee, pops, that's an awful gloomy expression on your face. I'm just trying to cheer you up. To bring you something sweet to hear even though some of it is lies, like most news of the world is.'

'Iowa, I'm so cheered up just by seeing you. And sad that anytime may ever come that I won't.'

'Ah. You know, guys dealing in lingerie somehow exude an old world charm. Seeing so many tits and asses all the time, they know exactly what a girl wants to hear. They get so they're just glad to have you hanging around. Like girls like to do. Plus I guess it's not like it's a case of being more and more admired with each layer of clothes a girl takes off.'

'God Iowa, just to hear you talk.'

'I am talking aren't I. And here, a poem I wrote. Just let me get it out. A present for you:

> Go for the grass greener
> Till it fades
> Just like the grass you left
> Because there may never be
> Grass that green again.'

'God, Iowa reading these words. "Go for the grass greener." Am I going to be left. As I am already the grass faded.'

'No, you're not faded. And when I first came in and said tears were welling in your eyes I got the feeling that no one had ever been really kind to you before.'

'Iowa, you've been kind to me.'

'Pops, I apologize, back in time, taking off more and more for my acting classes. And I guess with the films but really the part in this play it just suddenly without warning paid off. This sounds so awful, doesn't it. If I could I would be here more often as I am right now. You know, for no other reason other than it is just nice to be here. I lost your phone number. Feeling that you always welcomed me barging in. Fact is I came looking for you. And loyalty, anyway, is the only thing worth worrying about in the world.'

And I did welcome her. And more than anything in the world wanted her to be around, anywhere that she could be. Closer to me.

'Pops, I guess you might know that things are happening. The play's playing at the Orpheum Theatre, Second Avenue. And I'm sorry. Really, not to be doing anymore modelling photographs for you. I mean I know nobody really sees our advertising publicity pictures like the wide-scale population would see somebody in a movie. OK. The cat's got your tongue.'

The cat indeed had got my tongue. And the noises in my life were now getting so loud I didn't want to hear.

'On the billboard outside the theatre, it says, *Iowa not only a state in the union but a woman you've got to see on the stage*. Oh god, pops, especially to you, I can't believe I'm bragging.'

And although hiding her magic look of honesty, she was so proud to tell me she was the toast of the town even just walking on Second Avenue. Her hair flowing back over her shoulders, every head turning to look at her. And here she was. Her grass greener. Just inches away. The clock forever ticking towards the moment when she'd be gone. And never in the history of silence has any ever been so thunderous. Stop listening. Reach out and touch her before it was too late. But I was a married man. Of whom it could be said was happily married and faithful to his vows. Except minus once. And even as Iowa and I had grown closer and closer together, it seemed we were being held apart, even safer and safer from each other. Especially in this room. Yet one did have the desperate thought. Just say it straight out. Let's go to a hotel. Discreetly large. Discreetly cosmopolitan. Uptown. The Biltmore or Grand Hyatt. And somehow I know it's all too late.

'Pops, to stand there in the glare of footlights taking a bow, the perspiration ready to roll down your cheeks, and the clapping reverberating in your ears, with the whooping sounds and whistles. I can't tell you how wonderful it is. Little glints of tears, like diamonds in the audience's eyes.'

I sensed that more than just applause and wonderful and flattering words on a billboard were changing her life. But there seemed still some doubt lurking in her voice, since she'd been so dramatically discovered. Already offered movie roles. Beckoned to Hollywood and back. Which could, and in her case had, in an instant make her a member of America's only true aristocracy. Feted, adored. Her autograph collected. And nothing like a poor lingerie operator raising her salary would keep her.

'I brought you a not-half-bad chocolate cake I baked. I could be arrested for being an un-American woman. Slaving over her hot stove in the kitchen. You see the limits I go to, to try to impress you. Just, on the off-chance, grabbed a cab downtown in the hope that you might be here. So now what about some tea?'

'Iowa. My god. Or rather my goddess. You betcha.'

'Sure, why not. Goddess. For you I'll aspire to that anytime.'

Within these four walls enclosing a floor I remember first measuring twenty-six feet long and twenty-four feet wide. And at first plenty roomy enough for most things, even a refrigerator, but now with bookshelves up the walls to stack magazines, photographs and newspapers, one still had to navigate through obstacles on the minimum floor space left. I tried to be host. For this up-and-coming stage star. Who had with such few words reawakened and enlivened my life, some bit of emerald to add brightness to my faded green. There she was watching me, in my kitchen corner, filling the electric kettle, my hands trembling.

'Pops, my god, the kettle overflowing and this electric cord worn through, you could get electrocuted. And sorry to allude. That bed. The sheets need changing. How are you surviving here like this.'

'That's what I ask myself each day. Perhaps I'm just keeping myself aware of one's transient mortality. But if it brings you here, just as it's done this one last time, it's worth it.'

'Oh pops, I'm going to miss you.'

But now her words, so totally endearing, and despite this soothing relief of her visit, were filling me with a sense of finality. As if she were preparing me for a further shock. An emotional upheaval, which would, at the end of what she had to say, not only leave me shocked but shattered. Her sleeves pulled back, her wrists so slender, hands so elegant, capable and strong. Her fingers going into the handle of the teacups as she lowered them on their saucers. With all the things she brought how did she manage in a cab and she must have known somehow for sure that I would be here. Desperately waiting to take this taste of tea upon my lips.

'Hey, pops. God. Grasping at all I can get from life before it leaves me, I don't know how I'm going to say all the things I've still got left to say. Some of them could be *très* moribund. Bursting out from hiding deep down in what is commonly called the soul. But before I say anything more, let me say that what I really like about you, as older than me and wiser as you are, and of a generation, or is it two generations, gone by. Oh gee, pops, let me rephrase that. You're still like you're a young guy. A contemporary human being of flesh, blood and bone, ha ha, just like me.'

'No I'm not, Iowa. The flesh is accumulating wrinkles, the blood requiring regular infusions of champagne and the bones I guess may hold out a little longer.'

'Oh come on, don't forget I see girls giving you the come on, all the time.'

'Iowa, the truth is, with no finishing line, I'm heading for fifty and at such a speed I've already gone way past that signpost.'

'*Quel* hell, pops. I hurt your feelings. No. No. This is getting like a requiem. Just darken a little bit those traces of grey hair and you could smilingly pass for forty-eight and a half. Ha ha. I mean thirty-six. But don't let the glooms and doldrums enfold thee. With me expressing my inspired opinions. I should shut up. Especially as I always end up saying all the absolutely wrong things to say.'

'You don't say the wrong things, Iowa.'

'But pops, I do. And here goes. Are you in love with me? Whoops. You don't have to answer that unless you want your silence to speak volumes. I should explain that my world has fallen apart so often that I've reduced it down to just keeping myself glued together and just depending upon the definite things I know, but don't totally trust. Because, who knows, the world could one day suddenly go crashing down around us. Leaving us sorry forever that we didn't ask the question to which we so much wanted to know the answer. OK, you're not going to answer.'

'Iowa you're not going to slide down.'

'Pops, I may. Just like the tears I see in your eyes could any second go down your cheeks. God, at least I asked. I shouldn't have. But that's all over now. So I won't mention or suggest all the other things that are supposed to go with love. Like that white picket fence that can lock people up in respectable misery. Kids' toys on the front lawn over which you hope no one breaks their ass. I know you've never asked, or even hinted as guys before long usually do, for a girl to open up her legs for them. Jesus, pops, I hope this isn't an unhappy subject, those aren't more tears in your eyes. It isn't as serious as all that. That's why I want to sort of cure you. Untie our attachment a little bit. But not entirely. That's why I'm telling you these things. Not to leave you bleak. That it'll seem like I'm good riddance after I'm gone.'

'Iowa, I'll be more than bleak.'

'Pops, you're going to go on meeting hundreds of girls like me. And do you really like my cake?'

'It's truly wonderful cake.'

'Women are not supposed to bake. But I speak now as an aficionado of the relentless promotion of the American female dream. Not to be domestic slaves. I also speak as having been the briefly conspicuous girlfriend of the star of our high-school football team and learned that enough publicity can cure people of not liking you. Then a boy who was in love with me and had a limp invited me to the senior prom and I said I was already pledged, and he, the night of the prom, was found on the highway dead, hit by a truck. Pops, you see why maybe we're having this conversation. Or rather more me having it. You never even once asked me about a single statistic in my life. And I never told you that a bit of Omaha Indian blood flows in my veins. Just a trickle. From my father. And maybe I shouldn't say anymore. Before the bones of the skeletons in my closet start clacking like the loudest castanets of haunting memories you ever heard. That then might make you not like me anymore.'

'Nothing, Iowa, that you could or will ever tell me will change anything I think about you.'

'OK. My resumé. I was for a while the highest-paid topless dancer anywhere. I was, too, other things. I made what was to me a lot of money. But then there were spooks floating around in my brain. Taking every venereal precaution I had affairs that would last seven weeks followed by five weeks of celibacy. The best baseball player, best football player and even hockey player. If the guy was nobody in particular it was always a longer romance and longer recovery. Shoved out of school, out of home, out of town, then came an abortion. I tell you this, pops, so that later on you can never find these things out that maybe might make you not like me anymore.'

'As I've already said, Iowa, nothing you can say or ever do will ever stop me liking you.'

'Pops, you were one of the first people who ever looked into my eyes instead of at my tits and waited to hear what I had to say. I almost thought you would ask me to sit down and play a game of chess. Or examine the hallmark on a piece of silverware. Anyway, there are all the things I haven't told you about me yet and I won't tell you now. Not that my father tried to fuck me, or that I broke his eardrum socking him on the side of the head. Sent him tumbling down the cellar stairs. Then when I ran away from home, my father committed suicide in the worst possible way you can imagine. Instead of carbon monoxide. By snakebite.

Locked himself in his car. With the worst breed of rattlers. So people wouldn't know he took his own life. Maybe I imagine it now that my father was so beautiful. My mother was beautiful too. But it was also my father's ancestor who was a pall-bearer at Beethoven's funeral. My mother married again. Someone very rich. And that's how I got sent, as my mother was, to a snooty school to pass social muster and become a lady. Now. Do I denote eyebrows up again? Yes I do.'

'Iowa, you've never told me anything of any of this before.'

'I know. Ha ha, I didn't want you to feel inferior. Knowing I went long enough to a snooty school to feel superior and to cause resentment among women. Now you know why I love your toadying to being British. And pops, this will kill you. Not perhaps stone-dead but kill you all the same. I went eight months to that Swiss finishing school before they politely suggested I withdraw. I stayed just long enough to know who Adolf Loos is. And then, to avoid becoming a lifelong snob, I beat it to Paris. Took up residence in the Hôtel Raphael in order to knock around the cafés and nightclubs on the Left Bank. Have I told you enough yet of my emotional history unearthed from the subterranean wilderness of my subconscious, which I guess they say is your soul.'

'Iowa. Iowa. Oh god. You mustn't cry.'

'It's so funny, isn't it. I'm crying. And the last thing I perfected from acting school where I've now stopped going, was how to, on command, cry a single tear out of one eye, the left one. But as you see I'm now using both. So pops, I should go, leaving you, and more than probably for the last time. Well I know you're shocked. But you see, I really appreciated your social climbing. And now at least you know plenty more about me, if not all about me.'

'Well perhaps I'm a little bit shocked. But I think, as I hold on for dear life, that social descending is a better description of me.'

'I hope it hasn't all been a mistake to tell you. Because I know you haven't told me any lies. I guess maybe I was lying a little bit pretending not to know about the Orient Express and the London season. Then I was nearly tempted to confess when you were so sympathetic when I first told you how they blew up my dog Gesundheit. Christ there I was, the sagebrush tumbling across the prairie, back in America. My stepfather describing it as taxpayer's purgatory. Me referring to lawns as the sacred cloth of respectability over which you flew the stars and stripes. But I loved my country's flag and I did try to teach Gesundheit to be a good American canine and not go relentlessly pissing and shitting on other people's front lawns.'

'Iowa, please don't get yourself upset.'

'Jesus, pops. I did so adore that little mutt. His brains all over the grass where they shot him. After that I taught myself how to screech like a lioness and raise my hands in claws. Scare people away. Then the bastards wrote me a letter. The poisonous fumes of the words came right up at you off the page. Even with my couple of aristocratic artistic connections to the past, there were no pall-bearers at Gesundheit's funeral. Just me. I dug his grave in the middle of the night and buried him on the little front lawn of the shack of the furnished house I rented. Collected a sack of my things. Disguised my looks. And in my dowdy clothes jumped on a Greyhound bus. Half way to New York in South Bend, Indiana, I changed my mind. To go back west. Telephoned the only friend I had left behind. A waitress I got to know in a lunchroom. And I learned that a tornado had come and flattened everything and killed the people who blew up Gesundheit. For the first time I thought evil deeds are sometimes revenged. I hopped back on a Greyhound bus again. And that's how I ended up here, in New York. Practising my accents and vowels, trying to make an honest go of my life in the lonely friendless beauty of these canyon streets.'

'Iowa. Life is a kick in the ass and happiness is finding out who did it.'

'You know, pops. I've only got the nerve to tell you now. That a couple of times with this key you gave me and in order to avoid a wilderness of troubles out of my past from an unwelcome caller and without enough money for a decent hotel, I came here and I slept on your floor observing all the protocol of my Swiss finishing school not to desecrate the privacy of your bed. Nor did I snoop in any of your papers. Oh god, are you shocked at my presumption? Promise me you're not mad, are you?'

'No. I'm delighted.'

'Well you know how people hesitate and then fish around for things to say when they want to answer and maybe even want to get rid of you.'

'Iowa that, believe me, is the last thing I'd ever want.'

'I see by your grandfather clock that it's nearly four thirty-eight minutes post-noon Eastern Daylight Time, so now in the further words spoken in my best British accent, I must I think, hasten off. You know. Tiny bit of shopping to do. Buy an apple to eat during intermission. Got to be in the theatre by six thirty. Curtain up at eight.'

'Iowa. Thank you for tea and your chocolate cake. These couple of hours have totally transformed my life.'

'Pops, let's see, I came just after three, so one hour and thirty-eight minutes has transformed your life. God, that little bow of yours. You can be a prize of hands-off politeness can't you. Peck you, cheerio my dear, on the cheek. My life's sailing off into uncharted waters. Oh god, this is all too chaste. Oh please. Give me a hug, pops. You're such a gentleman. And knowing you're such a social and intellectual snob would make up for it, if you weren't. And I've shocked you too, haven't I?'

'No you haven't.'

'Pops, I'm going to remain what I foolishly am because of the spiritual pain and fear I get when I'm not. That's why I hid my background all this time. But now bring you up to date to see that my pedestal is made of mud and I'm sitting on it in the pouring rain. Oh god, here come my intellectual name-dropping pretensions that I won't drop but maybe also, in the near future, before my *jeunesse dorée* is over, we can meet and discuss nonconformist subjects on a walk or over a pastrami sandwich in a deli somewhere downtown in the depths of Second Avenue. And at the same time, if it's still running you can come see me in my play. Toodle-oo.'

The door closing. One could hear the noises that break the celestial silence left by her leaving. The bothering sounds you never bother listening to. The faint constant moan of traffic on Sixth Avenue. The cranking and clanking freight elevator in the building that creaks floor to floor and makes it faster to walk up the stairs. Siren of a police car. And not a further sound able to come out of my throat. Even to say goodbye.

'Hey you. I shouldn't have been so abrupt and said toodle-oo goodbye. I can't leave you like this. Why don't we let's instead go right now real quick get you the hell out of here. Quaff a glass of champagne at the Pierre. Come on. You're fine. Up out of that ragged old chair. You're dressed perfectly for it. Even wearing that tie with the funny winged foot on it. I'm in mufti. I can fake it. Let's go. A real quick quaff. Our woes can fade away in the wonderment of pleasure. And it will give me a further chance to stand on top of my emotional ruins and moan like hell.'

The whole upside-down world and me right side up again. Together taking the creaking elevator down. Out the door and onto the street. I thought at least I would now outside and walking along the sidewalk to flag a cab, maybe manufacture the excuse to be able to hold Iowa's hand and have the opportunity of giving her fingers a reassuring squeeze. If of course she squeezed my fingers first. But in my haste I headed in the opposite direction, leaving Iowa standing. Till she gently pulled me back by the arm.

'Pops, hold it. Stay right where you are, sweetie. We've got a ride. All we have to do is to wait right here and it shouldn't be longer than a minute.'

And in the passing minute, so hard was it to imagine being in Iowa's company and in another's command going somewhere. That I obeyed her without question. The word 'sweetie' echoing in my ear. I was anticipating having her any moment suddenly remembering she had an urgent appointment with her voice coach that she'd forgot and expecting that she, getting into a taxi, would vanish, her flowing hair disappearing beyond the taxi door.

'See what did I tell you, pops, twenty-eight seconds, here comes Willard.'

A long black limozine slowing down to stop at a space between the parked cars and in front of Iowa. It was a vehicle you would look at twice and looked like the same limozine I'd seen take her away from Goodwin's funeral, and also collect her from the Pierre. The chauffeur Willard jumping out opening the car door for Iowa. And as I climbed in, saluting me. Even a couple of passing pedestrians stopping to take notice. A frisson of fear, striking. What if I were seen in Iowa's conspicuous company by one of Muriel's friends.

'Here you are, pops, let me sit you down, my junk is everywhere, clear you a space.'

Iowa removing a cell phone and a purple vanity case and what looked like an overnight bag on the car seat for me to sit. And if my eyes did not deceive, the black leather holdall had the letters *Iowa* written on it in diamonds. Then I found I was sitting on a copy of *The Wall Street Journal*, folded open to stocks and shares. Red ticks and arrows, and scribbles of numerals. A circle drawn around 'commodities', and 'The London Bullion Market'. And so with a mass of thick glass closing us off from Willard, this was in fact the other side of Iowa's life I was facing. And the only solace that it could offer me was that I was being invited into it.

'Guess you're wondering, pops. OK, I lied unashamedly. I said I came to see you in a taxi. And I didn't. Willard, you see, where he can't park and wait, just drives round and round the block. Listening to Sibelius. And does sometimes keep driving even when he can park. So when I'm leaving somewhere, except these days at the theatre, all we have to do is be patient a minute or so for him to appear and we step out from where ever we might safely lurk, then, and as we say in our better English, we motor off. But gosh, will they on second thoughts, even as a bolt out of the blue let me into the Pierre looking like this.'

'You look stunning, Iowa. And a glamorous asset to anywhere you choose to appear. And stepping out of a bulletproof limozine doesn't exactly make you undesirable.'

'Hey, pops, I wondered when you were going to notice. And I guess, isn't that what we're all fighting not to become. Invisible lives without notice. So I may as well pretend to be glamorous. Now that I suddenly have a lawyer, voice coach and agent. But still taking everything with a grain of salt. Still letting the hair grow under my armpits, becoming an indoor recluse while I still try to remain an outdoor girl. Still being a hypocrite waging war against hypocrisy. And to all the law-enforcement agencies. Whoever in the past gave me a parking ticket. But now. Suddenly, and just a fledgling actress, it's all different. Guess I'm presently a little shell-shocked and left most pleasantly spellbound cut off from my assorted roots. Ready, as a shareholder in munitions, to proclaim a ban on all war. And you, pops, for three whole blocks in traffic, haven't now said a single word. OK. I won't either.'

We were now coming up to Columbus Circle and the corner of Central Park. Sitting silently next to each other. And I was in fact simply speechless as simply I could not imagine such terrifying bliss. Cocooned in the armoured luxury of this car, the newly unobtrusive city outside passing nearly without sound. Nor could I say a word because I knew now for a certainty that she was gone. Out of my life. Could tell immediately by the windows and the sound of the car doors closing that this limozine was bulletproof. One more reason not to enquire any further into Iowa's life. Or her scribbles on *The Wall Street Journal*'s page. Treating all as just another repeat of a New York lesson as to what one already knew beauty can do. Produce options arising on all sides. Help yourself. Take what you want from the biggest giver. Yet Iowa was anything but the biggest taker. Not a miniscule of greed or grasping in her behaviour or character.

I didn't yet have a bulletproof limozine. To take me where the waiter at the Pierre now delightedly remembered Iowa. And I reassured myself that it was from our last visit, and not that she'd been in and out of this room a dozen times since, with others. The waiter nodding a smile and whispering the word 'champagne'. You could nearly sense him thinking that no other wine need be considered with this treasure being in one's company. In a city where everyone, as Iowa said, tries not to become invisible and so desperately wants to be even vaguely familiar. Provided it's not associated with embezzlement, rape or murder. Maybe murder was OK. It made people think you meant what you said. Iowa beseating herself like a nun and sitting back like a queen. Toasting our champagne I was tempted to say, Here's to Hollywood you're my inspiration to opening up a lingerie outlet on Rodeo Drive. But I quickly thought better of it. Even to remind oneself of somewhere three thousand miles away made Iowa seem already with a first-class ticket flying west. But then came her words.

'Hey, pops. Why don't you open up a lingerie operation on Rodeo Drive. Go for the grass greener because there may never be grass that green again. Remember my poem. A girl getting what she can before her looks begin to fade.'

'Iowa, I remember and your looks are not going to fade. If anything you're going to be more beautiful than ever.'

'Pops, what would really make you lose your cool.'

'I guess if the words "no" and "don't" were said to me too often. But why are you looking at me like that.'

'Well you see, since this seems to be honesty hour continued, I'm just making the most of it. And I was just wondering if you would look so benign sitting there as you are if you were instead sitting in a courtroom and we were fighting each other and I was either the plaintiff or defendant.'

'Holy Christ, Iowa.'

'Ah. There goes a bit of your cool. Never heard you blaspheme before. But we're not fighting. Never will. Just a random thought. Just someone I know in that predicament which seems a lot of guys are. And you seem so marvellously content sitting there savouring your champagne, happily married with a big house, which I've heard is like a palace. Of course I shouldn't have said such a stupid thing. Hey, pops, come on. Return to normal. You were one of the first guys who ever set an example for me. Elegantly individualistic. Those beautiful bindings you've got on some of those books in your hideaway. And you know how people were in the twenties. Canes, long dresses. Black Chantilly lace. Homburg hats. And the strange formality of your umbrella, rain or shine. Why haven't you got it with you.'

'It got stolen.'

'Pops, I know you're kidding me.'

'Yes I am. And of course in my nervous state, I forgot to bring my umbrella with me.'

'It was you who taught me that it was worthwhile to look at the buildings and streets of New York. Things nutty. Like the Flatiron Building. The peace you could find in the city's churches. Especially the mostly empty Protestant ones. And maybe by accident encounter organists and choirs practising their music. But even something far more important. The homeless. Down on their luck.'

'Iowa, I wish I'd known I was under such beautiful scrutiny.'

'Well I feel guilty now telling you but when I did follow you those times, I thought, Is this guy for real. You'd take something like a little packet out of your pocket and drop what looked like a book of matches or something. I couldn't tell what it was. Oh god, you're embarrassed. So when you disappeared I waited and found out from one of these homeless guys that it was a five-dollar bill wrapped around a half a dollar. And do you remember one day we were having this shoot in this sound studio when all the other studios were booked. It had a grand piano parked in it. Everyone had gone home and I was on my way and I suddenly heard this beautiful piano playing. My whole being seemed affected. I went back and looked through the glass and there you were playing this song called 'Gloomy Sunday' as I later found out. That's when I thought, Jesus, these guys hustling lingerie, they're cultivated too, follow this guy. So I'd disguise myself a little and get on the trail. Ah you didn't know, did you. You see, I know a lot more about your life than you realize. But why are you smiling so broadly.'

'The only thing, Iowa, you may have wrong is that the bills as I recall I dropped upon these chosen homeless guys had upon them a picture portrait of General Ulysses Simpson Grant, eighteenth president. Who was also the best horseman in his class at West Point.'

'Oh god, that's wonderful to hear you actually laugh. For the first time. So, it was fifty and one half bucks you dropped, no wonder these guys lied. Those who would say anything at all. Well that's it, other than learning your interest in Anglo-comfortable habits and the game of cricket. Sticky wicket. LBW caught in the slips. Bowled an over or something. When you mentioned a long time ago that someone had a first in Greats from Oxford. I was floored. Since I knew what it meant, I knew you weren't just a simple old, I mean older, guy getting a thrill out of making lingerie. And your saying it made me feel like the elitist intellectual snob I quietly relish being, meeting another one, and that we really had something in common. Even though, if I'm honest, down deep I didn't know what the fuck it really means.'

'Iowa, I really haven't a clue either.'

'Gee, at last we're both laughing.'

The feel of evening approaching. Wanting to wrap my arms around her brain. Kiss it gently. And it was at that stage of our conversation that just when you most entertain the pleasure of each other's company, and on the pouring of our third glass of champagne, that Iowa's mood grew more sombre. As now another couple were parked in this almost secret room. Their curiosity directed at Iowa and Iowa silently staring at me. A strange look in her eyes. As if she contemplated a disaster.

'Pops, I did you a disservice. Cheated your gesture of generosity of forty and a half bucks.'

'Iowa you cheated my generosity of forty-five and a half bucks, but who's counting.'

'Oh and I don't know why I'm saying this, but don't ever let anything awful happen to you. Promise. Gee, I don't know why I suddenly said that. I feel I'm on some kind of rocket launching pad. Could go up into the sky and not come back. It's like locusts gathering. In just one week I suddenly end up with a retinue. They smell just a faint scent of fame. And it's you need a manager, sign this, sign that. And so far I haven't signed. The people that were not that long ago distaining, now chasing after you. With not a single discouraging word. While I'm wondering where I'm going to end up. God, I don't mean them to be but these are doom-laden remarks. Maybe this isn't the time or the place to talk about such things.'

'Iowa, there will never ever be a better time or place.'

'Pops. Sometimes I think I've got so spoiled. Guess I momentarily need some sort of spiritual guide leading me by the hand. Like you. But would you ever have anyone murdered. You don't have to answer that. I was going to tell you something now I'm not going to tell you. Because it might change everything you have ever thought about me. Let me first take a good swallow of champagne. But I am going to tell you. And I suppose I'll spout a lot of excuses.

'I was a hooker. I could tell you a lot of shit about how, when I got back from Switzerland, my stepfather stopped my allowance. And that the fact of having or not having money could become everything. And instead of pretending to be an elegant lady I became a dealer in body parts. Cheap at first. Then an extremely expensive one. Then my stepfather threatened to stop my life. You know how everyone is looking for or already knows about some sure-fire contract killer. So I thought of killing him. Simply on the premise that he wasn't nice to me. I got for a while to hate human beings. Then as a selectively brilliant hooker I came within a hair's breadth of deciding to remain an outright permanent one. You're shocked.'

'Iowa I'm …'

'Have you ever been to a prostitute.'

'No.'

'Well then you don't know and I shouldn't be telling you. What can happen. The downmarket kind of conversations you have with tricks. Trying to get rid of them as fast as you can. You've had yours, buster. Then the moment when, handing over money, the philosophy comes. What's a really beautiful nice girl like you doing something like this. A reply I did make once was, that this really beautiful nice girl is for hire for the money just paid by dumb hard-up jerks like you. I got my nose broke. Ended up three days in hospital. Was out of work. A hooker has always got to be looking her best. Evicted from my apartment. I became one of those homeless people. Kept a sliver of soap. A comb. Would try to keep looking respectable in order to go sit in the public library. Forty-Second and Fifth. Hungry, battered and climbing those steps between those two big sculptured lions.

My finishing-school imperiousness intact coming to the fore. And nearly a couple of months recuperating. That's how I got hooked on quantum physics. I thought, OK it's all down to a matter of waves. And that's what decided me to straighten up and fly right. Like Amelia Earhart. Who disappeared into the wild blue yonder. I even tried to become a Mormon. Thought if I could get the gift of tongues, I could solve my fucked-up life, if not the nature of the universe. Oh god, pops, but I better get the hell out of here before this confession conversation further ruins our relationship.'

'Iowa, nothing has or will ruin our relationship but something else has happened that you're telling me all this.'

'Yes, pops, it has. But I can't tell you about it now. All I could think of back in those days was waving goodbye. At least with the universe it's beginning to look like there's no goodbye or even hello. Duration without beginning or end. Space limitless. Nothing too small, nothing too big. Matter eternal. Nothing created, nothing destroyed. As far as philosophy has ever got me is that you put a little bit more mustard on your hot dog before you eat it and maybe add a little sauerkraut because you like the taste. While meanwhile I'm remaining in the here and now thinking of the all-American girl whose white picket fence I've defiled. Figuring out, according to my time clock, the supposed right way to go. Kidding myself that I'm indulging a hiatus of freedom before marriage and motherhood. Like my other big decisions in life back during my brief sojourn in public high school, when I became a cheerleader, go, go team go, ending up dating the high school's football star. He also played basketball. Can you imagine, such a dumb game.'

'Iowa, I may need a moment or two to think about that. I do watch a game or two occasionally with a degree of enjoyment.'

'Well I bought this jock a jockstrap for a present with a specially reinforced area. He thought it was too personal. When I thought it was such a nice thought to protect you down there.

So I told him getting on top of me to get his rocks off was too personal. Then without knowing I had another half-brother and sister I only find out about when they both got killed in a crazy car accident on a sunny day in which you could see where you were going on a straight flat road that went for miles to the horizon. The story of their lives so garbled that who knows, maybe they were really murdered. And people getting in your way. Maybe that's why I asked you, would you ever have anyone murdered. But now when enough misery has already been stirred all around in your life and unless you don't know any better, you try to change things. And I better not drink anymore champagne. And I've told you as much as I have because I don't want you to entertain the impression I'm some kind of saint. And maybe that's why I'm trying to be an actress. At least for a while I can look at myself and pretend I'm not me. A chance to tell the world all about yourself without ever letting them know a single thing.

   'Now, pops, I've got to get to the theatre on time. You're not to move. Please. You stay here. Finish the bottle. Willard will be right out front waiting. But remember one thing. I hope without being sentimental about it, that whatever remains between us, will always remain. Guess it might not be much after what I've said. Come on, before we all get computerized out of existence, give me a hug goodbye. And I know you won't forget to tip the waiter extra large, for liking us both so much. And last but not least. I know I haven't hit a home run with you. But I don't want to strike out either. Because I want to die in your arms. So bleak heart, bleak heart, don't be bleak.'

SIXTEEN

IN THE VOID and vacuum left now in this secluded room, the devastation of her words. To mean such a thing. Die in my arms. When death would be so welcome if I could instead die in hers. And now with her gone feel bleak that my life had been dumped on a scrap heap. This was to be the last time I would ever be at the Pierre. In its strangely lonely elegance. Or sit in peace and quiet admiring the configuration of this room. Sure now, too, that I would never see her again. Unless from a seat sharing her with an audience. The waiter who saw me off with a gracious bow, I did tip extra large. Leaving now from Iowa's world. Back into my own life, thunderstruck. Down the corridor, past these hotel guests. Telephone Blueberry Hill. Boris had a degree of anxiousness in his voice. Muriel held a firework display at the lake. A few mishaps on the farm. Another tray dropped. A political argument erupting among the staff. Nothing fatal. But then the good news came.

'Sir, madam's guests have departed.'

'And Boris, is the chandelier-cleaning finished?'

'It is indeed sir, and everything is in sparkling fine fettle. And madam is planning to spend a day in the city and much wonders as to your exact whereabouts and as to the day of your return.'

Boris full of discretion, and anxious to be cheerful but knowing I would not be back until Muriel's guests were gone, as were my own children gone too with their own friends and three thousand five hundred dollars, skiing in Aspen. And sometimes you think of the contrast at their age, selling lingerie door to door. A husband or boyfriend chasing you down the street trying to kick you in the ass. Instead of worrying about waxing your skis. And teetering on the edge of gloom such thoughts did imbue upon the spirit, one especially welcomed and appreciated a parting nod and smile from behind the reception desk as I passed heading out the Sixty-Seventh Street entrance. Reeling out of the Pierre.

'Have a good evening, sir. Nice to see you again.'

In the street walking east on one of the city's least-used sidewalks. I know because I used to choose it deliberately to get to the zoo in Central Park. Recalling again Iowa's words and snatches of conversation. Wondering had one been duped. By this free-spirited angel. Coming in and now passing out of one's life. Hoping against hope it wasn't true. Wanting to remember only those things she said with her innocent smile. And that she meant. Die in my arms. And not wanting now to remember anything else she said. How could New York be so lonely? To cross eastwards the few blocks to Midas Towers. Try to conjure up again the privacy of peace and quiet that could be enjoyed again at Blueberry Hill. Meditate in the library on the soothing beauty of some old-master and nineteenth-century paintings. And in the company of my wife. Who had always stuck by me. Except maybe when first showing her Blueberry Hill as her birthday present. And she was about to get me wrapped up in a straitjacket to be taken to Bellevue. But she did in our marriage and in our early financial struggles deserve and get all my tender attention. Washing the dishes, scrubbing the floor. Killing the cockroaches. Statistics say that people can only stand fifteen years of each other. Muriel and I have lasted nearly twenty-four. And to think now that I would dare do what I did. Give in to the temptation of Iowa's company. But then Iowa did come out of the blue just to see me. But taking the risk of being seen with her, in a place of fashion, was to say the least unconscionable. As my footsteps fell on the sidewalk I sank in gloom. And remembering that Iowa also said, 'Pops, seems people find it easier to believe stories of tragedy. Maybe I'm biased in telling them.'

And I had already got news of a small tragedy. Muriel had found the copies of the *Social Register* in the library and gone through the pages to dig out the identity of reasonably local folk to whom to send an ad hoc invitation. Printed up by Tiffany's.

Choosing those with the longest list of clubs after their names. Come for a cocktail. *Mrs Nathan Johnson at Home*. With Hal and his wife gone on a trip to Paris, not a single other person came. Except someone who got past and who wanted permission to visit the cemetery. Newt stationed at the gate to keep out gatecrashers. Boris, who had the hors-d'oeuvre dishes full and the champagne chilled, kindly suggesting that the *Register* was years out of date. Of course I was nearly left wondering when I might get my invitation. To come visit where I lived.

Cross now over Madison Avenue, maybe named after a president, has no Nathan Johnson Lingerie. Which put me again wondering, daring myself, would I go see Iowa in her play. I'd already found from my office that I'd have to wait. Three weeks. Every seat sold out. And presume that due to fire regulations no standing room. Instead, I bought tickets to a musical to take Muriel for when she gets to town tomorrow. Book a table at La Grenouille. In grand elegance. What the hell. And I'm feeling serious enough to think it. When you have your own dear wife radiant in her form-clinging electric-blue gown. Even without her tiara she looked dazzling. To make you wonder why, with a woman like that at home, guys still chase other women. And another *bon mot* from Iowa. 'Pops, variety is, as they say, the spice of life, and you try not to let the pepper get in your eyes.'

And I had Flatbush too again on my mind. Rumour of a story brewing to appear in a local newspaper. Goodwin's widow. Would I go visit her again. We could talk. But about what. Drive out there. As I nearly did again. And in fear turned back halfway. At a traffic light the blaring music from some boom box held up against the car window by some kid trying to nearly break my eardrums. And reminding myself that if I hadn't made money, instead of living in a palace with a grand staircase to descend upon, I could have ended up on one of Flatbush's desultory streets.

So to discourage creating your own unnecessary nightmare and more gloom in life and a broken ass, or even fucking a widow, I turned around and drove back to Manhattan Island. Went to the Game Club, took a steam bath and a swim. Wrapped in sheets, lay back to rest outstretched on a steamer chair. The familiar faces of members and the less familiar naked bodies walking by to the spout and hot rooms. The water-polo team working out, waving their arms in the air and treading water up and down the pool. While I politely asked god that with Iowa gone to please protect me from discouragement. And the vast void to be left in one's life.

And now with her total disappearance from everywhere, my days would go by in a new loneliness. Tempted to grab my toothbrush and stay in a hotel on Central Park South. High up in a suite. From where I could look down and over the great spread of spaciousness across the treetops far up into distant Harlem. And if one could ignore the occasional mugging, rape and murder beneath the boughs of those trees, you could think of this great space as a freedom to cherish. Where people could have an opportunity to pretend who they are, or even better, who they could become if given the chance. But yet, to feel right now, that as Nathan Langriesh Johnson I badly need somewhere familiar. Even Midas Towers. Sprightly sail in the big glass doors.

'Good evening. Long time no see, Mr Johnson. Been travelling.'

'Yes. Been travelling.'

'Nice picture in tonight's newspapers.'

Seems that after you've been shocked out of your complacencies in this town you never have to wait long for a new jolt and surprise. What picture? What newspaper? Get out of the lobby. Ascend to the apartment. Twisting gently my key in the lock. The picture in the paper could be one of one of the cliffs of the Grand Canyon at sunset. So go straight along the hall and into the living room. Find it strange how you'd forgotten how thick and soft the carpet is. To cross. To stare out the window.

Between the buildings just catch a glimpse of Central Park and its trees to remind me of Blueberry Hill. And erase a newspaper headline of a rape leading to murder emblazoned on the news stand on the corner.

In the kitchen, from the refrigerator, I helped myself to a glass of milk with a dollop of maple syrup and had a cookie. I finally picked up the phone and called to the lobby. The words 'nice picture' mentioned by the lobby boys could mean nothing else too bad was being said. And the lobby spokesman said, 'We'll be right up with the newspaper, Mr Johnson.' In this city where you have to blot out a hundred images a second and where the end of the world was coming to at least a thousand people a day. And here it is in my hand. The newspaper. A picture of Iowa. Looking ravishingly beautiful as one might say in those somewhat hackneyed words. The headline read out painfully slowly by the elder statesman of the lobby boys. And now in front of my eyes:

FORMER LINGERIE MODEL FOR NATHAN JOHNSON
MAKES IT TO STARDOM ON THE STAGE

'Gee Mr Johnson, we didn't know you were a celebrity. A real luminary.'

I didn't answer as I might have liked. That's right, you nosy bunch of bastards, I'm a real luminary. Not the pitiful, harried-faced lonely tenant you see shuffling occasionally through the lobby. But all that the celebrity recognition did was make me pronto want to return to Blueberry Hill. Out of the maelstrom. Relax back into a semi-quiet life. But to hear my own name mentioned in the same breath as Iowa's. That was something. Made me catch my own breath and thank the lobby's elder statesman and gently, slowly, close the door. Muriel due in town tomorrow. Bury the paper in my own underwear drawer.

But it's amazing what just the sight of your name in the newspaper does for your self-esteem. And on the gossip page.

Except that if Muriel sees it. And one be instead asked questions. Guilt written in the answer all over my face. That could send a suspicious wife to a lawyer. Reginald to whom I placed a call on other business, was always ready with advice, and had already seen the photograph and story. And his suspicions aroused, was already jumping to conclusions as I was scratching the back of my head trying to be casual. The upshot of his comments being that although there was nothing much you could do about a blatant reference in a newspaper, any explanations volunteered always dug your hole deeper. Especially as I had already made Iowa a beneficiary under a trust.

'Nathan, maybe in the nature of the male some men have an above-average sex drive to make their sex behaviour unpredictable. And they should always remember that the smart move is business must come before love in order to keep the love and not lose the business. Wives are always in a hurry, but their ace in the hole is to wait. Catch him. And Nathan, when that verified complaint from the Supreme Court of the State of New York comes down the pike and gets shoved in your hand, there's no rest from worry. It sure blasts the shit out of you. More money is being spent on divorce in this country than is spent to run the United States Navy. And that navy costs plenty. Six hundred ships cutting through the waves full steam ahead around the world's oceans.'

'Reginald, the way you put it, sounds pretty rough stuff.'

'Nathan. You bet your life. And your wife. I know. It happened to me. Picture it. Now the divorce is all over. You have a paper bag with a salami sandwich in it, which was all you could afford. Someone in the guise of a sheriff's henchman saying, Hey, let's go, buddy, you don't live here anymore in your palace Blueberry Hill, or in your spaciously luxurious apartment high up in Midas Towers. You're evicted. Thrown out on the street. Homeless. Not even able to live in the back of one of your own stores. Hopping and skipping around your lobby in high dudgeon isn't going to help you, or shouting out I'll sue the shit out of the bailiff. Or screaming that your big deal's on the verge of closure with the first few million due on signature. You nearly beg. You ask. Where's your human kindness and mercy? Tough shit, buddy, I'm the bailiff, it has nothing to do with me. I'm just hired by the city to do my job.'

Arms practically wrapped around my head, going off to sleep I naturally, after Reginald's words, went ready to endure a nightmare. Which, wouldn't you believe it, came with a vengeance. How do you loudly utter in a calm civil voice that you're innocent of all wrongdoing. That you're nice and you're kind. But that you did bear bitter grudges. And I woke myself up. A shout coming from me. Dreaming I was at the counter of the deli. Asking for credit, to pay later for the pastrami on rye. And refused, I was terrified now to ask for an extra pickle with my order. Screaming I live in a castle and have a goddamn brilliant butler, Boris, who was already ready with a wheelbarrow to wheel the stacks of hundred-dollar bills to the bank. Along with blueberries, peaches, pears and plums. To dump them in the door. Here you are, you bastards. And Boris who once worked for a duke, said His Grace, the duke had chiselled on his gravestone an epitaph:

> THERE IS NO GLORY
> THERE IS NO GREATNESS
> GLORIOUS OR GREAT ENOUGH
> TO STAND
> AGAINST DEATH.
> SO WHY SUFFER
> ANY INCONVENIENCE
> WHILE YOU LIVE?

But the stubborn counterman in the deli is shouting back that no one in America gives a good goddamn what dukes think or have as their epitaphs. You're in New York, buddy, and the bailiff is already tugging at your heirloom furniture, still parked up in your apartment, busting armrests off the sofas as they pull stuff out the door as you're protesting that such possessions are of astronomical sentimental value. I grabbed the counterman over his glass case, socked him one. Said, as the bastard lay on the floor minus his bicuspids, that the stuff sold at auction would clear the debt for the pastrami sandwich and two pickles, ten times over. But nothing in my nightmare made any difference. This counterman was a particular son of a bitch. Had someone call the police. And holding an icepack to his jaw said, That's right, buddy, you and your sentimentally valued possessions are all standing together in the middle of a great big zero along with the rest of your lousy junk, which nobody could sell and if we threw it all out on the street we would have to bribe the garbage collectors with their college degrees to take it away. Then a voice, Iowa's, in my dream. Woke me up. 'Oh pops, you don't want to be tired out, worried and battered and have no one to whom to go where you can find solace and safety and someone to gently cradle your head.'

I sat up in the middle of the bed in a sweat. Fists clenched. Ready to fight. Wondering how theoretically close I was to disaster. Making sure to remind myself that this nightmare was only a dream. Stirred up from a piece in the newspaper about a former employee. Whose sudden catapulting into fame might even be good for business. One is still breathing. After having successfully avoided a very brief but very nervous breakdown. A sigh of relief. That you're still solvent. Returned to your own apartment high up above the city of teeming millions. Your palace still in the country. The newspaper was already in my hand. Iowa's picture. Don't read what it says. Rest secure, safe from the world, until tomorrow's headlines again intrude with murder, rape and mayhem. And the constant threat to world peace. One's real life is safe. If there's no real story about this former Nathan

Johnson Lingerie model now actually playing her role on the stage looking and dressed like a debutante going to a ball. Described as so young, elegant. And of all things, according to the report, sporting a perfect English accent.

Waiting now this morning for Muriel to descend and to perhaps, put bluntly, finally wipe away the hopeless visions I seem to endlessly have of fucking Iowa. To imagine what she would say flesh to flesh in my ear. But then Muriel had her moments. Which, had to be admitted, were not many now. As used to be. Of planting an unpremeditated kiss on my lips and making an uninhibited grab at my privates and with a squeeze and a tuck of her fingers, to whisper, 'Hey big boy, if you're not too busy making all the money you make, I'd like some of this.'

SEVENTEEN

TODAY to go visit the uptown office. A task one commonly avoided week after week by delegating Reginald. Just barge in, in an arrival unannounced. Dressed neatly for the occasion. Life back to the way it used to be. On an even keel. Check the mail. That's all you need to do is to let a day or two go by, shutting yourself off from the world and before you know it, you can imagine yourself into what you hope is only a temporary state of terror. People cheating you. Plotting to take over your business. Steal your designs. It could get you to thinking it's about time I came to the end of my fucking life. Keep the life and bury the fucking. And this waking-up panic attack of getting kicked out on the street hit just as the sunshine flooded in the window from Long Island, bringing dawn daylight to Brooklyn, and flashing off the sheer sides of Manhattan Island's buildings with their tens of thousands of windows. But Jesus, who would believe I was having emotional trouble with my fucking life as a multimillionaire. Images of last night's dream still floating around in my brain.

One remembers every move one makes. Because you know you'll start to knock over your coffee. Spill your orange juice. While you try limbering up exercises for the brain to keep you smart. To get up now. Put on a dressing gown over one's monogrammed black silk pyjamas. My black leather travelling slippers. But to inspire action. Put on casual clothes. Loafers and sweat socks. Make it to the kitchen. Have a glass of pure orange juice and coffee and crumb cake for breakfast. Maybe even knock off a Danish pastry on the side. Take the newspaper. Crumpled up well by the lobby boys. Look at Iowa again. Hope against hope Muriel doesn't see her. In the bathroom try to resurrect a new day. Go out. Make my tour of the homeless, before I pack up and go upcountry to Blueberry Hill. Make up a few packets but I've nearly run out of fifty-dollar bills. Last night even thought I could read myself to sleep with the Bible Muriel had placed in the bedside drawer, insisting it should be near at hand for a guest to dwell upon. But which book had never really been opened by anybody. And another funny thought came into my head. Someone said in the annals of someone's history. Give me publicity or give me death. And their death following shortly thereafter, came with plenty of publicity. As I now plan to go scour the papers in the quiet peace of the Game Club library to keep track of Iowa who did once voice disquiet over her future. 'Oh pops, wish me luck as I go prostrate myself on the altar of success and pray that I don't take to drink or drugs to blot out failure, as I offer myself up to be added to the myth of fame.'

Remembering everything Iowa said, it was as if she was still with me and not gone. Strange how something can make you go to the most unused room and bathroom you've never used before as if you didn't want to be where you were. Enjoying the peace without Ida on one of her now more frequent stays in Brooklyn. None of her banging to make a noise somewhere to make you think she's hard at work. Here in the twelve-by-twelve guest room, prints on the wall of Paris, with its own toilet and all its marble embellishment to be added to all the other toilet bowls I now own. Or rather my wife does. Remind myself that I am still Nathan Langriesh Johnson sitting on one of his many bathroom thrones. Open the newspaper, fold it over. Look up new locations in the ads. Each headlined *Perfect For Profit*. If you listen out right now to the drone of traffic, sirens of police and fire engines, it sounds like a strange silence. A reminder that there's no goddamn shortage of folk who this minute and second are at each other's throats. And others who can't take it anymore. Are taken away. Filling up Bellevue Psychiatric and the morgue where, tags on their toes, bodies wait to be claimed. Please don't leave me because I'm dead. Revealing the truth of all those abandoned bodies unclaimed. A loneliness in death so great no loneliness is greater. While other hearts go on beating. While nothing stops. No time to catch your breath before something else begins. Like Iowa's picture in the paper. Hearing once from Reginald sitting there leaning back as he does in his leather chair. Stacks of papers covering a big desk. Now executive vice president of the burgeoning Nathan Johnson Lingerie empire. Piles of Internal Revenue forms, a couple of squash racquets leaning up against the wall, his diplomas and citations. Went to an OK college. Phi Beta Kappa, and family portraits behind him on the wall. And apropos of nothing else at all, said it like it is. Because there was no doubt he long ago knew about Iowa.

'Nathan, I know the girls come and go on their way bettering their careers. But sometimes there's one so outstanding one might like and can afford to take a temporary domestic detour. And I know you well enough not to suggest to be careful nor remind you of an unpretty picture but as you know, every guy in this city who's met his wife downtown, or maybe they went to the same college, laid her, got her pregnant, got married and then is breaking his ass trying to make a living if not piling up a nice pretty little pile of money and ends up agreeing with her lady-ship's demand to move to the suburbs to the big house where she has in the sylvan surroundings three cars and a swimming pool, bicycles and computer games for the kids. And your nice, reason-ably successful guy commuting each day, and still struggling to pay for it all. Always knowing that hanging over his head like the sword of Damocles is divorce.

'Then while wanting and needing a bit of praise and love in response to his business boasting, elbows on a bar, makes that fatal mistake. Convinces a doll he's a big deal, unattached. Hi honey, I'm a film producer. They step out of a taxi, go to an hotel or her apartment. In a flash of two seconds, a friend of the wife spots them. As a supreme favour from the friend, the wife is told. Or a private dick already hired on the trail gives his report. The husband pleads it was an urgent business conference and he missed the last train. Bam. He's served with papers. Whammo. Supreme Court of the State of New York. Locks changed on all the property he thought he owned. Award plaintiff exclusive use and occupancy of the marital residence and its contents. Lunch hour at his job he may lose any second, he finds he's out sitting in a non-conspicuous atrium. And he ain't got enough concentra-tion left to be able to scratch his head. He only feels a little better when he breaks down in tears.'

Although I kept wanting to turn to see to whom Reginald was speaking standing behind me, one had to take on board Reginald's austere warnings. Especially as they sounded as if they came straight from the horse's mouth. He said such observations came across his bow more than he cared to count. And that's what it was. Counting. The costs that could be bitter. I had just come back from the bad news of Iowa's departure and her long message she left on his answering machine that he played over and over again and could remember her every word. And perhaps glad he should be that now Iowa had moved further out of his life. Because that life was your children. Your wife. And if you made a big bundle, a reliable companion into the retired luxury of old age.

But blot out such dreariness. Put the day's newspaper up in front of your face. Before I take one more last look at Iowa. Hear a sound. A door opening and slamming shut. That could be Ida back from Brooklyn or even Muriel down from the country. Or with the sound of more doors opening it could be a burglar in this burglar-proof building, where all visitors must be announced and every door is monitored or watched. Sound of another door slamming. Christ whoever it is, is making plenty of noise. Someone in the kitchen. Something just smashed that sounds ceramic. Each door opened. Slammed closed. Christ, what's going on. Hold my seat on the throne. Footsteps fast down and along the hall. Could be somebody with a gun. While I'm in the middle of a bowel movement with the shiny brass doorknob turning in front of my eyes.

'Hey, hold it. Don't come in. Is that you Muriel? Oh my god, it's you Muriel.'

'You're goddamn right it's me, you bastard.'

Nathan Johnson looking up over the newspaper. And past the headline. More millions of fraud in the twilight world of Wall Street. The glint and flash of the long blade of a kitchen carving knife. The sharp tip aimed arching through the air. Coming down. Remembering the moment I bought it. To last a lifetime. One of his first expensive purchases on Columbus Avenue when they lived over on the West Side of town. Advertised as the knife edge so keen it cuts through the uncuttable. And right now goes slashing through page thirteen of the newspaper with a searing pain. The stainless-steel blade sinking into my shoulder. Followed by a crumpled envelope and a page thrust through the air into his face.

'Read that. A letter marked "personal".'

'Holy Christ, Muriel, you've stabbed me. Stop. Stop.'

'You shit. So this is what you were doing all those days ten years ago in Atlantic City. You bastard. I'm going to kill you.'

'Muriel stop. You've stabbed me. Put the knife down. Stop.'

Another glint of the knife, plunging through the newspaper, smashing into the hardness of his collar bone. And burning deeper into the side of his chest next to his heart. Must. Have to. Pull out the knife. Inches deep in my shoulder. Raise myself off the lavatory. Hold on to the envelope and page thrust in my face. Muriel turning and running knocks over something in the bedroom. Feet thumping down the hall. Sound of the apartment door slamming shut. What the hell's gone wrong with her? Out of her mind. What the hell does she mean Atlantic City? Oh Christ. She means days gone and dead. Ten long years ago. That's what she means. Light goes off in your brain. Urge it back on again. Be able to think. The blood gushing out. Save your own life. Could be dying. Strength already beginning to ebb. Hold on. Tight. Pull up my pants. The British call them trousers. Close the buckle on my belt. Grab a towel. Blood soaking through my shirt. Drops on the bathroom floor. Get my legs to move. Get out of this bathroom. Across this bedroom. Get to the kitchen. Oh Christ, I'm really hurt. Throw the knife in the sink. Remembering when I bought it thinking this goddamn knife could kill you. Turn on the tap. Shove it under. Clean it. Get rid of the blood. Put it back and away in the drawer. Hide the blood. Grab my jacket get another towel. Get fast to the hospital. An ambulance. Be dead before I even get down and out of the service elevator. Then out of the garage and out on to the street. Atlantic City. One of my most successful stores opened there. Oh god. Whatever in god's name has gone wrong with Muriel, shoving an envelope and piece of paper at me that I may not be able to read so blotted as it is now with my fingerprints and blood. Someone's handwriting. Postmarked

Philadelphia. Envelope marked 'personal'. Addressed to me at my uptown office. Can spot the words. Top of the page. My life's more urgent than words now. Go careful. Step by step. Into the service entrance. Took the service elevator. All the way down to the garage. Wait. Drops of blood on the top of my loafers. Waiting. Hurry up elevator. Strange how you remember. Loafers were first invented by Norwegians as slippers as something comfortable to wear. Then a young American called Alan Kuntze ancient times ago in the Bronx saw them advertised for sale as slippers and started wearing them as shoes. And here I am while I bleed to death watching mine get coloured in blood. Red blots on my sweat socks. Got to stop it flowing. Eternity is right now. And is still now while the elevator doors open. Lets me in, closes. Descend. Hurry past the floors. Got to go out this way. Into the gloomy chill of the garage.

Nathan Johnson, his arms wrapped around his chest crossing the basement garage. Nearly empty of cars. A nice gloomy place to die. My Daimler. My racing-green car gone. Muriel had a set of keys. Her station wagon still parked. Get out across the cement floor. Beyond the pillars. As a vision of darkness passes across my eyes. The brain begins not to think. Except that I can see out of the dark garage towards the light of day. Christ, can I get there, up and out the incline. Past the barrier. Slowly. Step by bloody step. One foot in front of the other. Move. My own two feet doing the travelling. Could I be dying? Or already dead. Thinking I'm alive in some dream beyond life. Clutching this envelope and what I just can see with my blood smeared fingerprints over it, starts out with the words, *My dearest Nathan*. Your dearest Nathan stumbles forward. Must keep the shoulders back, the head up. Try to look like a single respectable citizen in this city. My heart thumping at least means it's still beating. I'm a perfect victim for a mugger. Already wounded. And now if asked he would have to explain how he already had a towel to staunch the blood. But this looks like a Good Samaritan approaching. Can't answer any questions. Got to get by him.

'Hey, are you all right.'

'Yes thank you.'

'Are you sure. You're dripping blood.'

'Yes just a bad cut. I live just in that next entrance around the corner where I'm going. Thank you. Thank you very much for your concern.'

Watched now by this rare good citizen who stops turns and waits and still watches as I turn to look back and turn the corner. Choral music is wafting through my head. Like I'm already at my funeral. Which if it happens now won't be at St Bartholomew's where I'd like it to be. Now take these last few steps. And in the doors of Midas Towers. With at last a story for the lobby boys they can discuss into next month. Or year. And their children into the next century. As I go now hoping not to drop dead at their feet.

'Holy shit, Mr Johnson, what's the hell's happened.'

'I got mugged just around the corner. Please call an ambulance.'

'Sure thing. Hey Fritz. Get a chair you dumbbell, over there, right away for Mr Johnson. He's hurt. Hey Patrick, call the ambulance and the police.'

'No please, the mugger got away in a taxi. He's gone. Just call an ambulance.'

One's head starting to feel heavy on my neck. And now could be another story in the newspaper. Resident of a prominent millionaires' tower, aptly called Midas Towers, mugged and robbed outside his building. And there was now the rest of my story to tell those to whom it may concern. The lone mugger came from behind threatening with a knife. I handed over a roll of cash, a couple of hundred dollars. Then he stabbed me.

'Don't worry Mr Johnson, the ambulance is straight on its way. Sit back now nice and quiet.'

Nathan Johnson tucking the reddened towel under his arm. For the first time ever sitting waiting in the lobby of Midas Towers fumbling to straighten out the blood-stained and crumpled envelope and sheet of paper. Reading the words.

Montrose Apartments
Columbia Ave
Philadelphia
Pennsylvania
15 September 1999

My dearest Nathan,

I know as I write this you may still not like that name which has always meant to me, as it does in Hebrew, 'gift', which you in your gentle kindness were and remain to me. And I hope that this letter will still find you far away as you are in your own life where no one else calls you 'gift'. Knowing your sense of your own privacy and apartness, I have hesitated to write more times than I can think of. But then loneliness can get the better of you, plus I thought I was already a person who in a small way had gained your trust and earned the privilege to breach such a long silence. And I guess too that such is the memory of what we had together and could communicate to each other, that it kind of breaks down all of my reserves that as you know I pride myself in having. Even though I was brazen enough to enter my first beauty contest coming second as Miss Nebraska, thinking then I guess I'd be crowned Miss Middle West America if such corn-belt contest existed. God, the dreams you can still have at the age of nineteen.

And now as I fracture my grammar, it is just to somehow let you know I am still somewhere with only a few photographs, reliving that all-too-brief a time in Atlantic City. Walking along the boardwalk holding hands, listening to the waves thunder in from the sea after that big storm we heard raging all that night. It was for me at least, a time of having your strong and loving arms to guide me through in my fears. In my utter happiness of those nights together was also our future I thought we could have. How can things so simple be so wonderful and then so complicated at the same time. Even though it is nearly ten years now from that very September Sunday we parted at the bus station, those days of that wonderful week remain the ones that I shall never forget. And I did laugh too, as you might remember, when you told me Atlantic City was where they invented the money game of Monopoly and that the boardwalk they built to keep the sand out of your shoes was a place on the Monopoly board where you could find yourself moving to when you threw the dice. And I still laugh a little remembering your remark, 'I'm just an ordinary guy with elegantly exotic tastes.' And so that you can indulge the latter, I'm glad to see the Nathan Johnson empire still prospers and grows.

My own life now seems lost as if I am on a desert island, and how grim and gruelling it can be. I gave up modelling when five years ago my mother and father got killed in a car crash. It was not their fault and although they were insured, which let me finish graduate school, there was very little to fill the vacancy left in my life, and I still miss them so. Eighteen months ago I finally divorced and left the brutal man I married back in Nebraska and moved to where I now live in Philadelphia at the address above. I have a good job working in a supervisory capacity at a bank. Not the most inspiring work but it pays well I have a pleasant apartment near Temple University and knowing you were intrigued by the game and liked things English, I often go to watch cricket matches at the Philadelphia Cricket Club. I know it is brazen to ask but would you like to come with me one day?

And I know as so much has happened in my life that much must have changed in yours as well. But I would, I so honestly would, love to see you again. The worst of it all is, in spite of our briefness together, I still after all these years, love you. As the tear blots I leave on this page most sincerely will tell.

Jane

The echo of the name Jane. And having read the letter, I must have lost consciousness. But remember the ambulance arriving. The lobby doors of Midas Towers opening. The white coats and wheeled gurney entering. The frightened look on faces. The ambulance siren. Then woke again on my back with a mask over my face. The paramedic in the ambulance, giving me oxygen. Makes senses alive and alert again. Speeding west across the city, to Roosevelt Hospital. The envelope and blood-stained letter clutched in my hand. Takes all my strength to lift my arm to hold it. Clutch again the envelope and sheet of paper.

'It's all right, sir. I'll hold it for you. Don't move.'

And Jane's face. Each day after being separated a few hours in Atlantic City, when we met again, there were always tears in her eyes. And the sight of me now could produce sobs. My senses alerted again by more oxygen. To know where you're going in a city. By centrifugal force. That we're speeding around Columbus Circle. Having come along my favourite boulevard, Central Park South. With an elegance all of its own. Shall I ever go hither again? Without knowing. My focus fading again. The paramedic helping me.

'Just raise your head a little, sir.'

As it may be the last thing I do before I die, raise my head, try and read the address again at the top of the letter. The words so neatly written on the page. The blood-spattered paper. Meant words of love to me and betrayal to another. That face I briefly knew. And even, if briefly, loved. The smile. Tresses of black hair. A vision come back at the last moments before death. While you still live. You can hear choral voices. An organ playing. And Jane. All those years ago. Her wonderful gurgling laughter. Her arms around me as I woke from sleep. And here I am near death, awake. The moment nigh. Meet my maker. Enthroned in his heavenly clouds. Consoling. Nathan. Oh Nathan. Although you don't believe in me. You did try so hard. To administer around you kindness. Devout agnostic although you are. You must. At least take comfort. That I know of all your charity. And remind you. About at least one good thing in the lingerie trade. That at least in keeping women warm you don't have to worry about the flimsy fabric you use.

'Sir. Sir. What's your name, sir? You're in Roosevelt Hospital.'

'My name is Nathan Johnson.'

The aromatic, clinical smell. Just as it is in my brain. Faces looking down. All hues and shapes. Jane's words float back. Strong and loving arms to guide me through my fears. *Love to see you again.* Life seems lost as if on a desert island. How grim and gruelling it can be. Yes Jane. Yes. My wife read your letter. And now that she's tried to murder me, I don't have to worry about what Muriel says about my umbrella and waistcoats and other little Union Jack affectations. Nor, in aspiring to be a squire, the idea of wearing a monocle over my weak left eye. Wheeled along corridors to a hospital operating theatre with my British dreams. Transfusion. Replace the loss of blood.

Pockets emptied to find what proof I had I could pay. Semi-comatose three days in a ward. Regained enough sense to negotiate with a large cheque a private room with a sliver of a view of the Hudson river. Entwined with tubes and wires, punctured with needle holes, pain between my lungs. Bedpans. Leaving you mortified in your helplessness. Stare out at the white-coated world of strangers. Reassemble pieces of my life. All disappeared off the map. Questions. Who is your next of kin? How did you get your wounds? Have the police been informed? Hold the phone. My office not taking my calls. Reginald unavailable. No one worried or concerned I was missing. Iowa's telephone disconnected. But someone phoning back apologizing that Reginald would be there in the morning. And he was.

'Hey, pal. Are you all right. Took us a while, but not nice to find you like this.'

'No. I guess it isn't.'

'I understand you'll need a bit of convalescence but will make a full recovery. But by the looks of it, at least your appetite's OK. That's some breakfast you've got there. But I don't know how to tell you what I have to tell you, ole pal. But the only way is to start. Nathan, this is one of the worst moments of my life. I know something happened that we won't go into. But I told Muriel it was your brain and brilliance and constant dedication that built the business into what it is today, and that with you gone, things could just as easily not continue the successful way they've been going.'

'With me gone.'

'Yes with you gone. Yes. I know, pal. Only too well. And I told her so. Everything could go bust overnight. Nathan. I'll be frank.'

'I'm listening.'

'Well Muriel wouldn't. No matter what I said. You've been shut out. Wants a divorce. The children have merged their shares with Muriel's. Your fifteen per cent shareholding of Johnson Lingerie leaves you with nothing other than that. She's winding up the beneficial trusts you established for employees. Goodwin's widow left out on a limb. And I'm finding this particularly difficult to say. Relevant locks have been changed and you're no longer welcome at head office or at any lingerie outlet. Your papers have been sequestered and sorted to return to you those strictly personal to you. And I have to tell you, some of them along with certain photographs have been destroyed. Access to Midas Towers is subject to an injunction and as you know is exclusively your wife's property, as are all the cars. Down to a broken old bicycle at Blueberry Hill where you have no access. Also Blueberry Hill with its contents and land exclusively your wife's property. Your personal effects have been removed from both properties to storage I've arranged. As is her right, all funds have been removed from the joint accounts.'

'A clean sweep.'

'I'm afraid so, pal. And Christ, nobody feels more bad about everything than I do. That all this, no matter what's happened, is unwarrantably unjust and undeserved. That there was some other way we could and should go. But it came from her own lips. I quote: "I'm going to see him vaporized and sent down the memory hole." I'm afraid there's a guy right now waiting outside in the hall who, as soon as I leave, is going to serve you with papers. Pal – sorry, I mean Nathan – I've done everything I could to prevent this. Goddamn for this to happen to you. No one I know deserves it less. But I can't help you. My job wouldn't be worth it. But let's say on a strictly confidential basis I'm available for further information. And gee, pal. I hope to find you soon back on your feet at the Game Club, playing squash or something. And after those good workouts we used to have, having a beer in the taproom. At least she can't stop you doing that.'

'Well it sounds a hell of a lot like she can if I can't go on affording to pay my dues as a member.'

Reginald leaving closing the door gently. As if not to further disturb my peace of mind. Could tell as he spoke and kept glancing at my bandages, that he knew what had happened. That instead of sending Muriel to the women's prison on Rikers Island, I was shielding her. Who was in the process of ruining me and had already done so quite literally overnight. Starting with my cheque made out to the hospital already bouncing. I could just catch sight of the tweed sleeve of Reginald's jacket as the door opened again for the next waiting gentleman. Who, before I could disappear hiding under the bedcovers, held out the papers for me to take into my hand.

'Are you Nathan Langriesh Johnson.'

'Yes.'

At least this process server was wearing a jacket, collar and tie. And as one does when socked silly, I courteously nodded my head in an acknowledgment of receipt. Thanks for the additional stab wounds. From the Supreme Court of the State of New York. The words in capital letters plunging in the knife thrusts. Get up out of your sickbed and fight. And you can't. Might be better to just stay here and die. And suddenly. Reginald standing again in this open doorway of this hospital room.

'Just something I want to say to you, ole pal, before I go. That it's nice to know that there still are a few of you left in this city. I can't always say that it will get you somewhere or that it's the way to win. But at least it means something to be able to say to you that you are a gentleman.'

Amazing how few need be the words spoken to re-sow a little spark of hope back in one's heart. For a few seconds remind that maybe not everyone's an enemy. Yet it's still battle stations. Across a desk. Lawyers' faces. Start their clocks ticking at their hourly rates. Bills arriving bigger and better. Making you, right at the start, already broke and defeated. My fifteen per cent of one hundred per cent long ago put in trust for the children. As a nurse comes with files Reginald left near the door. 'I'll just put these over here, sir. My, we are busy, aren't we. And here's your newspaper.'

'Thank you.'

Success rises in a pinnacle and defeat descends in an avalanche when the pinnacle gets shoved up your ass. How do I tell people I'm not anymore the Nathan Johnson they may think I am? Not even in my soul. If there's now such a barren place. Where there's nothing left. Nothing to feel. And all you can do is recall. Ten days in Atlantic City. And a letter marked 'personal' turns my life into Horrorsville for what looks like being forever. In the locker next to my bed the crumpled and bloodstained sentence of death. Brings tears to my eyes to read it again. Then tried for a fleeting moment to conjure up a reply.

My dear Jane,
So nice to hear from you. And yes. If it can be ignored that I am wiped out and a sad and defeated figure wrapped up in bandages in a hospital and bankrupted with hospital bills, I would love to attend a cricket match once I am recovered from my financial and physical wounds and would so look forward to seeing someone knock a cricket ball for six.

Still too weak to rise from this bed. Unable to reach my arms to my face. My sprouted beard growing longer. And nothing I need do about my beard. Everyone else was shaving theirs off. Not a single friendly soul left in my life. And how do I stop the useless recriminations coming tumbling into mind. Back when Muriel and I had only just moved into Midas Towers and an incident one evening should have warned me. Thinking I was alone, I was intending to have my favourite meal. Fried eggplant in olive oil. Thought it needed a bit more oil in the pan. The bottle slipping out of my hand. A large dollop spilling on the kitchen floor. Suddenly the sound of footsteps announcing that Muriel was home. Muriel, angry over something else, holding out in front of her a tray of newly acquired Baccarat wineglasses. Erupting as she saw the oil on the floor. 'Now what did you have to do that for, clumsy.'

Nothing ever said to me before could have ever been so wounding. Nor could such unappetizing words ever be spoken that I wanted to hear less. But sometimes you never know when instant retribution might strike. No sooner were such words out of her mouth when whoops, she took one awful skid, upending and falling out of her loafers, flipping backwards on her ass.

A thump amid the expensive tinkle of breaking crystal. Scattering everywhere. And I let loose my mirth. So what? Let's laugh. We're plenty rich. We can get more Baccarat. But you'd think that all the time she'd spent on ice-skating at the Rockefeller Center, her balance would be such that she'd avoid skidding for a loop and landing whammo in an innocent little puddle of the best Italian olive oil.

'You goddamn bastard, how dare you laugh.'

It seemed getting richer didn't help us one bit in treating little accidents as inconsequential. Muriel also saying that I had a suspicious trait in my character in that I never split my sides laughing my head off. It was true. My sense of humour was not easily stirred as it always seemed strangely inconsistent in a profession where depression could be endemic with the constant worry of trying to turn a profit. But on this occasion, as she stood up again and started screaming, I had doubled over in such a vast upheaval of mirth that I also slipped and flipped on my ass. Boy it didn't take her long to laugh and split her sides in stitches in one of her instantaneous mood swings. Just as she must have undergone in making her stabs into my shoulder to semi-paralyse my left arm. Leaving me on my back, destitute in a hospital. With my trusted former accountant Reginald quoting chapter and verse of my demise.

EIGHTEEN

BUT IT WAS time to leave the hospital. And with nowhere to go except my redoubt, I went. Hobbling out to a taxi. Two weeks soon gone without speaking again to Reginald. Who at least had already paid my astronomical hospital bill. Knowing, of course, that I was no longer health- and accident-insured by the Nathan

Johnson empire, and that my cheques would bounce over the Empire State Building. Which news and the cause of my condition could make a stink of publicity. Free of my wires and drips and needle punctures, the last thing I did from my bed was to write to Iowa. Crossing out and amending sentence after sentence trying to find the words to say. Stabs of pain in my shoulder trying to write and crumpling up each sheet of paper and brushing it away onto the floor. Until I did get down in a scrawl the only three words that mattered.

Dear Iowa,
   I miss you.
   Yours sincerely
   Nathan

But then nowhere to send it. I realized I was now living in a vacuum and that my life had crashed into a haunting loneliness. Even though my shoulder was at last seeming to mend, nothing in the future made the silent weeks going by worth living. Playing myself on a chessboard and re-enacting famous games. Removing the last bandages to reveal the scars of nice neat puncture holes. I was now holed up a month in my outpost. On my first practice walk out of doors I circled the block once. Then next day twice. And the following day, three times. Then took the subway north to Columbus Circle and walked the rest of the way to stand and stare up at Iowa's apartment windows. Now with Venetian blinds and clearly occupied by a new tenant. Except for my anger and resolve not to die, it was as if the whole city had become meaningless. Then this voice from the past echoing. 'Gee, pops, I did, I used to follow you downtown.'

And I actually turned around just hoping her ghost would be there, still trailing me. Sign of encroaching insanity. A walk, the longest, all the way downtown to Battery Park. Pausing to re-catch my breath on every second street corner. Through the garment district along Broadway where I mattered no more. Finally the remaining half of the way I had to take a taxi. Then at the ferry somehow, I couldn't get myself to take that lonely ride. Before it got too dark went instead and read the names of the war dead in the park. Then throwing financial caution to the wind, took another taxi and visited the theatre on Second Avenue. It was almost as if I expected Iowa to still be there. Instead of a new play installed. But this is where she'd been. Stood on the sidewalk with tears in my eyes. Somewhere read something I couldn't bear to read. That she hit Hollywood like a hurricane and was like a sex bomb blowing it up. The wonderful willowy Iowa. Truly gone. And just as well. She sure wouldn't want to know me now.

Next damp chilly morning. Worrying about each penny spent. Forced myself in the interests of cheering the spirit to dress presentably and go out for breakfast. Toast, coffee and bacon and eggs, sunny side up. Had the paper. Turning to the business pages. Announcement of new Nathan Johnson stores in Brooklyn. New stores in Atlantic City. Rumours of plans to franchise in every state in the Union, and in Canada and Mexico. And it was no rumour that I was in hand-to-mouth survival. Breakfast to last to the next day. Planning my afternoon. Go look for a job. Founder and ex-chairman of the board of fourth-largest lingerie retailer ready to roll up his sleeves again. Read up on divorce law at Forty-Second Street Public Library. Found little to encourage. And even less when visiting my new lawyer. Wondering how I was going to pay him. While across a desk his face informing me, 'Your wife is suing you for income support, Mr Johnson. By the way, I read in the newspaper that Nathan Johnson Lingerie is going public.'

Reginald as good as his last few words, kept me informed but would not meet or confer. But also in the newspaper, Muriel in a legal battle with the children. Suing her and each other. No consolation, to say it serves them right. Greed. Tearing them to shreds. Until Reginald another month later finally reported that none of them had anything left of the Nathan Johnson empire, except massive lawyers' bills. Shares now a bargain. The children I brought up to be straight shooters, shooting each other and their mother shooting back. Alienation seems to run in the family. Muriel's relatives didn't want to know me when I was flogging lingerie front porch to front porch. Then when I was a squire they sure came around quick enough knocking on my door. Or at least trying to get up the drive through my locked gates. In school, in ninth grade I played Scrooge in Dickens' *Christmas Carol*.

Nathan Johnson physically fully on the mend. But spiritually maimed. Mornings having to force myself to get up from bed. The television having already announced what new disaster or misfortune had happened in the world. Lying there staring at the ceiling. Finally tear the bedcovers back. Brush the crumbs from the sheets on to the floor. Wash a shirt, wash socks. Days now approaching four o'clock and just reliving times with Iowa. Resolve that nothing was going to stop me. Walk all the whole way down to South Ferry. Five miles as the crow flies. One foot in front of the other. Knowing nearly every building. See a familiar face sitting over a cup of coffee on a stool in a diner. Then someone pushing dresses along the street who recognized me. New York never totally anonymous. And especially when you don't want it to be. You go to the same places, to reassure yourself that the human spirit needed this familiarity in its struggle to survive. As a ghost. Lost. Go out on the grey dark water and across Upper New York Bay.

Nathan Johnson, staring out across these bleak cold waters remembering that he was once squire of all he surveyed. A butler dancing attendance. And now estranged from all that. When in the redoubt, as he now called it, looking at the walls lacking a servant's bell to press and seeing at pictures of Blueberry Hill, its elegance, beauty and grandeur, its lake and forested space, tears fell on the photographs. No more the freedom to wander the woods conscious that each tree was yours and could be cherished. And now knowing that each day it was growing increasingly certain that I could only take so much more isolation. The lonely pain which was now my life. The tiny catastrophes. Becoming major. A button missing on my coat and two off my shirt. My broken coffee percolator. Threatening notices now shoved by force under the door. That once not long ago were just little reminders pleasantly dismissed and only remotely came to attention. Now bills unpaid could cut off the little that was left of the outside world. No telephone, no electricity. Stacks of newspapers left unread. With all the time in the world to do so. But each day now determined to venture forth and pursue predetermined destinations. And by staying alive maybe something better will happen.

Walked up Madison Avenue and over to Park. Dressed in a suit and tie to go hear a choir sing. Their voices to cheer me. Reconnoitring first the massive lobby of the Waldorf Astoria. Got an inviting look from an attractive young lady but with a spirit so low I could only smile and bow slight appreciation. Having to quickly remind myself that she might only be for hire. Seeking solace in the nearby sanctum of this church, St Bartholomew's. Taking comfort from the names commemorating benefactors and the dearly departed. No poor people here dead or alive. But at least one place left in this city to find sanctuary to make one feel immediately heartened. A nod and smile from the curate who'd seen me there before.

Out back on Park Avenue again, in view of the haunting windowless walls behind which the tennis courts were housed in the Racquet and Tennis Club. Could never convince Muriel that women were not members. And that I was unlikely ever to be. Went back to the Waldorf Astoria where both men and women were allowed and finally summoning up enough courage to ring Reginald. Muriel, in her recently straightened circumstances had taken up with a boyfriend. A polo player. Landing in a helicopter at my former palace. Lounging in my drawing room and study. Maybe even barking orders at my former staff. Quaffing champagne, smoking my cigars, sipping my Armagnac. Thoughts to sap the little enough strength I'd just resurrected. Wondering if Muriel will end up with a venereal disease. Doctors with their stethoscopes pressed over your wallet. Lawyers with their time sheets. Even walking to the Forty-Second Street Public Library, felt the sidewalk could jump up and bite me. And trying to avoid passing a newsstand I did trip into somebody.

'Hey look where you're going.'

I was. But apologized. Thought that I had caught sight of something about Iowa. Now a celebrity with me now nothing but a cipher. My new social position as a loser who has finally lost. Although I must have done so I can't remember ever making her laugh. Maybe made her gurgle a bit. Yet there were times when my jokey ways could highly amuse Muriel. In the Midas Towers kitchen throwing up an orange and catching it behind my back. However she'd only laugh when it hit me on the head. Yet, there was that one superlative moment of our life together. On the terrace of Blueberry Hill. Sound of crickets in the soft evening air. The sea of treetops to the horizon. Clinking our glasses together with our first sip of champagne in our palace. Memory which comes now that I can't even have my old bones buried in what I once considered my own cemetery. Which if it ever had my tombstone, my epitaph, in big chiselled capital letters would read,

I'M GLAD IT'S ALL OVER

Yet it was another day lived. Supine on my bed back in my redoubt, both my arms able to fully move again. Getting up, throwing sparring punches in the air. Bringing a hint of hope that life could come back to normal. At least cogitating I had the strength to make-believe I could knock an insulting taxi driver's front teeth out as I was finding a way or ways somehow to buy back shares in the company I single-handedly created. Then came without preamble. Catastrophe. With a piano aboard the old rickety freight elevator crashed. Plummeting three floors to the basement and sending an earthquake shudder through the building. Morning bringing jackhammers eight out in the hall, raising the dead. And even the deeply depressed. Dust sifting through the slivers of space around the door. Carpenters rebuilding the staircase. Electricians. Engineers. Hoisting the elevator up again. And it falls. Three times. A struggle now even to go in and out. Making way for wheelbarrows. The management snooping. An aroma jeopardizing my tenancy. The smell of my frankfurters and sauerkraut cooking the last straw from a haystack of straw. Comes a notice of eviction. My redoubt not suitable for human habitation.

At wits' end, it helps to whisper to oneself, *You're under siege fella, you're under siege*. But before your last gasp's gone, you know you've nothing further to lose. So fight. Rage against them. Even if it's only to pretend to be inhuman. Doing a jig of the insane. Frightens muggers in the street. Never surrender. Even when you feel like an insect pinned to a board. Struggling to get free again. Battling even when you know there is a time you can't take anymore. That this is down and out for good. And you've got to decide. Comfortlessly knowing no one is left to care that you're gone. Yet strangely, that there is vanity after death. Not to be found ignominiously. Already in putrefaction face flat having tripped over my biggest stack of newspapers. Something more dignified is required. To be discovered sitting in an armchair, attired in the cerulean blue velvet of one's smoking jacket. Half-drunk glass of vintage port to one's left, half-smoked Havana cigar to the right. Open upon one's lap at a very erudite page in a scholarly tome about beauty.

Now if I die in this room I'll be unclaimed and collected. Like the amputated arms and legs from the city's hospitals. Brought on my last journey stacked in a box on a barge riding through Hell Gate on the East River. To final rest in Potter's Field on Hart's Island. Lain there deep down. Because I've been there and seen it, an employee down on his luck. And you felt you could not leave anyone there unacknowledged in such abandoned loneliness under a granite cross. Bearing the inscription,

HE CALLETH HIS CHILDREN BY NAME

And perhaps death was better for poor old Goodwin. But after hanging himself he at least had someone to whom to leave a note and make an apology. And who maybe even loved him when they modestly lived in their own little palace in Flatbush. He could have come to me and admitted all and I would have given him a break. But he's far better off than I am now as I'm broke. Have no palace left. Have nowhere to go. Except to be homeless on the street. Like one of the addicts, or an aged vagrant. Or like the crippled or infirm. Nor I guess, except for Iowa, do I have anyone to whom to leave a single sentiment. And even to her I would not so presume. All because of ten nights in my life ten years ago. And she was Jane. She was plain nice. Her purring softness. Her whispers of love. Someone in my arms who wanted to be there. And now shouts out in the hall. I'm being called. Respond with my best English accent to bangings and demands at my door to vacate before they broke it down.

'Holy shit, there's a limey in there.'

Voices still out in the hall. Never mind daydreaming. My eviction continues. But even thinking of Iowa made me now go as if jumping up out of a trap, back into the battle of life. Nearly making a fist at the bailiffs as they came back from lunch.

'Hey look, Mr Johnson, sorry the door's off the hinges. But you just go back and forth as you like. Save as much stuff as you can. You've got a couple of hours.'

And swift and silent like a burglar, I went back about my business in my redoubt. Opening drawers. Sweeping the contents out to leave them all strewn on the floor. Kicking piles of junk like a football across the room.

Nathan Johnson tearing open the last of the cupboards, pulling down the stacks of lingerie samples. Thongs, brassieres, rompers, bikinis. Strew them around the goddamn room. Yank out this last drawer and be finished. Chuck out this cigar box. And oh my god. Totally forgotten. Full of my half-dollar coins. Nearly spilt them all over the floor. Kept to be wrapped in fifty-dollar bills. Seems years ago I dropped such upon those whom you could always tell from the hunger shown in their eyes were the genuine homeless. The pleasure I got, even abiding now. Myself soon wearing the look of the dispossessed in my own eyes. What did I do with the fifty-dollar bills? Can't remember. Upend this last drawer. Full of photographs of models on the catwalks of Europe. And one priceless picture of Iowa in a lingerie catalogue. Her mischievous smile. Covering, oh my god, what's this? That stack of brand-new crisp notes hidden and put here months ago. Still sealed in bank wrappers. Easily more than a couple thousand bucks.

Nathan Johnson looking up heavenwards at the cracked plaster in the ceiling. View for the last time this chamber. Leave Reginald to collect what remains. Shove the banknotes into my L.L. Bean yachting bag. Take it, my initials N.L.J. written on the side, put it in my locker at the Game Club. An oasis of safety in this city. From which for the time being I need no longer resign. And where my suit can be pressed. Buttons sewed on. Shirt express laundered. Now stand at attention. Shoulders back. And whatever I do don't forget my umbrella tightly rolled. Get my hair cut by the club barber. Shampooed. Fingers manicured. Always detested the discomfort of a frayed nail brushing a delicate piece of lingerie. This present afternoon becoming a strange journey. Coming away from death. Being like no other moment, minute, hour, or day of my life. Reverberating words Reginald once said.

'Pal, when everything else gets confused, money when you have it is the only comforting thing in life that really makes sense.'

NINETEEN

NATHAN LANGRIESH JOHNSON is the name. The United States my nation. From Maine to Florida. From New York to California. I am its loyal citizen. And before I am homeless out on the street, I am, without slipping and breaking my neck, going to wash my face in semi-cold water. Dry it with my last clean towel in a warm room. Grab what I can to wear. My unironed shirt conforming to the Game Club dress code as best as can be expected under the circumstances. A pinstriped suit with a waistcoat, collar and tie. Used to make Iowa smile.

'Hey, pops, you look respectable but two million miles out of style.'

Have my trusty rolled umbrella at my side to make everyone think rain or snow is on its way. Alas, goodbye to my windowless, dusty, downmarket sanctuary. Slip a few fifty-dollar bills into my wallet. A little salute for the bailiff.

'Hey Mr Johnson. Now you're talking.'

In a taxi riding north to the Game Club, envisioning as I am at the moment, the last fifty dollars of my crisp notes being gone. Providing the conclusive end to all I'd ever worked for. At least I'm having a good minute. Looking forward to having a good hour. Or even two or three. Starting right now as I head nonchalantly through the gleamingly elegant lobby of the Game Club. Past the list of names in bronze of those who fought and some who died in a war. Glide upwards on the silent elevator. Check into the locker room. Get my key from the cage and be greeted by a familiar deep gravelly and friendly voice.

'Hi Mr Johnson. Long time no see.'

Walk past the aisles of these grey tabernacles of athleticism. Dedicated to amateur sports and exercises of every kind and to the encouragement of physical culture. Open up my locker. Place the bank-wrapped packets of notes into safety under cover of my old sweat socks. Take a moment at the window. To gaze in silent relief out over the treetops of the park. Do my first routine. Sit-ups, then take a quick run around the track. Beat some of these other slower gentlemen while more beat me. Competition is in the soul and never ends. Unless someone beats you to a pulp. Meanwhile, take my first shower in weeks. Wait another day before I punch the boxing bags and take a swim. My transformation nearly complete. From down and out. To up and at 'em.

Nathan Johnson booking a room in the Game Club high up overlooking the park. And going to investigate this apartment in its perfect location nearby. Sedately out of sight and with all that was needed. The deposit paid in cash and casual mention of the Game Club membership soon to be paid. Reginald did rescue into storage a pan and pot or two. And along with a few other items of my remaining goods and chattels. So with nothing much left to move, I moved. Plus got a couple of champagne glasses for whenever I would be able to celebrate again. And could find someone to do it with. Thus did I squeeze into my new room-size apartment. When you think you need a lot, you learn how little you need.

'You play a hard game friend.'

'Thank you Tom.'

Christ, encouragement was good to hear. A compliment paid by the club champion Thomas M. Gill with whom I was now able to play squash every other day. The resounding report of the ball against the wall in the chill white barrenness of the courts seemed to defy adversity. Just as did my stock of crisp notes, for the time being hold back doom. My spirit temporarily rehabilitated. Going careful crossing every street corner. With life again ahead of me it was now a matter not to get mowed down by a car. Even in my losing games of squash they were getting more closely lost. Perhaps because Gill, a sporting gentleman, always likes to give you the impression that you had a chance of winning. Until with the final ball cracking the wall like a bullet, you finally lose.

After squash, Nathan Johnson heading for the baths. A few askance looks from fellow Game Club members. Word travels fast about business matters anywhere not going well. To substitute for previous bonhomie there were nods. Anyway, I much preferred avoiding such camaraderie. Or smiles. Or handshakes. A steam bath much better. Commended the spirit anew. Then following a swim. Swaddled in soft sheets. Reclining in peace on a steamer chair. A rest between rounds in the boxing ring of life. Come out fighting. The splashes of the water-polo team practising in the pool. Wait for the little old Spanish doctor to go by who lived in the club. On his way wrapped in towels to the steam room he went spouting his worldly advice up at the swimming-pool ceiling. And often stopping in his tracks. By a glint in his eye I know he knows I'm there pretending to be asleep but am listening.

'Hey. The world's going into the next century. Hurry, hurry before we get hit by a big meteorite. The solution to a happy life. Tell your wife that sometimes she shouldn't talk so much. After she divorces you for unreasonable behaviour, blink your eyelids. Play your vocal cords loud as you can. Don't drink coffee in a place called Chock Full o'Nuts. You could get arrested for being insane. Go home. Scrub the kitchen floor. Work hard enough to need to rest. Cook. Be hungry enough to eat your spaghetti and meatballs. Two helpings.'

As two weeks then three weeks went by, the vaguest sense of optimism arising and Nathan Johnson now running a mile on the track. Doing fifty sit-ups. Skipping rope three hundred times. Punching the body bag in the boxing room. And then taking a routine trip to the baths, visiting the sauna and steam rooms and listening to the Wall Street philosophers before I go lounging again by the side of the pool. The spirit mending, the soul floating at last in peace. Then nodding off in a nap, waking hearing the doctor's voice again as he passes.

'Hey. You want another solution in triplicate for happiness. Cheat the actuarial experts. They expect me dead at eighty, over ten years ago. I fool them. Based on statistics they give you a form. Fill out in triplicate. Sign in triplicate. I tell them. Go shove it up your ass in triplicate. I'm going to live to be one hundred.'

In the Game Club taproom. Watching TV basketball games. My tonic water with grape juice and a squeeze of lime. Steak and salad. Apple pie à la mode. And returning to my new tiny apartment, doing everything just as the little old Spanish doctor advised. Muscles at work reminding me of everything my body was able to achieve in times past. But I didn't feel much like blinking my eyelids, or reverberating my vocal cords loudly enough to annoy the elegant if slightly eccentric neighbours. Of whom it was noticed one or two sported tailoring from Savile Row. And who gently nodded to my passing presence and tap tap of my brolly. God it was wonderful to be a snob again. I scrubbed my black and white tiled kitchen floor. Just a little as the Spanish doctor had advised. Ignored the dishwasher and washed and dried the dishes. Shined my few pieces of cutlery till gleaming.

Routine was helping me keep my spirits high. Taking an evening stroll along the boulevard. Hookers plying their trade on the corner of Sixth Avenue and in the shadows of Fifty-Eighth Street. Tempted a couple of times to try my luck and choose one of the attractive ladies with a college degree. Or one engaged in graduate work. But then thinking of my continued good health, I went instead and had a pineapple ice-cream soda. The little old doctor's wise words always spoken with enviable light-heartedness had included an additional reminder that there were a litany of venereal diseases about that you could catch.

'Hey. You want old diseases. Or new ones. There's plenty for everybody. Chlamydia. Gonorrhoea. Herpes. Nonspecific urethritis. You hear enough. There's plenty more. Watch out.'

My stab wounds grown fainter but still visible. Able now to stretch enough to touch my toes. My arms were still in some pain. But my fitness improving a little bit, like magic. Also magic, the speed at which my crisp fifty-dollar bills were disappearing. Could also think now of all the asses I could shove things up in triplicate. Especially a verified complaint entered in the Supreme Court State of New York. Citing an illicit cohabitation the defendant perpetrated upon the plaintiff. Demeaning the marriage. And to grant the following relief to the plaintiff. Directing the defendant to pay any and all uninsured medical expenses incurred by plaintiff and to maintain life insurance coverage on defendant's life with plaintiff to be designated as irrevocable beneficiary. Monthly expenses included twelve hundred dollars for dermatology. And one read no further. In a dream last night in my little cubbyhole of an apartment, I stood on a rampart of Blueberry Hill, staring out into the endless moonlit darkness, a balmy breeze upon my brow. I was shouting out over the trees, 'You fucking goddamn bitch, Muriel. No one is going to use my stables or my straw and graze their polo ponies on what is justifiably my grass, which I bought and paid for. And then you bunch of bastards drink my Château d'Yquem out of my Baccarat wineglasses.'

And it was with relief that I awoke sitting upright in bed, raised fists clenched. My own shouts waking me up. The window out on the atrium slightly open. My voice echoing and maybe trembling neighbours windows. Making me realize in no uncertain terms that I was still in a pretty bad way. And needing to affirm new resolves. Another chukka. Fight the battle again. Run fifteen laps on the club's indoor track instead of eleven. Swim half a mile instead of four laps in the club pool. Breakfast on a large glass of freshly-squeezed orange juice. Buckwheat pancakes sprinkled with wheatgerm. Ham, sausages and bacon. Doused in Canadian maple syrup. A strong cup of coffee with the morning paper, delivered at my door. What's new with the world? What's new with New York? Pages turning. Get to the business section. And tucked down in a corner column of the newspaper. In a bigger than modest headline, stating in unmistakable words.

NATHAN JOHNSON LINGERIE
BECOMING UNSTITCHED

TWENTY

NATHAN JOHNSON instead of a club workout taking a bleak early afternoon walk down Seventh Avenue. Back again on the slippery slope to doom. Life suddenly again celestially distant away from solitude. Drums beating to the tap tap tap of my brolly. Once more enveloped in the blazing nightmare without boundaries. To make me suddenly stop in my tracks. In front of this hotel. The Wellington. In an affirmation of my British affectations, I go in. Must call Reginald. Wait and wait. Twenty minutes trying to get him on the telephone. Sound of disaster in his strained voice. Muriel held a recent cotillion at Blueberry Hill. White tie and gowns. And you betcha, nobody from the wrong side of the tracks.

Then came the further news. Each word a searing spear of pain shoved through me. Stab wounds to end all stab wounds.

Reginald's voice hoarse and hesitating. 'Pal, as of at the close of business today, the cash reserves of Nathan Johnson Lingerie are exhausted. The auditors are called in. There's been fore-closure by the bank on Blueberry Hill for the borrowing out-standing. The new stores just opened are closing down. I'm afraid that the shares of the once-prosperous Nathan Johnson Lingerie empire made public not that long ago are in freefall. Are you still there?'

'Yes.'

'Pal, with all my heart I know how you feel. I'm feeling the same. All my own eggs are in one basket. I have two kids just beginning their last year in college. The nice little company we so successfully put together and was ready to be franchised around the world is now past even being on the brink. Are you still there.'

'Yes.'

'And that's not all, pal. If you ever want to talk sense into the situation, save your breath, because all you'll get is an unrea-sonable response in return. Seven law firms are already involved in the suits brought by your children against their mother and each other and her counterclaims. Should say eight. Because I'm being sued. Pal, whoever invented the word "crash" to describe financial disaster sincerely knew what they were talking about. I'm sorry I don't have better news.'

'Well that news, Reginald, is enough. It sure seems sometimes that children will never forgive you for being nice to them.'

'You said it, pal.'

Nathan Johnson hanging up the phone. Walking in the direc-tion of the bar. Passing slowly across the lobby of this hotel. Towards the sound of clinking glasses and the prosperous-looking, going about their business. A girl I recognized previ-ously as one of my models I could have said hello to and for distraction suggested we have a drink. But instead alone, have a cognac. A double. Bolster one's suddenly unbolsterable crushed spirit. Iowa who asked why didn't a very busy guy like me have a couple of cell phones so that you could telephone somebody in an emergency. I said I didn't because I didn't want to have to be a busy guy. Or find it possible to get bad news all day. She also said, during one of our afternoon tea sessions, that there was rumoured to be a star beyond our universe as big as our whole solar system and burning brighter and hotter than a million million suns. Maybe it could come closer. Like the meteorite the little old doctor said could smash down. Burn us all up. And right now, in a world for me that could never be colder or darker, I could use the warmth.

Nathan Johnson huddled in his coat on this chill damp evening. Traffic thick on this street. A cold front had hit New York. Beginning to snow on Seventh Avenue. Nearly found myself looking for somewhere to sit down on the kerb and put my head in my hands. My family. For all of whom I had provided. Attended to their necessities. And even though it was sometimes little enough, some money was always there. Sent to the better schools even when I couldn't afford it. Skiing solving a lot in their lives. Now battling each other. A family consumed in a blaze of greed. When once about me could be said, 'Gee, pops, wonderful how it must be, you a happily married guy with your family all grown up.'

I shouldn't have done so. But I did. Walked eight blocks to stand across the street from my very first Nathan Johnson Lingerie store. Located over a basement that might have been used for underhanded intentions by the previous owner. But acquired cheap. Now a prime location in a street that had slowly but surely come upmarket. The windows shrouded in brown wrapping paper. Signs. Closing-down sale. This is it. It's all over. Except for the tears. Once I heard Iowa's voice say, 'Hey, pops, modelling lingerie is at the very bottom of the female social ladder and only one small step up from being a hooker but you've bestowed upon it a magisterial bent that I'll be proud to acknowledge in all my publicity if ever I become a star.'

Nathan Johnson trudging back up Seventh Avenue. Going into an ice-cream store. Indulge the last act of sheer luxury left in my life. Have a strawberry ice-cream cone. Finish it before I reach the Game Club. So this was the final chapter reached. Just stare ahead to avoid the never-ending stream of people. And back in the lobby the detour and go look at how my name would appear posted in the list of recently deceased. And as I looked. Under the legend,

IT IS WITH DEEP SORROW THAT WE RECORD THE NAMES OF OUR MEMBERS RECENTLY DECEASED

There it was. And like everything else now catching me. Catching me unawares. The name. Of the little old Spanish doctor. On his merry way to spend one hundred years on this earth. Listed last among the four members recently deceased. And I suppose leaving to anyone in his wake who would listen, all the things he knew. In triplicate. A tear fell down my cheek as I entered the elevator. His death as bad as the worst that I had already learned this day. Ascend to the darkened ninth-floor lounge of the Game Club. Stand at the window. Flakes of snow swirling. Look down and out all the way to Harlem. The doctor may have come from some faraway place. Like Rochester, New York or Dayton, Ohio. Or even somewhere in Spain. But he was a true-blue New Yorker. Deserving that I come to attention at this window. Salute him. To say to the little old Spanish doctor. In triplicate. Goodbye. Goodbye. Goodbye.

Solitary with a glass of tonic water, grape juice and a squeeze of lime. A small dish of biscuits and soft cheese. Riders on galloping horses go chasing a fox in a painted scene behind the bar. With their drinks, and louder voices of bonhomie, pals gathered. A last look out this window to watch over the avenue and see pedestrians waiting for the traffic lights to change from red to green to cross the street. Rush hour is nearly over. Other thoughts come for thinking. At the dawn of darkness on the death of day. Within the distant sound of massive mountainous waves tumbling on the Atlantic City shore. A woman briefly loved. My life without warning ended. In a letter. Sent to me in tears.

Nathan Johnson leaving the Game Club by the back-door entrance into this shadowy street. Wait for the lights to change. Walk my way back to the apartment that I've not yet even gotten used to. Struggle to view the future. And knowing one cannot wait any longer. Do I believe in god? Keep my options open. Wait till I get there. To heaven or hell or wherever. Arrears in rent ready to loom. Write a letter of apology. Just as Goodwin did. Leave enough to pay a month's rent after I'm gone. And any excess paid to the landlord donate to Traveller's Aid and to those lost in the journey of life. Then I'll take a taxi halfway and walk the last mile down to Battery Park and the ferry.

Reginald once said, 'Pal, if you tell people you're finished and washed up, they'll believe you. And if you tell them you're the cat's meow and the world's latest sensation they want to see the proof. So best to keep your mouth shut.'

My pockets sagging with the weight of the coins I still have left. Chuck them to any homeless. The many times I've thought of doing what one should dread. Umbrella in hand and with a couple of dumbbell weights in my overcoat pockets. Sink me down into the deep. Where the Atlantic Ocean meets the Hudson. With no tombstone over my watery grave. Wending down from Schenectady. I grew up where the Mohawk river adds its flow to the Hudson. And lived my first young stories of sorrow. Waiting in trepidation in high school. To find the nerve to ask the nicest prettiest girl to the senior prom. She could have just said go and die.

TO WHOM IT MAY CONCERN

Let these following words suffice in being all the further that I have to say. Except that it meant something to me to be a gentleman.

> *Yours sincerely*
> *Nathan Langriesh Johnson*

Leaving these words on a white sheet of paper on the table in the apartment that must have been meant to be a desk. Go down in the elevator, nod to this gentleman also aboard and go out now into the chilly mist. The man in the elevator did look at me twice. Who knows. Maybe he sensed my despair. As you would recognize a wounded dog.

Go to my now abandoned private office around the corner from the Flatiron Building. In that shabby windowless chamber my few last things. Photographs, high school and college yearbooks. Encyclopedias and music. All that he still had left in the ownership of his name and among which he lurked too many long hours in desolation. Not to sleep, not to wake. Waiting for the telephone to ring. Just to hear another voice.

No need to remember anything of these last remaining hours because upon the final moment everything is to be gone and forgotten. Imagine I hear St Bartholomew's choir. Decorate my death with my obsequies. Not even Iowa left to say goodbye to in a telephone call. Nor would anyone but her return one.

AFTERWORD

Bill Dunn

THERE WAS, indeed, a letter marked *Personal and confidential.* It gave J.P. Donleavy the seminal idea for a new novel in which an unexpected letter, delivered late in the narrative, unleashes chaos and sets a new course for its intended recipient.

Bob Mitchell,* a good friend both to Donleavy and to his son Philip, visited Levington Park, in Mullingar, County Westmeath, during the late 1990s. Over drinks, Mitchell told the true story of a hard-working visionary who sank millions into a risky venture that succeeded beyond expectations. His wife and their children were given shares. Life was good. Then a letter addressed to the husband, marked *Personal and confidential,* was delivered and promptly opened by the wife. The sender was a long-ago lover the guy had not seen or thought of in over a decade. The wife

---

* Bob Mitchell, a New York entertainment lawyer, was a partner with Philip Donleavy in Donleavy-Mitchell Productions that secured the film option on *The Ginger Man.* Bob died in 2017 at age sixty-two.

reportedly went ballistic. She and the children pooled their shares, took control of the business and ousted its founder – a generous and loving husband and father.

Donleavy was captivated by the anecdote and spent several years writing the novel, *A Letter Marked Personal*, begun in 1999 when he was seventy-three. As with his previous works, the principal characters are composites of people he'd known, including the person he knew best, himself, mixed with pure invention and feelings and experiences that are echoes of real life.

While he was not the inspiration for Nathan Langriesh Johnson, Bob Mitchell's father, Adrian, was the source for detailed information about the lingerie industry used so effectively in creating the colourful backdrop for the novel. Adrian was a partner with his brothers in Mitchell Brothers, Inc., a leading American manufacturer of intimate apparel for ladies, headquartered in Manhattan. Fascinated by what he learned of the rag trade during their periodic transatlantic phone conversations, Donleavy no doubt asked Adrian as the novel progressed for additional details about the glamour and grit of the lingerie trade in New York, with its temperamental designers, self-absorbed models, hard-charging sales reps and executives battling cut-throat competitors.

New York City is vividly summoned up by Donleavy, a native son, in his description of streets, landmarks and neighbourhoods: Johnson's penthouse in Midas Towers on the East Side, the crowded Garment District on the West Side; his one-room hideaway near the historic triangular Flatiron Building at Broadway and Twenty-Second Street, the area where Gainor Crist – inspiration for the main character in *The Ginger Man* – had a flat in 1952; the Game Club, clearly the New York Athletic Club where member Donleavy learned to box; and north past the urban Bronx where he grew up onto the leafy suburbs of Westchester County.

The traits of Nathan, forty-nine, grown more grey and reflective with age, are vaguely similar to the septuagenarian Donleavy with hair thinned and gone white but trademark beard full. Both had succeeded in tough businesses yet maintained a gentlemanly air, enjoying vintage wines and classical music, favouring tweeds, dropping British phrases into conversation, with the same English car, a Daimler, in the garage. And like Donleavy, Johnson would buy a country house with stables for horses on a wooded estate overlooking a lake.

The manuscript grew to more than 400 pages, written in classic Donleavy style and unique syntax. There are stream of consciousness riffs, shifting voice and verb tense, drawing the reader into story. In case you were wondering, 'limozine' was not a spelling error that slipped past copy-editors. That's how Donleavy insisted on spelling it. As for interrogative sentences, Donleavy had his own idiosyncratic rule understood only by him, closing some such sentences with the expected question marks, opting for periods to close others.

By early 2005 Donleavy had a complete draft of the novel, including his version of the life-altering letter. During those years a steady stream of reporters and columnists came to Levington Park to profile the ageing literary lion; he was always ready with opinions, anecdotes and recollections of bohemian Dublin. The resulting articles invariably made passing reference to J.P.'s work-in-progress, *A Letter Marked Personal*, fuelling the anticipation of fans around the world, hungry for a new Donleavy novel.

Despite the manuscript's promise, the author abruptly put it aside to resume work on 'The Dog on The Seventeenth Floor', a short story written in 1993 then filed away and forgotten until its discovery over a decade later. This swelled into a novella and then took on the heft and size of a novel, with many reworked pages and dozens of pages of notes on where the novel-in-progress was going. It diverted his attention from *A Letter Marked Personal*, to which he intended to return but never did. Work on 'The Dog' eventually slowed and then stopped.

In his last years Donleavy lacked the energy for long stretches of writing and editing, jotting down notes and sketching instead. His early artistic efforts were at the easel, and he always found painting and drawing relaxing. He had a few favourite spots at Levington Park, built in the 1740s and visited by a young James Joyce circa 1900. Donleavy would sit at the kitchen table by the fireplace, in a wooden Windsor armchair made comfortable by plumped pillows, listening to RTÉ's Lyric FM classical music station. Or he would sink into a low, overstuffed, oatmeal-coloured armchair by the fire in the living room. On spring and summer days he enjoyed being outside, sitting under the porte cochère or in the sun, surveying his fields and his grazing cattle, beech trees swaying in the breeze. James Patrick Michael Donleavy died on 11 September 2017 at the Regional Hospital, Mullingar, after suffering two brain aneurysms. He was ninety-one.

J.P. Donleavy lives on in his work. *The Ginger Man*, his 1955 first novel, has achieved classic status, been translated into two dozen languages including Mandarin, and has sold more than 45 million copies worldwide. On the first anniversary of his death, The Lilliput Press published *The Ginger Man Letters*, Donleavy's correspondence with Gainor Crist and A.K. Donoghue, friends from Trinity College Dublin days who inspired the characters Sebastian Dangerfield and Kenneth O'Keefe respectively.

The typescript of *A Letter Marked Personal*, notes and early drafts were stored in the library at Levington Park. Lilliput publisher Antony Farrell and I read the text and agreed it should be published, needing only judicious cuts and a final polish. *A Letter Marked Personal* is the third of what Donleavy called his New York stories, preceded by *The Lady Who Liked Clean Rest Rooms* (1996) and *Wrong Information Is Being Given Out at Princeton* (1998). These independent stories are all set in Donleavy's home town. The first two books carried the subtitle 'The Chronicle of One of the Strangest Stories Ever to be Rumoured About Around New York'.

A Letter Marked Personal is the last novel Donleavy completed in his lifetime. It is his fourteenth work of fiction and first novel in two decades. Published on the second anniversary of his passing, it is a worthy addition to the Donleavy canon of twenty-eight books, including his plays, works of non-fiction, collections of short pieces, correspondence and memoirs.

Bill Dunn, a Donleavy friend and archivist of his papers, is editor of The Ginger Man Letters *(2012)*.